GOING HOME

GOING HOME

TOM LAMONT

ALFRED A. KNOPF

NEW YORK

2025

THIS IS A BORZOI BOOK
PUBLISHED BY ALFRED A. KNOPF

Copyright © 2024 by Tom Lamont

www.aaknopf.com

Knopf, Borzoi Books, and the colophon are registered trademarks of Penguin Random House LLC.

This is a work of fiction. All incidents and dialogue, and all characters with the exception of some well-known historical and public figures, are products of the author's imagination and are not to be construed as real.

Library of Congress Cataloging-in-Publication Data
Names: Lamont, Tom, author.
Title: Going home : a novel / Tom Lamont.
Description: [New York] : [Alfred A. Knopf], 2025.
Identifiers: LCCN 2024006497 (print) | LCCN 2024006498 (ebook) |
ISBN 9780593803240 (hardcover) |ISBN 9780593803257 (ebook)
Subjects: LCGFT: Novels.
Classification: LCC PR6112.A533 G65 2025 (print) |
LCC PR6112.A533 (ebook) | DDC 823/.92—dc23/eng/20240510
LC record available at https://lccn.loc.gov/2024006497
LC ebook record available at https://lccn.loc.gov/2024006498

Front-of-jacket photograph © Stockbyte/Getty Images
Jacket design by Jared Bartman

Manufactured in the United States of America
First American Edition

To my mother,
and in memory of my father

GOING HOME

Joel was in the park. He had to save all the dandelions—they were at war against the birds. It was so good, this game. His name for it kept changing. Today the weather was green. Today (he pushed out his tongue to check) the weather tasted of fresh. He was allowed fifty pushes on the swings. He couldn't ask his mum for more, it was already such a lot.

At home, later, they were going to watch a tiny bit of TV. They were going to have a tiny bit of chocolate. One of Joel's hobbies was to collect sticks from the park. If anybody saw a stick and it was shaped the same as a sword, or a gun, or a gun-sword, Joel wanted to know about it. Shout.

He collected answers to your questions. Joel Woods. Two! Salt-and-vinegar flavour. If you asked him he would admit that he was scared of wild animals, robbers, monsters, some robots but not if they had kind eyes. His mum was his best person, even when she was a tiny bit ready to stop playing. Joel knew how to count to sixteen. Beyond that he knew how to guess. It was his birthday next July. He had none brothers, none sisters, none dads. He did have a bedroom of his own, and a religion, and a favourite cartoon, which was about another boy who was secretly magic. Joel's hope was: in the future, him and this other boy would meet.

He had none cousins, none grandparents. His mum said, I worry I'm not enough for you. Their favourite dinner was baked potato. Joel lived in the London borough of Enfield, in England, in Earth. If he ever got lost at the park he was meant to find another grown-up with a child. They wouldn't know many facts about him. It would be Joel's mission to tell them the facts: his name, his age, what crisps he liked, what he collected, the enemies he was scared of, where he lived, how many turns he was allowed on the swings, what exactly had been agreed about TV and chocolate, all the conditions of his big life.

Joel saw another bird. Right, you.

He was the fastest boy alive—when he needed to be. He collected sound effects. He looked forward to later. He liked that it wasn't later yet.

SPRING
TO
SUMMER

ONE

TÉO

The North Circular Road was a threshold. As soon as Téodor Erskine crossed those four lanes of traffic and drove into the London suburbs on the other side, he felt he'd left the city behind. It was misty tonight in Enfield, winter's dregs turning his childhood neighbourhood a colour that was grey-green and miry as seawater. When he reached Ben's road, Téo, obedient to rules, squinted to read a sign that laid out the local restrictions. Thirty minutes to wait . . . then he could park for free. He hesitated.

Park anyway.

That's what Ben Mossam would've said. Meaning, I've got the cash in my pocket. I'll cover any fines you get.

Park anywhere.

That's what Lia Woods would have said. Meaning, who cares about a sign? What *sign*?

Lia was their group's one girl. He hoped she would join them later in the pub; she still lived on these roads. Decision made, he carried on driving, ready to use up half an hour in the nearest shop. He asked himself, will I buy the expensive beers to remind them that I'm doing well in my job? Will I buy those thicker, better crisps?

"Don't—I'm thinking. You're someone's son."

"That's right," he said.

"Don't tell me."

Téo understood. He was almost memorable. Middle-sized and not athletic, he was shorter in the world than he was in his head. If he were ever shown a menu of genie wishes, he meant to add five inches to his height and leave matters there. He looked all right in photos. Especially his chin: it had a rare central dimple. At the age of thirty, Téo kept his hair short against the threat of it spooling out coiled and unruly, which he had been famed for and lightly teased about at school. For clothes he favoured zips, pockets, your lasting materials. He was loyal to his colours. He wore the same pale blues or charcoal greys or over-washed whites, whether for work or a weekend in Enfield or only to hang about doing nothing in his rented flat by the river.

Téo was sure that London had taken the measure of him. London had reached its decision. He was average as a citizen. And in among his responses to this (some frustration, some self-pity) there was peace. Where he lived now, in Aldgate, near London's financial district, nobody expected much of him. Neighbours on his floor called him Tee-oh instead of Tay-oh, leaving out the Polish stress. He could escape the building with nods in reply to greetings, silences not chats. He hadn't made many friends since he moved in from the suburbs, a deliberate fending-off of additions to the guilt they could still exact from him at home. He had been careful to arrange a life in which he could leave obligations at the door of his flat, next to the coins he saved for Ben's poker nights and his shoes that were comfiest for driving.

Téo went home once a month.

He heard complaints if his visits became any less frequent than that. Instead of taking the train, north out of Liverpool Street, he liked to drive—slowcoaching up the A10 on a Friday after work, light to light, passing bars and pubs and cemeteries, later the hospital where he was born. This far north, the suburbs touching countryside, one location was always quite far from another. He felt better bringing the car.

"I'm Vic Erskine's son," he told the shopkeeper, "Téodor. People call me Téo."

"Ah," said the man. "Been ill, hasn't he?"

"Who, my dad? Yeah."

"He's got Parkinson's, hasn't he?"

This place!

"It's something like Parkinson's," Téo explained. "One of the surname diseases. Your slow declines. I come back to see him as often as I can."

They had verbal contractions, specific to this suburb, that were rarely heard anywhere else. Along laddered roads of terraced houses, on estates or mansion roads, they spoke a muddled Londonese that was everything: part Irish, Asian, African, Mediterranean, Jewish, Eastern European. It sounded good tonight. Téo was excited, suddenly, about seeing old friends.

He was asked by the shopkeeper, "How far away do you live these days?"

"D'you know Aldgate?"

He had ferried some beers to the counter. He chose crisps.

"Only Aldgate," whistled the shopkeeper.

"Bit east as well. You might call it as far as Whitechapel, yeah."

"Not that far though."

"I hear you. I should visit back more often. There's no excuse."

Except this, thought Téo, the grief, the guilt.

"Boys," he told them in greeting.

Cards were being shuffled. Stacks of one- and two-pound coins were being put in order on the table. Téo sat in an empty chair. There was that armpit stench of raw weed and their same sixth-form favourites played from a speaker on the kitchen counter. It was about to be a Friday session, the format of which hadn't changed in a decade. Poker at Ben's then pub. Before anything else the crafted spliffs, held for the next man around the table with the stub pinched carefully, like something of interest found on the floor. Téo (big on the diplomatic smiles, not about to judge them so soon) passed around the offered spliff without comment. There was some teasing tonight about his major career decisions. He joined in where he could.

"Where did you leave us for, T? Car college?"

Snorts, as cards were sent skimming around the table.

Gathered in by player after player, these cards were examined for their value. People had a habit they copied from Ben. They put their cards on the table and they pressed their fingers down on top, as if each card had a mind of its own, as if each card might choose to flip over and reveal itself if not properly held in check. Ben's voice broke first out of everyone. He was tallest. He seemed to snooze through the arrival of his muscles. Thanks to Ben they all learned the unbestable social move that was the no-show, its consequences for others, that chilly redundant feeling that ran through you as soon as you realised you were the dickhead left to wait. Téo was irritated to feel it tonight. He asked, "Where's Ben, if we're starting already?"

They were in the Mossam house, seated around a Mossam-owned table, but this was no guarantee of Ben Mossam's company. A roamer, Ben stashed house keys in the gardens front and back, free for anybody to use. Properly described, the house belonged to his parents. It was left to him one miracle day in the new millennium when they had graduated from school. Ben's mum and dad were about as eager to sack off Enfield as Téo. They flew out to their second home in the Mediterranean and rarely came back, leaving the house in their son's care for a term without limit. It was lofty and many-bedroomed. It had a lift. Ben figured out his economic advantage soon enough. While the others in the group went to college or took jobs, settling for the agreed patterns of a swap whereby hours of your freedom went out one door and what came in the other was meant to be the stuff of life, a broader mind, your opportunities . . . while the others knuckled down and worked, Ben never did. He never had to.

"Will he be at the pub?" Téo asked. "Will anyone be there?"

He was winning at cards for once. A sullen quiet had settled over the table.

"Pub?" they asked. There were pouts. People shrugged.

"It'll be the same lot as always in the pub."

"The usual lot."

"*You* lot, yeah," Téo said. "Anyone else though?"

Finally a few of his friends smirked. As a group they had a note they could hit, an elastic, elated "Oh-h-h-h-h!" that meant some suspicion of theirs had been confirmed, some trap fallen into. "Téo's like: he comes back to see *us*."

"When in fact."

"He wants to know about Lia Woods."

"He wants his second chance with Lia."

"Second chance!"

"More like ninth chance."

"Ninetieth."

They roared, well pleased. Whenever Téo was away from here, commuting to his job, eating takeaways and watching episodes, these friends at home receded to become a distant choral voice in his emails and his message threads. They weren't important. They weren't always distinguishable as individuals, with their teases and repetitions, their limited repertoire of jokes. Some of them weren't even *in* the group the last time Téo lived in Enfield. They'd only been absorbed by default, for reasons of having hung around long enough he supposed. They adored Ben and relied on Ben's energy and ideas, his money. This Friday night would feel undercooked till Ben showed up.

"Oh-h-h-h-h!" the group was singing.

"I'm here to see my dad," Téo corrected them.

So they took pity, and Téo felt guilty about using his dad to deflect a cuss.

He said, "I haven't seen her in a few months. How's she doing?"

"Lia?"

Téo waited.

"She's the same. She isn't any better."

"You know Lia."

"She might be out tonight," someone said.

"If she's up to it, she reckons. If she can find someone to mind the boy."

Téo had met Lia's son Joel a few times. He had done a bit of babysitting. There was a teenager Lia relied on. She had an elderly neighbour waiting on the sidelines. If either of those options fell through, and if Téo happened to be back for the weekend, Lia asked. He had made her promise she would ask. Summoned over, three or four times so far, he got a hug by the door and maybe a compliment, about how he was the only one in their group who was mature enough to be trusted like this. But his babysitting hadn't amounted to much. Whenever Lia left him alone, Téo sat on her sofa for a few hours, alert and suspicious, expecting some test of his ingenuity or his reflexes. He was apprehensive about the business with the nappies and the milk, the telling them they couldn't eat any more sweets and such. Was it water you did give small children or never gave them? In fact, every time Téo had gone over there to babysit, the boy just slept. Occasionally Téo ventured into the dark and pungent bedroom to make shushing noises. That was it. He wondered whether parents didn't hype up the difficulty, their innocent joke at other people's expense.

He hoped she would be at the pub, if only so that he could try some of the kinder, wiser enquiries this crowd would never stretch to. He looked at his cards and he bet big by his standards. The track that played was kind to his moment, cresting into a breathless explanation of a rapper's big win. "Phew," Téo said, when the remaining players showed inferior cards. He claimed his money, dragging a mess of coins towards his lap.

From the front of the house there was the jangle of an opening door and a slack, shouted: "Yo." Everyone sat straighter. Téo criss-crossed his hands to clear them of the feel of touched money.

Ben Mossam was pharaoh in this crowd. Be your good fortune (you understood) to get an audience right away. Téo watched his old friend as he entered the kitchen, moving slowly and deliberately around the table and placing his hands on everyone's shoulders as though to press them back into their chairs, no need to stand for me, no need . . . How long-limbed he was, thought Téo, how restless, with the insect energy. Ben had had terrible skin at school, thank God. For years there was lots of conspicuous defusing work going on between his chin and his skullcap. Those problems had long since cleared. Ben was handsome.

The last around the table to be reached in greeting, Téo rose out of his chair. He timed it awkwardly, right as more cards were sent skimming in his direction. One of the cards slipped over the side of the table and fluttered to the floor: a valuable king.

Téo knelt to retrieve it.

"Didn't see, didn't see," Ben protested. He showed his palms to underscore his innocence . . . and Téo—it was ridiculous—he flinched, not meaning to. Ben said, "Think I'd hit you? Come here for a cuddle."

It was a fluke of administration that made them friends. They were put next to each other for carpet hour in primary school. By secondary school they were touching fists after collisions in lunchtime football matches, to demonstrate that theirs was an impressive bond. Aged fourteen or fifteen, Ben was kindest, substituting himself out of a game he was winning to lead Téo to the medical room. Absolute warhead of a shot. No chance of ducking. Téo's nose went click like two fingers, like pay me some attention over here. Older, aged sixteen or seventeen, they learned to be mild rivals, reading insults that weren't intended. Even saying hello they wound up in shambles, one stretching out his hand to shake when the other meant to embrace. Tonight, following Ben's clear lead, they embraced. The others around the table chimed in:

"Lovebirds."

"Let each other breathe."

Everybody was happy. Ben had come. He had a handful of money out his pocket and he thumbed through it, asking them, "How much will it cost me if I'm buying in late?" Generous terms were offered. As if in celebration the ingredients for another spliff were brought out. Ben would assume the manufacture of the next one, not because he was the group's leader but because he had a signature style; he made his spliffs tautest, neatest, skinniest, how the group preferred them. After tucking and massaging his creations into shape, Ben would apply the final seal with a wetted thumb, never a lick. He was much imitated in this.

Always, Ben could conjure what was fashionable from the invisible air. He used to do tricks with a football you would not believe. He was the immediate first choice of any playground captain. Presuming the universe smaller than it was, they guessed that B. Mossam would become a striker in the leagues—as soon as exams were done with and school would let him loose. It was a shame, Téo felt, that Ben had done so little with his talents. But tonight he was charmed, same as everyone at the table, to see Ben roll and fidget one of his excellent spliffs into shape. Téo whistled with the rest of them, agreeing, "It *is* nicely done, Benno."

Swept up in the mood, he decided he would leave his car where it was for the night. He'd walk home after the pub. Live a little. He'd come back and collect his car in the morning. Settled on this change of plan, Téo went to the fridge for a second beer. The group cheered it. They stamped their feet. They must have been paying more attention than he realised.

"That's Téo in for the night."

"Oh Téo's committed now."

"Someone call the police."

Ben said, "He *is* the police."

"You become police, Téo, since you left?"

"You know what I am. I'm like an instructor."

"Of what though?"

"Traffic laws. Speed awareness. It's about being responsible on the roads."

Téo was distracted. Yet another perfect hand had been dealt to him. He pushed forward a substantial amount of money, trusting that at least one of the group would misread his aggression as a fib and bet big in reply.

There was a notion, a notion built on truth, that Téo was incapable of tricks.

"Fold," they said, surrendering their involvement in the hand.

"Fold."

"Fold."

Disavowed cards were placed on the table. Téo's heart banged. It was only Ben to decide and Ben muttered, you know what? He was all in. He was matching whatever Téo had staked. He was putting in the rest of his money as well. "Let's get this done," Ben yawned, "then we can go to the pub."

"What do you mean?" said Téo. He tried to laugh it off. "What d'you mean by 'get this done'?" Staring at his excellent cards he did his sums again from scratch. It was beyond him, excepting moonshots and miracles, how anyone else could have the better hand.

"You in," asked Ben, "or you folding?"

"I fold," Téo said.

The mist had cleared. At the far ends of straight roads, where facing houses were brought almost touching by tricks of perspective, Téo could see tall leafless trees rising out of their park. Behind and above these trees, banks of pale cloud remained visible in the night sky. He thought of tsunamis in films. He thought of dust brought up by stamping.

All the way to the pub there were those in the group who wanted to point out posters advertising excellent raves, raves that Téo had missed. He sucked in the Enfield air, trying to remind himself, I have the key to a car in my pocket, I can escape whenever I want to. They pushed inside their usual pub, which always smelled of ripe ale and bleach and aftershave. The place was busy: a hundred in at least. Even so, Téo picked her out immediately. Ever since they were at school together Lia had fiddled with the cuffs of her jumpers so that the material fell away in strands under either wrist. Her limbs were often crossed, inventively.

She scowled as a matter of course. In the group's mass descent on the bar, Téo ended up too far away to say hello without a scene. Instead he stood on the fringes and faked an important text to write. He was handed a pint and drank it fast, dosing to the necessary state of give-a-fuck required to be this close to her and not panic.

They caught each other looking.

Few times actually.

Once he thought that Lia offered him a silent question, her chin lifting, you okay then? He folded his lip in reply (I'm so-so) and he bowed his head, miles-highing the eyebrows, meaning: are *you* okay? Lia turned away. She leaned an elbow on the bar behind her.

Over their years in classrooms together, shouted quiet by the teachers, they had learned how to communicate silently, widening eyes, scratching ears, talking under talking. Could be, Téo had lost the knack for it. But when Lia shuffled sideways, deliberately exposing a piece of the bar behind her, it seemed to him an invitation: come and join me then, dickhead.

At the bar they touched cheeks. Her overriding scent was the same, flavoured salve, a substance that Lia applied to her lips all day long, a substance she used to graze from, nibbling it off her finger like a snack. She smelled as well of her leather coat, of nicotine, and something faint and metallic, a side effect of her medication, Téo thought. He asked her, casual as he could manage at a shout: "Who's looking after Joel tonight? The teenager or the old dear?"

Lia had no living parents, no family. He would hate to hear there was a boyfriend. "The dear. She's more expensive," Lia shouted back. "So this. Talking to you. It's all adding up."

He took a moment to catch on. He laughed too late. The noise in their part of the pub was of amplified conversation, people yelling their own part of a story as though that part mattered most. The rest of their group had started on tequila shots. It was all part of the format for a Friday. Standing in a crescent around Ben, they downed their drinks. Triumphant, tearful, they told each other, "Hah!" Over heads, hand to hand, a shot glass was sent in Téo's direction.

The lights had lowered since their arrival. The music in the pub was loud enough to make the little glass sing between his thumb and forefinger. Despite it, he could hear and see Lia completely, his every receptor, his skin, tuned in. "Not drinking that?" she asked.

"Wasn't sure you'd welcome it. Right in your face."

"Look around," said Lia.

Téo nodded, there was nothing to be done, a night out in England, an attractive woman, she was going to get some prick breathing his beer in her eye.

"How've you been?"

"Bad on the whole."

Her style hadn't changed. Like it must be teasing, the things she came out with, like she was daring you to guess. Téo tried looking amused. He meant to prove he could read her and that he remained a connoisseur of her ways. "I'd like to meet your son again. See if he's grown."

"I could ruin that surprise for you now."

"I mean how he's grown."

She drank off some of her cola. She asked him, "You back for a while this time?"

Téo thought of the forty-eight hours he'd allotted for the visit.

"Nothing's definite," he said.

"I suppose you could take him on for me."

"Take him on?"

"Babysit again. During the day this time."

"While you do what?"

"Whatever I want to, man."

Lia met his stare. She stirred the ice in her glass. They used to spend Saturdays together in a burger emporium on one of the high streets. Icy drinks. Zero meals of substance. If they needed food they abused the condiment station, stealing ketchups and mayos in packets that only wanted a sharp-toothed tear in the slippery plastic, a squeeze into tilted throats, and there was hunger dispelled for another hour. She used to tell him about her boyfriends. They were always older. Téo used to smile, biding his time. "All right," he said, "I'll take him on for you, yeah. I'd like that."

"Tomorrow," she said.

Which was pure Lia—leaving no room for the wriggling-out.

She took the shot glass away from him. It was full of tequila he hadn't drunk yet. She placed the glass on the bar for somebody else to go second helpings on. "You'll get some sleep tonight, promise?"

"Promise."

Their friends were restless again, intent on a change. They wanted to escalate and improve this Friday night and they discussed a desperate-sounding club out by the motorway. Apparently it had a rope, an executive rope. Ben was proposing he pay for this rope to be lifted. "Got my winnings from the poker," he said, glancing at Téo.

Lia left them to it, escaping before last orders and so avoiding the worst part of an Enfield evening, in Téo's opinion, which came when the pubs started chucking out. Then you had to stand around between the upturned picnic benches and the ant hills of dropped cigarettes. Often there would be talk of travelling into central London, trying casinos or strip clubs . . . more likely they would drift back to Ben's. They would smoke there. Take pills in his front room. They would dance on his carpet till Saturday morning, Saturday afternoon, this part of the weekend having its strict format too.

Téo was done. He declined to drive them to their club, wherever the hell it was, repeating the no even when Ben took him aside and used his special persuasion voice. They clutched hands goodbye, pressing their shoulders together, with Téo happy to pretend he wasn't noticing the mocking faces of the others. He walked home by himself, only the foxes and the billboards for company. Traffic lights continued on their no-end loop even though they'd fewer and fewer cars to boss. It was after midnight when he opened his dad's front door and snuck in.

The Erskines owned the flat on the end of a long, low communal block. They had an entrance to themselves and a slice of garden that amounted to a thin, impractical curve of grass, running from the front of the property to the back.

Téo stepped in over leaflets and circulars. Victor hadn't bothered bending to retrieve them. When it was a kingdom, this flat, when Téo was younger and much smaller, the hallway seemed endless. Now he crossed it in a few strides. The hallway gave on to a lounge which in turn gave on to a kitchen. A bathroom upstairs matched the kitchen's dimensions. They had a couple of bedrooms. Téo could hear his dad in one of them, coughing while he slept. He went up himself. The walls of his childhood bedroom were bare, stripped years ago of his football posters and his tacked-up photographs of friends. Shelves that used to house Téo's DVDs were empty these days. Lying full stretch on the bed, it took a few minutes of wriggling negotiation to get a plausible covering from his junior duvet. Their building was constructed in the 1920s, made out of a mealy, resonant brick that carried in every sort of sound from the other flats. He lay there, disturbed and excited by his conversation with Lia, listening to the neighbours. There was the gist from someone's talk-radio station. A dishwasher, completing its cycle, beeped for attention. There were barks as dogs wound down their own Friday nights, asking each other, why aren't you sleeping yet?

Where Téo lived in the city it was all poured concrete. The odd murmur leaked through the walls or floor, a chair's scrape, a slammed door . . . but you never caught the bleed off a neighbour's stereo, like here, like tonight, like this morning, he meant. The music was conveyed to him in pieces so that he heard a steady insect click for drums, an ogre's grumble for bass, mistakable lyrics with hardly any meaning left. When he was younger he found it a comfort, this sharing of sounds and smells, the garlic that breezed in the open windows at dinnertime, the scent off somebody's candles, their bleach, their bacon. This morning Téo distinctly smelled coffee from a stranger's pot.

He had slept a few hours anyway. He rose and he dressed, putting on the same clothes as the night before. Downstairs, trying not to disturb Victor, he washed himself in front of the kitchen sink. Before he left the flat he gathered up the scattered leaflets in the hall and he left them on an arm of his dad's favourite chair. Outside, the cars, courtly as dance partners, bobbed into empty bays on either side of the road. They flashed each other: after you. The joggers were out early, also the shul-goers, a few Saturday shoppers. By the time Téo made it to the park the weather was starting to cheer. It was the last day of March and the spring wanted it known, she was almost ready, she wouldn't make them wait long. Squirrels dashed across the paths, competing in their mad mini races between bins. He found Lia and her son in the playground. He was punctual to the minute.

It used to be carpeted with woodchip, this playground, but now it had the vulcanised rubber underfoot for that bogus sensa-

tion of a stomp across a mulched forest floor. There was a wob-
bling bridge made of slats and rope. Children tested their nerve
by crossing the bridge at speed. Others messed around on mon-
key bars or waited for their turn on a roundabout.

Amid all this, one boy was playing by himself. As Téo
watched, he hiked the polished steel chute of a slide, as though
this particular piece of playground equipment did not understand
what it was meant for and had to be taught.

Joel then.

Téo did some maths. He must be about two and a half. Téo
watched him risk his small body within reason. The limbs were
wayward, chubby. Joel's stomach was stout and proud as a granddad's at the beach. He had untidy brown hair, wet at the back
with sweat. He had unreasonable eyes, toad's eyes, massive and
monstrous in relation to the head, just gorgeous.

Lia was sitting by herself on a bench. She had cried that morning, it was obvious. He dropped down beside her and shouldered
her, playfully. She shouldered him too. Lia had once described it
as "the black," that was all; she went to the black sometimes. It
was a thing people knew about her, mates, teachers, the neighbourhood rabbi, doctors at the local surgery. Since she was small,
Lia had been visited by spells of depression. This was Téo's own
word: spells. It comforted him to use it. If they were spells they
were something neat and occasional, of finite duration and threat.
At school they could tell when Lia was in the middle of a spell
because the form teacher would skip her name in the register. A
few times, Lia had tried explaining to him that no, these were not
spells, not flurries, not bouts. She lived in her head. For her this
was always, this was landscape. Téo nodded, keen to show he was
getting her, he understood, when really he was just flattered to be
trusted with an intimate-sounding explanation. At an age when
disillusionment was figured to be romantic, even enviable, Lia's

illness lent her an aura at school and made her seem more worldly and informed than the rest of them. When they were seventeen or eighteen she missed some crucial exams. She never got the letter grades everyone knew she was capable of. She never left.

"You showed up."

Téo nodded, he did, he showed up. Duty was his thing. He was convinced that Lia was deciding something important, something about the two of them. Ready to press any advantage he said, "I'll take Joel till the evening if you want? Leave him with me however long you need to. Just keep your phone beside you in case I have to text. Otherwise get some rest."

"You sure?"

Joel was waved over to be introduced, or reintroduced. He stood in front of Téo, pocket-sized . . . that is, as tall as Téo's pockets. He only looked sceptical. Soon he ran away from them again. With a butterfly's spirit of inquiry, taking random-seeming routes, Joel went everywhere around the playground. He was wired for stunts and hazards, that much was clear. He went looking for raised surfaces to jump from. He landed two-footed, in squats or on his hands and knees, pausing for a fraction of a second as if to ask himself, am I stunned? Satisfied, he moved along to another source of potential danger.

Since they'd distracted him from his games, an argument had begun. A game had soured, over by the rope bridge, and instinct for scandal made the other children gather around. Joel hovered too. It looked like your classic struggle for advantage of imagination, with some of the bigger children insisting this bridge, it was in space. Others said no, it was underwater. It was a prison. It was the past.

On the bench Lia pinched her eyes.

She exhaled and she said, "Six o'clock or something?"

"However long you need."

Lia went over to catch and collar her son. "Téo will be watching you today," she explained. She knelt. "And you watch out for Téo, yeah? Help him. Remember what we always say."

"Because is grown-ups," Joel tried.

He hooked a finger on his lower lip, stumped.

"Cos grown-ups need looking after as well . . . I love you, okay? Hey. Joel."

It didn't look like a satisfactory goodbye. Perhaps the boy would have consented to a proper hug without the other children around to see. But here in front of a crowd, he did not want to be held any longer than he had to be. He bowed his head for a hair tousle, the most he could offer.

Lia tried one more time. "Joel. I'm telling you goodbye."

Vexed, vexed. As if he had to say this sort of thing so often. "Bye——!"

"I love you," she said.

He was gone, off in the direction of the swings for his turn.

The Erskine flat was explored till it held no more surprises for Joel. He had worked out the most reliable skidding zones, his best den, his second-choice den, and several fall-back dens after that. He spent a lot of time under the sink, rearranging the cloths and the boxes of powder. Then he returned for a second stint by the door, peeling up the welcome mat and calling it disgusting. Triangulating clues—Téo marvelled—Joel was able to figure out where to drag a kitchen chair, better to clamber up on the counter and reach the cupboard that held the biscuits.

He called this *his* cupboard. According to Joel they were Lia's sofa cushions. A ring of keys that Téo let him fiddle with, "Mama's keys." But it was allowed to be Téo's toaster, this appliance brought to Joel's attention at the time of his mid-morning snack. It was allowed to be Téo's bread and Téo's jam. "Is my butter," Joel insisted.

"What? No. Belongs to my dad, that butter, everything here, the cutlery, the light switches . . . This is my dad's home, y'see."

Joel repeated, "Is my butter."

"No. It can be yours for today if you like? Shall we make it Joel's butter, just for today?"

"Is MY," he roared.

And so they had their first argument, Joel's temper accelerated out of all proportion by the nuclear fuel of his questioned word. Téo made peace. Have it, the fucking butter. In need of a sit-down, he let Joel watch some of the TV he'd been pleading for. They put on a children's channel and the magnolia walls of Victor's front room turned pink and green, reflecting the palette of some hectic cartoon. "Happier now?" Téo asked. "We mates?"

The programme changed on the hour. Joel was absorbed to a different degree, hardly daring to breathe while the music played. Téo supposed this would be his favourite cartoon. He watched along for a minute, curious. The cartoon was about a superhero who was gifted with animal powers. The hero fought evil with the assistance of sidekicks who were animal-powered themselves.

Joel began to fidget. He stood and he copied some of the fighting moves, unable to remain a bystander. Soon he was ordering invisible teammates to do his bidding. He complimented them and he listened to their imagined praise with grace. He didn't seem to be paying much attention to the story any more. End credits registered though; as soon as the episode finished Joel sought Téo out, upping the pitch of his voice to ask, "One more tee-bee?"

"You've probably had enough."

Joel's response to this seemed unreasonable. He collapsed, he was on the carpet, he screamed his frustrations into the fibres. For half an hour he disagreed with anything Téo had to say. He ignored condolences, shushing, small talk, bribes, till he could only be shocked from his sulk by the clumsy descent of Victor Erskine, who was finally out of bed.

And just who (said Joel's changed expression) is *this* old wobbler?

"Well then," said Victor, "yes."

Perhaps the sound of Joel's tantrum had disturbed him. Perhaps he'd been awake in his room for hours, on the principle that his absent son could be made to wait. But Victor must have known there was company because he had dressed in what Téo understood to be a pullover for special occasions. The garment was clumsily stretched. It gathered in folds at Victor's belly and breast, giving him a faintly feminine appearance. Two white triangles (the arms of his shirt collar) would not stay tucked.

"Dad. This is Joel. You remember, he's Lia Woods's boy."

"Ah!"

"How you doing, Dad."

"Yes."

They had their hug while standing on the border between rooms. A belt of brass ran from wall to wall and divided the kitchen tiles from the front-room carpet. Téo stared at this familiar line as he squeezed his father, feeling him up and down as though checking for unseen damage, a supermarket customer inspecting fruit. After widowhood and retirement, old Victor had surrendered the care of most out-of-the-way features, his nostrils, his earholes, all but the frontmost teeth. He still paid for his hair to be styled by a barber somewhere in Enfield. The latest "do," maybe a few weeks old, resembled a polar bear's claw that clutched Victor's head from behind. Lately their telephone conversations had become more of a chore. Victor lost focus.

He sometimes needed reminding where he was in a subject. He remained an expert, a consummate pro, when it came to the practice of guilt.

When Téo tried to apologise for the racket they were making, Victor raised a finger. "A little noise is welcome," he said. "It's been quiet in this home long enough."

"I came last month, Dad. And the month before that. The month before as well."

Joel was playing in the kitchen. Lia had put some toys in his nappy bag and a few spare clothes, as well as three square books, their pages made out of cardboard and sticky to touch. Right now Joel had a small toy car in hand. He dragged it over the kitchen tiles, tightening its clockwork gears till they crackled in readiness.

With some effort, Victor bent.

"And what's your name?"

Even Joel knew they'd already done that bit.

"JOEL."

"You'll come back and visit me, Joel, any time you like?"

"He's here now, Dad. Enjoy the visit now."

"I have a show-you thing," the boy decided. He waited till he was sure he had their attention: then he released the small car. It began a mechanical scuttle across the kitchen, emitting a steady grey noise that reminded Téo of the static on an old radio. When the car hit the metal border that marked the change in rooms it turned itself over. The wheels spun faster and fruitlessly expended themselves. Joel laughed at this. Victor laughed too. He lowered himself to the floor to fetch the toy car and toss it back in Joel's direction. Getting to his feet again took effort, even with Téo's steadying hand under his elbow.

"I can manage. I *manage*."

Dust and dandruff had gathered in stripes on the shoulders of his pullover. Téo brushed him clean then he took him to sit by the TV, where Victor switched between subscription channels, finding the news presenter he liked.

"D'you remember Lia, from school?"

"Oh yes, yes, I see her around."

Victor turned, stiff about it, and inspected Joel again. "You'd know who he belonged to, that's for sure."

Victor and Lia had been fond of each other once. They used to bicker when Téo brought her over. They left each other's company rankled and amused. For a while Victor even started keeping back cuttings from his newspaper, articles that were supposed to prove a political position of his—refuting, absolutely, one of Lia's. Téo usually sat off and let them argue.

"You offered to babysit I see."

"I offered, or Lia asked. What does it matter."

Téo tried not to commit to question marks with Victor. The man was a genius at taking questions and converting them into reproaches.

"Your first day back in weeks, and babysitting—never mind."

"She's a friend. She's having a tough time."

"Ah."

"I might be staying a bit longer than Sunday, anyway. I might take some time off work next week. It depends. Oi. You and me, we'll have our moment as well, all right?"

"*How* long will you be staying?"

"Don't know yet."

"So not long."

"I don't know."

Joel had appeared beside them, full stealth. He seemed to be acting out his favourite animal hero from before. On tiptoes, his fingers curled into claws, he was straining not to blink. "I leopard-boy," he said.

"I can tell. You want some lunch soon, leopard-boy?"

Joel purred.

"I'll put on the oven."

Téo with no idea on quantities. He covered an oven tray with nuggets, fingers, waffles and fries. He boiled them half a kilo of frozen peas and the same again of sweetcorn. Later, presented with this enormous meal at the kitchen table, Joel asked, "What for else?" They watched him drink his milk only to pause, gasping, and request another portion, what Joel called "more some milk," even while he had his snout in a half-full cup.

Téo messaged Lia. He wanted to put her at ease and report, Joel's eaten, he seems cheerful. He pictured Lia in receipt of his message. Meticulous, she'd be thinking: firm but fair, a good example for the child. Again and again Téo felt impressed by himself and his morning's work on her behalf. The value he was demonstrating.

Would he move back to Enfield to live with her?

Or would she move down to his Aldgate flat?

With Joel? Without Joel?

Think, dickhead, where else would a little boy go.

Téo pondered this game of parenting, which seemed manageable as far as it went. It was absorbing for stretches. There was legitimate satisfaction in the weight of the job, an authority you gained. But it was tiring and it was total. Minding a child was one of those stamina sports, perhaps, the kind of sport you looked forward to finishing more than doing. He checked the clock. He would like to have the boy's funny sayings to think over and appreciate in his own idle time. He would read, later . . . take a quiet drive . . . maybe visit Mum's plot.

"Damn," said Téo, snapping his fingers. "The car."

Left outside Ben's, his car would soon be ticketed, if it hadn't been already. Joel seemed accustomed to grown-up swearing. He reminded Téo which were the forbidden words. "Okay. Thank you. I've got them by heart already."

"King sake," the boy said. "King hell."

Téo informed Victor that he would be nipping out on a small errand. "Twenty minutes tops," he promised, explaining that he had to retrieve his car from Ben's before he got a fine.

"Tay-OH," Joel complained.

And Victor refused the suggestion outright. He waved his remote control in the direction of the TV as if lowering the volume on the news was some kind of sorcery. He said, "I'm afraid not." The Scottish pushed through in Victor's voice whenever he was holding a grudge or getting his own back. "You've taken the responsibility. It has to be you."

"Fifteen minutes I'm asking for. Ten minutes if I jog. It's called a favour."

Even so, Téo felt ashamed. There was an unwelcome whining note that entered his voice whenever they argued. "All you'd have to do is sit here. Same as you've been doing all afternoon."

"You took the responsibility," Victor repeated. He seemed satisfied how this was turning out. "On the first day of your visit you offered to help someone else."

"I was asked for my help. Now I'm asking you."

"And I'm saying no."

Téo scraped up his keys. "Come on," he said to Joel, "we'll run this errand together." Biting the keys between his teeth, both thumbs working, he wrote another message to Lia, asking her, can I put Joel in the back of my car? Without a child seat? If it's only a short journey? If it's sort of an emergency?

Joel stood his ground. "Don't want it, errand."

"No choice," said Téo, "I'm the one minding you today. I'm the prime minister, I'm president, it's got to be me. Let's go."

"You HAVE," he pleaded.

It was a surprise to Téo how much of the boy's language he understood already. "You HAVE": by which Joel meant you have to: by which he meant please. He said "I do" when he meant I am. "It's not" for no. Even while he muddled up the basics Joel could lift his chin and speak a complete sentence.

"I miss Mama," he said.

"I hear you. Couple more hours and you'll see her again, I promise."

Joel had to be led by the hand. He had to be persuaded on with chatter and distraction. He had to be carried for half a mile in Téo's arms, then put on the ground again so that he could lead. Téo coughed, thumping at a sore point on his chest to shift a blockage. He felt uneasy as he sent Lia a third message, because seriously, he needed to know. Was he okay to stick Joel in the back of the car . . . Inclined to expect the worst in most scenarios, aware of this as a failing and a handicap, just an unattractive feature, Téo made himself imagine a load of reasons why Lia had not replied. She'd be at a double movie. She was having a critical nap. He saw mislaid phones or used-up batteries. The closer they got to Ben's house, the more anxious Téo became and the more carefully he made them cross roads. He insisted that Joel peer in both directions, peer in all directions, up.

He explained that Enfield was known for its bad drivers. Your speed demons, your boy racers. The richer ones were the worst. Whenever they heard the nearing racket of an expensive car, Téo made them freeze where they were, shielded by trees or stationary vehicles. "Look right, look left," he repeated. He got them over safely every time.

"Be with Mama soon?" Joel tried.

It was maybe the fifth or sixth time he'd said this.

"Yep."

"Is promise?"

"Yep."

Téo took out his phone. He sent her another message, not meaning to hassle, only wanting an answer. Beside him, Joel sighed and sighed. He said, "I can't find Mama, everywhere."

They were in sight of Ben's. Through the big front windows Téo could see that some of his friends were still awake and dressed for their Friday night out. They held cans of beer and they jittered from side to side in a wary two-step, like people being forced to, like people afraid to stop. He assumed he'd been seen as well and he raised a hand. His mates were pale under their second-day beards. They had the night eyes, unnerving. None of them waved back.

Be a pity if Joel saw any more of this, Téo decided, as he hustled them on towards the car.

He found himself out of patience with Joel and they argued about whether the boy could sit in the front or not. When Téo finally persuaded him to clamber in, they had to argue again, this time about his seat belt, which rode uncomfortably high on Joel's chest. Téo was sure that people would be watching from behind their curtains. They'd be criticising, wondering why he didn't have the proper safety gear. He tried texting Lia again. He stared at his phone, willing a response. "Know what," Téo said out loud, "we'll leave the car here. We'll walk back to Victor's instead."

"No."

"I'll carry you."

Joel said he was hungry. He said he didn't want to be carried after all. His foot hurt, such a lot—he refused to say which foot. He wouldn't be helped by anybody except his mum now. Téo's thumb was missing the buttons on his phone. He did call her but it rang through. Joel said that he wanted to watch TV.

It was a story he needed.

A tiny snack.

"Tay-oh," Joel complained.

One of his shoes had come loose at the heel. "Keep still," Téo said. He was bending to help. It was better to sound stern than frightened. "Stop fidgeting. I'm trying. Please."

TWO

VIC

Their taxi moved slowly in the morning traffic. Commuters hurried by them on the pavements, blind to Vic Erskine, who sat facing his son and the sleeping child, the three of them hidden from view by the taxi's tinted windows. Like stowaways for the border, Vic thought . . . like film stars due at some bloody palace!

It was 9 a.m. It was time for jobs and school bells and the resumption of everybody else's useful lives. There were mornings when Vic's awareness that other people had obligations, still, made him so jealous he could only hide away in his bed. Today the situation was different. Today he had a reason to wake at a sensible hour, to dress with some of his former flair, putting on a smart black suit and a shirt. Before they got in their taxi, Vic swapped his usual stick for a grander one, the one with the curved derby handle on top. Not a visit to the doctor's, not today, and not a haircut. Instead he had an honest-to-God appointment, he had a funeral to attend. A loud snort of satisfaction escaped Vic's mouth before he could stop it.

"Dad," Téo complained.

He made a face: you'll wake Joel.

Mumbling apologies (Vic hadn't meant to disturb anyone), he propped his stick between his feet and turned to the window, continuing his study of the people outside. He believed he was connected to them all, the binding agent a sequence of letters and numbers, their postcode, which was enough. When you'd grown up without family, a postcode in common was enough. Since his retirement, Vic's status in the neighbourhood had diminished, that much was clear. To many of these people he'd become another old man, fumbling for coins, click-clacking along, requiring tedious chivalry. But not this week. This week Vic was a resident of consequence again, he was a wheel-spoke in a tragedy.

"*Dad*," said Téo.

Their taxi turned a corner and they came in sight of the funeral compound. Dramatic red-brick buildings straddled the road. Cremations on the east side, burials on the west. Most pedestrians walked by these buildings without a glance. They hardly seemed to notice the big chimney or the rows and rows of headstones in the cemetery opposite. Many were superstitious, the Jews of the community especially, who tended to pessimism in the fabulous and imaginative tradition of their race. Ignore death. That was his wife Sal's way of thinking. Ignore death and trust to be ignored by it in return.

Vic considered the sleeping child. Would Joel walk by this cemetery one day, trying not to look inside? Would he be put in mind of his mother if he did?

The police broke into Lia Woods's home on Saturday night. Joel had been staying with the Erskines ever since, a contingency measure agreed with the social workers who were assigned to his case. All the attention and concern that came with a two-year-old stray was a surprise to Vic, very different to what he was used to. The social workers visited often. Neighbours, rallying, left dishes of food on Vic's doorstep. Unsigned envelopes were pushed through his letterbox at night, the money sealed inside meant for Joel's temporary care. Sympathetic messages were sent, from real notables in the community, not-just-anybodies. The new rabbi came for tea. She huddled with Téo and the social workers at the kitchen table, where they talked slowly and soberly about Joel's future.

They had gathered that Téo was Lia's most responsible friend. Because of this, Téo was seen as one of Joel's better bets. The situation was dire; his social workers acknowledged that. There were only imperfect options. But Téo knew the local area. He was of the same religion as Joel. Vic, furthermore, had encouraged them to believe there was intimacy between the Woods and Erskine families. Only a mild exaggeration. Wasn't it Lia who left Joel in their care? By doing so, hadn't she expressed a choice? Whenever the social workers were visiting, whenever he could get a moment alone with them, Vic dropped such hints. Harmless stuff. Nudgings. His only concern was for the child.

Now he tapped his stick on the floor of the taxi, frustrated.

He had meant to ask Téo to buy more coffee. He had meant to request a larger quantity of milk, more than the usual puny pint. There had been so many interesting people in the flat. For as long as Joel remained a guest, Vic supposed, there would continue to be interesting people. It had been an empty home long enough.

He was coughing again. This did disturb Joel, who stirred and opened his eyes. He stretched in the cramped seat that had been provided by the taxi company. Vic admired him. The child was an easy passenger for sure, not one of those are-we-nearly-there children who fought against a journey, issuing unreal demands and playing the tyrant. Joel stared at whatever was visible to him out of the taxi's big windows. The tops of trees, was it? He'd put a thumb in his mouth when they set off from home and the skin there was mottled and sore-looking.

Joel had hardly mentioned his mother, not in Vic's hearing. Instead he napped. He played. He was patient. It was as though he had made a decision to brave the week, seeing it as an interruption to the normal state of things, a state that would surely resume as long as he feigned enough calm, as long as he remained agreeable. When the taxi was near enough to stop and let them out, Téo went around to help release Joel from his belts and his straps. "You ready?" Téo asked.

Joel understood there was about to be a change of scenery.

With some cunning, Vic thought, Joel tried his best to influence the change.

"Watch a bit of tee-bee?"

Téo was thrown by the request. "We can't watch TV. We're at the place, the funeral, remember? I'm sure we talked about this."

Téo hadn't been honest enough with the child. This was only Vic's opinion. Vic trusted he'd made his opinion clear. Joel was saying, "Tay-oh. One bit of tee-bee. I promise?"

"No, mate. Help me get these straps off, we're due inside."

He lifted Joel out of the taxi. He carried him across the car park. Vic found that he had been left behind. After an embarrassing wait for Téo to return to the car, then a misunderstanding (he was determined to manage), the taxi driver had to come around and help him out. It was a shameful affair. On his feet again and standing in a braced-for-anything crouch, Vic patted his pockets, hoping to recover some dignity by tipping the driver inordinately. He hadn't even any money, not even any cigs. Vic badly wanted to smoke. One of the old brands, those brands that meant business, raking the inside of the throat like sharp fingernails.

As the taxi drove away he squinted at his situation. Téo was nowhere to be seen. He must have taken Joel inside the crematorium chapel. Waiting around in the car park Vic saw a crowd of secondary mourners, their connections to Lia slighter, he believed. Some of them looked to be fellow congregants from the synagogue . . . yes, he recognised their faces. They had disposed themselves in a huddle near the chapel doors, presumably to wait for other relatives or friends to enter first. Vic aimed himself at the back of this group and he found a position for himself behind a stooped man, a front-row figure. Vic didn't know him well enough to chat to. He wasn't on speaking terms with any of the senior congregants, a form of elite, often described as generous donors who were essential to the synagogue's foundation and survival. Some of them had their names inscribed on bricks that were put down when Enfield Progressive was built. Although Vic was married to Salomea Kiryluk for twenty years, he had never formally converted to Judaism. He went to shul every week of his marriage and after Sal's death he carried on alone, conditioned to attendance, finding that services made him feel closer to her.

This man in front of Vic was sloshing about inside a suit that was much too large for him, cut years ago, Vic guessed, when it was meant to flatter a heavier frame. Next to him a wife, more stylish, wore a raincoat that was theatrically cinched at the waist. He listened to them gossip about the circumstances of Lia's death. From time to time he nodded.

They had started to take notice of Vic, acknowledging his presence. They turned to face him and they bowed. They even welcomed him forward, making room so that he could enter the chapel before they did. Vic was shy at first. But he manoeuvred himself with his stick quite smartly for once, walking between their ranks with composure and (perhaps) panache. They addressed him in the formal Hebrew. They told Vic his sorrow was shared and they wished him long life. "I'm grateful," he said in a low voice. "Grateful."

When they asked after the child he was able to tell them: "The child is coping." He was able to say: "We're looking after him as well as we know how to. He might be staying with us a while longer. Yes. Joel might live with us for some time."

Inside the chapel, Vic saw mourners waiting for the service of committal to begin. He recognised neighbours and several young men about Téo's age, school friends. He spotted Ben Mossam in the crowd: that peacock. Téo himself stood beside the doors. He was hand in hand with Joel and awkwardly accepting condolences on the child's behalf. To Vic's eye it was plain that Joel had no idea what any of this was about. Some of his questions since the weekend! They alarmed Vic greatly. Greatly. It was either that Joel was being kept in the dark about the death of his mother or he could not absorb whatever was explained. As Vic entered he placed a hand on Joel's cheek.

"My boy. I wish you long life."

"Sure, Dad," Téo said. "Listen, we'll need to wait a while after the service is over. That okay with you? Joel should probably be the last to leave."

Vic swelled. The last to leave.

"Your sorrows are my sorrows," he said.

"Okay: find your seat."

The rabbi had appeared. Sibyl Challis was a recent arrival in Enfield. She was kinder and more spirited than her predecessor. She was certainly younger and in Vic's opinion more interesting to look at. She had an open face and a tremendous swirl of coiled hair. For years they'd had an old boy at Enfield Progressive who drove in and out of the borough, handing off his more portable duties to volunteers while he attended to the competing needs of two other liberal synagogues around the suburbs. He'd a fine singing voice, Vic remembered; not much ear for language though, no talent when it came to the sermons and the intervals of chatter, parts that marbled religious services and made them memorable. An honorary Jew at best, Vic longed for ideas, for jokes, anything to salt the weekly portion of God.

Were that old rabbi in charge of this funeral, Vic felt sure, the manner of Lia's death would never have been mentioned. The new rabbi addressed them candidly. In her eulogy she spoke about the distant deceptive reaches of human sadness and the conviction that might take hold of any parent lost in such a place that their child would be safest, healthiest, happiest if freed of a burden. Lia was failed in life, the rabbi said, because she was not reached in time with help or with counter-arguments, with a hand on her hand. She would be failed as much in death were anybody to criticise her or blame her—ask, how could she?—without trying to understand that for Lia the question might have been, how could she not?

A taxi took them home. Vic had not been shy in reading and ranking the offers of assistance that were posted through his letterbox, nor was he squeamish about telephoning any of those neighbours who'd written, letting them know that in fact their kind offer of such-and-such a favour would be most welcome. He acted alone in this. Without a word to Téo he arranged it so that a neighbour who gardened for a living would pop over with some equipment while they were out at the funeral and have a go at the Erskines' overgrown lawn. While he was at it, the neighbour had agreed to tackle their hedges, those that bordered the garden on three out of four sides and fenced the property off from the road. As soon as they pulled up in their taxi, Vic saw that several large sacks of garden waste had been left out on the kerb. The lawn and the hedges were immaculate. Téo got cross again. He accused Vic of taking the piss.

"But a nicer garden he'll appreciate."

"He's only staying a couple more days," Téo hissed.

"That's yet to be decided."

"Yeah," said Téo, "by me, it's me they've asked, not you—it's me who'll decide."

He softened. "I would've mowed your lawn for you, Dad. I would have cut the hedge. Don't call in any more favours that are meant for Joel, okay?"

That afternoon, Téo did have his chance to labour for Vic. The early April weather had been bland, a pale blue dome overhead, but a few hours after the funeral it turned rotten, a blotched sky sagging above them like an old and untrusted ceiling. It rained and the sacks of cuttings on the road were overturned by fierce winds. Soon the nearest drains were blocked. When it was dry again, Téo and Joel went outside to see the puddles. Vic watched them through the front-room window. They poked around with sticks, trying to clear the caked grilles, Téo demonstrating for Joel which were the looser slabs of pavement and how he could step around them to avoid the water-traps and get back indoors with dry socks.

"Téo's go puddles," Joel shouted. He was taking off his shoes by the front door.

"I saw I saw," Vic said. He added in a whisper, "I spied on you both."

"Téo's go puddles," Joel yawned, a fact confirmed. It was one of his habits. He liked to catalogue adult movements, where adults had been, where adults imagined they were heading to next. "Vic's go work?"

"No. Not any more."

"Téo's go work?"

"He's outside, look, you can see him. He'll be in again shortly."

When Téo rejoined them they started to tidy away Joel's toys.

Vic made honourable gestures. He shifted a few reachable things from one surface to another before settling into his armchair to watch his channel for news. Joel sighed. "Always, always is putting things *away*," he observed. Later he said: "Téo's go work?"

"I'm here, mate. You're here. Victor's here. There's nothing left for us to do today, nothing except dinner and bedtime. Okay?"

"Tay-oh."

"Yeah?"

"Kiss-cuddle."

Téo remained where he was, on his haunches, frozen in the act of gathering up toys. He seemed dazed. Because of this, Joel took the initiative, going over to him and clambering on to his lap. Joel's tiny fingers played up and down Téo's sides. He wriggled his toes.

"You've probably been wanting to ask us some questions."

Joel was quiet.

"You've probably been wanting to know more about what happened to your mum."

"I miss Mama," Joel admitted.

"She loved you, which is forever. You understand what I'm getting at, don't you? She loved you, but it's— She's—"

Joel did not seem to think Téo's explanation was up to much either. He announced, "Kiss-cuddle finished," then he stood and ran circuits of the room, making train noises, exhaust noises, space noises, till Téo asked him to help finish tidying up.

Vic was thinking of an afternoon, was it the Sunday? It was teatime. The social workers were huddled in the kitchen with Téo. There were papers to go through, care orders to read and sign. Joel had been given a pristine colouring book and a packet of felt-tipped pens as a distraction. Vic was handed a leaflet which explained the importance of a wide support network for a child in Joel's situation. Undoubtedly the leaflet was an effort to

occupy Vic, as if he were a two-year-old boy himself. He eaves-
dropped as well as he could from his chair.

Téo was asked, not for the last time, whether he knew the
identity of Joel's father.

Did anybody know?

Vic sighed. For the most part he was impressed by these social
workers. But really. They were hard-worked, he granted. They
said they were under-resourced. The older and more senior of
the two was called Gil. Vic found her appealing, brusque, he
took from her a sense that all of human optimism was better off
checked in the first instance, that compromised solutions were
better than no solutions. Gil's colleague was younger, male, eager
to support whatever anybody said with smiles of encouragement
and murmured yeah yeah yeahs. Vic could imagine this younger
colleague disillusioned by his difficult work within a few years,
but for now he was hopeful . . . an Alex or an Alec or (bloody
hell, Vic thought, my memory) maybe an Alistair. Trouble was,
Vic had missed the introductions by the door. He was so determined to get around without a stick in their presence, he was
often a step behind the action.

Now he pretended to doze in his armchair, then he did doze.
When he woke again, Téo and Joel were on their stomachs on the
front-room carpet, piecing together plastic bricks. Téo stood up
stiffly, groaning as if he were an older man. He took Joel upstairs
and Vic heard the beginnings of their usual argument. Joel did
not want to go to bed. From an upstairs window he had spotted a trampoline in one of the neighbour's gardens. Broken apart
and rusted, this trampoline had been out of commission for some
time. Removed of its legs it rested upright against a fence, a great

disc of spoiled steel that rose about ten feet tall. Joel badly wanted the trampoline for himself. He pleaded again and again. "I promise you," he said.

"Promise me what? It's bedtime, be reasonable."

Vic climbed the stairs himself. He joined them in time to experience the full force of Joel's tantrum. He was flat on the bed, face down. Then he rose to glare at Téo, tired of Téo. "Go *away*," he hissed, adding with savage articulation: "I don't need you."

Downstairs, Vic said to his son, "Of course Joel needs you. Who else does he have?"

Téo was rubbing both palms against his face. He pushed his fingertips through his short hair. "I don't know how much longer I can hack this," he said. "In the night, whenever I go in there, he shouts the same things, 'I don't need you. I don't want you.' What am I even doing?"

"You're helping him."

"Joel sits up. He tries to figure out who I am in the dark. And he's not even frightened or sad. It's more like he's ashamed on my behalf. That I should have the guts to keep showing my face. It's like he wants to know, who *are* you to me?"

Téo twisted his head, listening for the sound of a disturbance upstairs. It was nothing. "The social workers say they need a decision. I'm meant to tell them yes or no, whether Joel can stay here for another couple of months while they try to fix him somewhere to live. They say there aren't any better options for the minute."

"And if you tell them no?"

"Either it's me who looks after Joel or it's a foster home, state care, whatever they can find as a stopgap."

Vic turned around in his armchair. "Let me tell you a story," he began.

"I've heard your story, Dad. You arrived. It was the middle of the night. A room full of beds and boys. You were scared out of your mind . . ."

"It was evening when I arrived," Vic corrected. "I still had the whole night to get through."

"Care's different now. I'm sure it is."

"Nothing is different in here," Vic said. He touched his temple. "Or here." He touched his chest. "In these places you're a child nobody wants."

THREE
BEN

"Lia fucking Woods," he proposed, suddenly solemn, so that the group stopped its talking.

To a man they raised their cocktails in hand.

"Lia Woods," they repeated.

It was the night of her funeral. All around Ben's house, big tubular candles burned. Bedsheets and towels covered the mirrors. Done properly, you were meant to go without cushions too, no comfort was the rule, along with no vanity . . . but relax, Ben thought, relax about the cushions. He didn't suppose potent fuming cocktails were a part of a standard Jewish shivah either. Yet here they were, a dozen of Lia's schoolmates, each with a stemmed glass, drinking martinis in her honour.

"And her son," someone was proposing, "we should drink to Lia's son as well."

"Joel," someone said.

Oh they were gutted for Joel, the lads agreed. Every one of them held up a glass again, to demonstrate the sympathy that struck them as apt. But whose toast was this? wondered Ben, sending around a very cool glare and telling them listen, of course

47

we're gutted for Lia's son. "Goes without mentioning, the son. Us lot? We'll keep him in mind as well as anyone. We'll watch his back from a distance, protégé-style. And the minute he's eighteen or whatever," Ben said, "I reckon he couldn't ask for a better group of mentors. To come out the shadows. Am I right?"

There were grunts. They closed and compressed their mouths.

Benjamin Mossam—! they'd be thinking. Spot on when he spoke, and touching your heart.

"But tonight's about Lia," he continued. "Our boldest friend, hard as nails and wise too. The first of us to go. We lost her, what, almost a week ago. Which is mad. Which is . . ." He trailed off. These cocktails had weight. He fidgeted inside his suit. "How the attractive rabbi put it earlier," Ben continued, "*she* got it right, there'll be no blame, not by anyone in this room. To Lia Woods. Drink."

"Lia fucking Woods."

"Lia."

"Lia," they said.

" 'Round three," Ben suggested.

" 'Round thre-e-e-e," they repeated.

At a later hour, when his friends had been hugged at the door and sent shambling home, Ben stood in the kitchen. He put his palms on the marble counter and he stayed there, bowed, for some time. When he straightened again he started removing clothes—mourning suit, sweat-dampened shirt, his socks, his pants—leaving the items where they fell so that Ben stood naked in the house except for a kappel, this skullcap held in position over his crown by a small steel clasp. Ben was the only Jew in their group who wore a kappel. He didn't believe-believe. He didn't buy into that proviso about covering your head to impress God. More, he

appreciated how it made women curious, and how it put men—
those he didn't know—on their guard.

Now he took some fruit and veg out the fridge, his thick
yoghurt too, and he blended together one of the midnight
smoothies he'd been trying to boost his resilience. A death in the
group. That reminded you. When the mixer finished its stop-
start racket, Ben took up the removable jar and drank reviving
draughts as he moved about the house. He went between interconnected lounges and a dining room, extinguishing candles as
he came to them, pulling coverings off the portrait mirror in the
hall and the landscape mirror that hung over the fireplace, mirrors put up by his parents to amplify the space and excavate new
territory in a house that was already, by anyone's standards, huge.

He wiped his top lip. He considered his naked body in both
of the exposed mirrors, chancing on himself and discovering the
view from unexpected angles, staring at a distance over thresh-
olds to see how this must look to the people he slept with. Ben
burped. Not yet admitting any serious strain, he expected to blast
through the next stage of bereavement how he blasted through
everything: with brio.

Téo called to tell him the news.

That happened on Sunday. Ben was in the upstairs gym at
the time. He was jogging and watching an action film. He was
calm in response to the string of unaccountable facts that Téo laid
out. How Lia was dead, no reversals. How she'd done it to herself
with hoarded pills. Her son didn't know yet. He would stay with
the Erskines for now.

Without a tremor in his voice Ben asked the businesslike questions back, articulating what a tragedy and a blow this was, without feeling it *was* a blow, not yet, without feeling anything, only
that his instinct was to end the phone call and unpause his film,
carry on running, putting away further consideration of Lia till

much later. Overnight on Sunday, the emotion did fetch up inside him. He had trouble sleeping. By Monday a low sulk was on him, tightening Ben's shoulders, limiting his lungs from their usual hungry complement of air and at the same time increasing his appetites and his recklessness, turning him twitchier and more glib. All that day Ben's thighs and calves prickled with something new that felt like vinegar between the muscles and the skin. His breastbone ached.

At some point he messaged the lads in the group, one by one, to tell them what had happened. He never anticipated they would have received the news already from Téo. At Lia's funeral Ben was stunned by his friend's elevation. Téo was a central player, one of the stars of the show, allowed to carry Lia's son in his arms for the duration and spoiled by sympathy that might have gone to others.

Tonight Ben *did* feel better. Ben was more his former self. He could imagine visiting a therapist in time and talking about it, how these events had knocked him before he blasted through and came out the other side with only a dull vacant feeling in his chest, with only this cotton-wool softness inside his head . . . Did therapists ever do house visits? he wondered. Would your mood doctors serve themselves up at the door like pizzas?

It put him in mind of his appetite. This had been terrific, non-negotiable, Ben keener than ever on food, liquor, your mischief in edible form, your uppers and your downers, the end-of-a-night zopiclones. He yawned and unclasped his kappel, leaving it in its usual place on a table in the hall. Top floor, in his gym, he caned a quick kilometre. Down a flight, in a master bedroom he'd long since assumed from his parents, Ben burrowed under laundered covers and opened his tub of zopis. None of his colourful dreams tonight, no flight, no stranger-sex, instead the more distant drugged oblivion, too far gone for dreams to reach him.

In the garden centre, 11 a.m. as arranged, he met up with Téo and Joel. They were there to buy the kid a trampoline. Ben had offered. Ben would pay. It was the least Ben could do. He came into the shop wearing sunglasses that hid the burning red ruin of his eyes. He had his credit card in hand. The idea behind the trampoline, Téo explained, as they rolled around a trolley, was to get Joel expending some of his excess energy. "Then hopefully we'll all start sleeping better at nights."

"How is it?" Ben asked.

"The sleep? Awful."

The trampoline they chose was middling, the one in the range they judged would fit in Vic Erskine's tiny garden, yet not so dinky that a two-year-old could give it the snub for being childish. Apparently this had become Joel's standard dismissal of gifts he did not want. Colourful plastic cutlery brought round by his social workers? Téo said it had all been refused by Joel and banished to a cupboard for the high crime of being "too baby." Same as donated items of clothing that had stars on them or moons, any clothes, Téo explained, with patterns that bigged up bedtime. Ben enjoyed hearing this. He drew in quick amused sniffs to show that he understood, he got it, childcare was a trial, toddlers were capricious, Joel had his chaos streak, it was natural.

The trampoline they chose came boxed, with what sounded like a billion pieces rattling loose inside. You had to assemble it yourself at home. Ben felt like a parent in an ad pushing this box around, the more so when Téo nosed the air, wincing, and dashed away with Joel to the car park, needing somewhere private to change a nappy. He heard Téo ask the kid, "Will this be a big one?"

"Mm-hm," Joel confirmed.

"Big as yesterday's?"

"What's yesterdays?"

After paying, Ben took the box out to the car. Téo's sporty hatchback was easily found, being the only car with its fog lights blazing, indicators on, the wipers squeaking and wheezing against a dry windscreen. As Ben approached, Joel buzzed open an electric window as if in primitive greeting. He was standing on the front seat in reach of the steering wheel and the best buttons. Téo was letting Joel "drive," distracting him like this while he ministered to a filthy backside.

Ben saw: a heap of wadded tissues on the ground and a fresh and abandoned-looking nappy, twisted out of shape, its application not a success. Téo held another new nappy in hand. A third one, its absorbent material yellow and engorged, had been balled and left on the passenger seat. Ben's seat.

He put down the big box. He hugged it beside him and he tried not to stare. "Or," said Téo, without turning, "you could help me."

"Repeat that?"

"You could collect up some of the rubbish."

"I'm looking after this," Ben said.

They were finished. Joel was wearing his tracksuit again and Téo was gathering the mess. While he went off to find a bin, Ben put the box in the back of the car. He bent to inspect his seat, freshening its surface with sweeps of a pulled-up sleeve. He sat and he reached for the lever beneath, croaking his seat backwards on its runners as far as it would go.

"Hey, be careful," said Téo.

Joel was seated behind. Ben turned to see the kid, buckled tight back there like some dangerous patient. He asked Joel out of curiosity: "Where did you drive the car just then, when you had the chance?"

"Africa."

Ben blinked. "You made it all the way to Africa and back?"

"YES."

"That's superb. It's a world record."

Ben showed the kid how to bump him on the fist to celebrate. Then he let his attention return to the dashboard for a time, the music choices, the air settings. Trampoline purchased and stashed, Ben wouldn't've minded sneaking away home in truth. Given a free choice? His preference would have been a nap and afterwards a heap of fried food. Here was Téo though—alert to possible shirking. Quickly Ben found himself locked into a verbal agreement to help them build the trampoline when they got to Vic's. A two-man job, the box reckoned. Téo's dad was no longer up to such feats.

Ben yawned. He had this image of Mister Erskine, years ago, twisting apart an apple with his hands for their amusement. Ben let his eyes close, pondering the body and how it should be used as much as possible before it started on the betrayals. He was shoved. His head bumped against the window. "What, what."

"You'll be snoring as well in a sec."

"I'm fragile is all," Ben sighed. With his hand he made a movement over his shoulder as if to say: it's last night's fault.

Téo said, "Ben went to bed late."

"Maybe is," Joel guessed, "Africa?"

"Africa's *far*," Téo said, "three a.m.'s late. Especially if you've promised to meet your friends in the morning. Especially if you've got a difficult day of DIY ahead."

"I'm ready," Ben said, "point me at any trampoline you want built."

Irritated by Téo's provocations, he was tempted to ask, but seriously, who d'you think paid off the parking fines on this car? Who do you think took care of the tickets that racked up when you left it abandoned outside my house for three days on end? Ben was glad he'd covered those costs: for a mate. But in with the gladness came this image of Téo finding out eventually and regretting anything critical he'd ever thought or said about Benjamin Mossam.

The Erskine home was ex-council. They had the garden flat in a block that was built for the neighbourhood's returning war heroes, whichever of the main wars that was, whichever set of heroes . . . Vic would have told them when they were schoolboys. Grunting out of deference to a parent's lecture (mostly wanting him to finish up telling them the history of his building and be quiet), Ben and the others in the group used to play computer games in Téo's front room. The room was low-ceilinged and cramped, on account of being modelled for those soldiers in the olden days, serious short-arses, Ben presumed, given some of the interior dimensions, the burrow-like corridors, the door-jambs tight around your shoulders, lightbulbs forever clocking you on the head. Téo's bedroom might have beaten out Ben's bed for scale. But not by much. Due to ancient habit neither of them mentioned these disparities.

Honestly, in their school days, Ben often felt a relief in the transition between his own home and Téo's. He liked to leave the pearly, carpeted, mum-fragrant mansion, hoovered and dusted with zeal by a small land-force of cleaners, and instead flop about with his shoes on at the Erskines' where there was no mum and no white furniture, where it was fine to fart, drink direct from a can, smoke the odd cigarette inside. Frayed rugs covered the floors. Cream paint chinked apart in hairline fractures on the walls and every faint crater betrayed a place where the door knobs bumped.

Joel kept close to Ben when they got inside. He wanted to play the tour guide, somebody who knew this property's enviable features. "Is my room," he was saying. "Is Vic's room. Is go toilet."

"And where's the sofa?"

"Sofa . . ." Joel said, prepared to reveal the information but needing a minute.

"It's through here, isn't it?"

Ben sat down in front of the TV, in reach of Téo's old games console. Out of habit he powered it on and handed one of the controllers to Téo. He hesitated, about to hand a controller to Joel as well. The kid would be, what, too young to get the gist?

"I play, I play," Joel insisted.

He sounded as if he was expecting to be refused and because Ben took pleasure in surprising people, he said: "Oh deffo. I could use you as my teammate." He lifted Joel off the carpet and placed him on his lap. "No fidgeting though. I'm serious or you'll cost me points."

Controllers clacked. Ben and Téo made quick administrative decisions on the games that loaded. There was simulated martial arts, a game they hadn't played together in a decade. Torturing the moulded plastic controllers, they competed in silence. Martial arts was the warm-up. Ben waited for Téo to load the next game. Loser's choice. Trading victories and defeats, they advanced through bouts of car racing, sniper murder, tank murder, ice hockey, go-karts, the competitions absorbing them and making Ben's jaw ache from clenching.

"Swap controllers next round," Téo complained. "Mine's broken, must be."

"See that?" Ben asked the room. "Did you see that win?"

Both of them kept a table of victories and defeats in their heads and not until this league was robust enough to provide answers about superiority did they let themselves talk about luck. "Nothing's going for me today," Téo said.

"Don't call this flukey."

"I'm on a nightmare run here, Joel."

"Did you see what I did there, Joel?"

There was a hiding place behind the normal minutes, a place that a hectic mind like Ben's could only reach when absorbed in something fixed and fake like this, something that had achievements to count, the messes to make, and none of that real-world necessity to clean up afterwards. Their rivalry pinned time to the wall, deleting a truer chronology so that Ben and Téo might've been twelve years old again, beardless, their voices high and unformed. They used to play the same games and repeat the same taunts and complaints when they were boys on the cusp. They had a plan. They would move to the city together and share a flat near the river. Then the words out of their mouths started to tumble down in pitch. Adulthood came and with it jobs, geography, Lia, all sorts of things that intervened.

They were playing at medieval duelling. Téo enjoyed two wins in a row. "Because," he protested, "it's about time." They both asked Joel, could he believe what he was witnessing? These skills? The vibe between Ben and Téo, which had moved from affection to hostility and back since the morning, was ambiguous again. The day might go either way. Before they played a clinching bout (and all square on points), they paused so that Téo could take Joel for another nappy change.

Left alone and hoping to distract his friend before the final contest, Ben had the amusing idea to lay out the receipts for those parking tickets.

"What's this?" Téo asked, returning.

"No big deal," said Ben.

"Oh. I see. Must have cost you a bit?"

"It was nothing."

Téo was always talking about things costing a bit.

"We'll settle up before you leave."

Ben said no. "There's nothing to settle."

"I've got the money on me."

"Do what you like," shrugged Ben. To be honest the joke

hadn't been worth it. He was relieved when their talk turned functional and snipped again. They focused on the game, simulated skateboarding. Ben removed Joel from his lap, better to concentrate. Joel complained and Ben shushed him. He played soberly, direly, the emotions tamped for one last push.

"Yes-s-s," said Téo at last. They both let their controllers fall to the floor.

Ben must have let slip a swear word because here was Joel reading him the rap sheet and reminding him about forbidden language. "Chill," Ben said, "chill with that. Before it becomes a habit. You'll start to annoy people." Joel looked hurt, so Ben explained, "I'm trying to help you. Nobody likes an accountant."

"Let's build this trampoline," Téo said.

They rocked and they rose to their feet.

Something: the vibe: it was perhaps the gaming or Joel's sulk. The day had soured after all.

Ben watched Téo unpack the trampoline with loathing. Before he would let them touch any of the pieces, Téo insisted on laying out the book of instructions, flattening its pages with spruce little movements of his fist and settling down on his knees to read it out loud. Backflips were forbidden on the trampoline, he reported. Somersaults too. The page that Téo was reading with such care, Ben saw, came under the general heading of HAZARDS. The world made room for every type of man, he thought.

As for Ben, he tried to be someone who let his gut advise. He had a way of understanding shapes and connections and this was why he knew how to send through a pass on a football pitch or overarm a crumpled piece of paper into a bin. He knew how to alter the line of his body so that it made the most impact whenever he entered a room. He had a feel for patterns, fit. Téo only trusted what was written down.

Joel, as if cued, waddled over to them on the lawn and he let them know he was ready for them to start making the trampoline now. "Such a long time," he was saying, "such a too-long time."

"Got to be patient," Téo advised.

"Till next year at this rate," said Ben. He had squatted on the grass himself. He had lit himself a cigarette. With the butt of it chomped lazily between his side-teeth, Ben took a closer look at these pieces of the trampoline. In any order, picking up whatever he found, rails, limbs, large steel plates, he wondered what might be done, how they might fit together.

"Slow down," Téo complained. He had his nose in the instructions still, as if this booklet was a more-ish novel.

"Nope," said Ben, "nope."

One by one he pulled a dozen steel springs from the bottom of the box, each spring about the size of a cigar. He pulled out bolts, washers, screws, all of them wrapped in polythene bags. Everything seemed reasonable. A certainty took hold of Ben and he ventured to think he could wing this in fact. He slotted a length of rail into one of the steel limbs. He deduced which size bolt was needed to secure it, then which washer, then which nut. As expected: a cinch.

"Now, Joel. Something I've learned about instruction manuals . . ."

"Don't," interrupted Téo, "not your world-wisdom, please."

"Different people, different approach."

"You'll never get it done with your approach."

Time would have to tell. Ben carried on with his method and at the same time he monitored Téo's opposition effort across the lawn. Cross-checking against the instructions, Téo marshalled his pieces into order, arranging a flatter version of the trampoline on the grass. Sometimes he stepped away, hand under his chin, to consider a bigger picture. Ben in his mounting annoyance about this was forced to hoard some of the pieces he'd grabbed at random, pieces which didn't seem so important to the overall effort but which Téo soon came enquiring about. "You seen that support strut, the square one?"

"A *support* strut . . ."

Ben frowned.

"It's there. On top of your secret pile."

"Oh the *strut,*" Ben said. He did toss it over.

"Cheat," Téo said.

"Prick."

"Cunt," he mumbled.

"Cunt," Ben mumbled back.

It was the same at school. Téo finger-reading a textbook, randy for method, while Ben dead-reckoned past him to the end of a task. They both got on well with their teachers. They were about as clever as one another. When it came to the younger men on the staff there was no competition, Ben was the favourite, Ben was elite, a corridor king, because he was the player who made the most telling and dramatic contributions to school football matches. They were both in the first eleven, Téo a defensive midfielder, Ben a striker and their star man. Téo approached a football match how he approached many things, going crabbily about an assignment, obedient to orders and pleased enough by marginal achievements: a useful tackle, the pass-before-the-pass. He would sit in the changing room after, tallying these meagre contributions. If Téo was unable to play for any reason they substituted in another player and that was that; it hardly mattered whether he was present on the field or not.

Ben Mossam though. Your Bens of this world! The Ben Mossams could not be replaced. Ben answered to an invisible muse. He didn't care what a teacher in charge had advised him beforehand; he went freelance as a footballer, he was a warrior and a poet out there, he played from his second brain, he couldn't have explained it any better than that. Inexplicable, he thought again, that Téo should have been the one who left the neighbourhood to live in town. Ben always thought they had an agreement, they would do it together, dominate central London as they'd dominated the suburbs, Téo with his caution, allied to Ben and his purer flair. He had received a text one day. Téo was moving on by himself. The rest of the friends in their group were no use when it came to talking about this defection. Ben stewed on it in private for months. The better part of a year went by before he and Téo even spoke. Lia Woods was the only one in Enfield who understood why Ben was so eaten up, who understood what it meant to be left behind.

"I'll get us drinks," Téo said. The cartilage in both his knees popped as he stood. He'd put a lot of the trampoline together by himself, beetling forward in typical fashion while Ben sat and daydreamed. The structure was now about the height of a bed and sorely tempting for somebody tired and hungover. As Téo went inside he warned Ben, "Don't climb on it while I'm gone."

"Is dangerous?" Joel asked, when they were alone.

"Nah."

To prove it Ben walked over to the half-assembled trampoline and had a closer look. Tentatively he climbed on and lay down, the mat yielding pleasantly to his shape. "Totally fine," he said. He took out another cigarette and he lit it, supine, blowing a tidy lance of smoke at the sky. "Thing is," he said, "grown-ups get to decide these things for themselves."

Joel was waiting at the rim of the trampoline, his arms raised, expecting to be lifted on board as well. Ben did as requested.

They lay beside each other on the mat, ear to ear, Ben careful to direct his smoke out of the far side of his mouth. When he rested his cig hand he did so at a remove, his fingers over the edge of the trampoline so that any ash would fall on to the grass. Once or twice the structure did creak beneath them. But they were fine; Ben had said so.

Joel put his thumb in his mouth and he made noisy metronomic tut-tut sounds as he sucked on it. He had his belly against Ben's arm. Ben could feel the kid's pulse, the young lungs and heart toiling away at an immense pace.

Joel removed his thumb. He complained, this trampoline, it wasn't meant for crying. Ben apologised. He took a needed drag on his cig and said, "It's maybe that I'm upset about your mum, more than I realised." He added, "You know what I mean? Like, the magnitude."

"Mama's go drive," Joel explained. "To Africa. Mama's come back."

"Nah," Ben replied.

There was no point bullshitting him. Grown-ups got to decide these things.

"Mama's gone Africa," Joel repeated.

Ben said, "No, she's dead. That means never seeing her. It means we won't have her around to talk to any more, we won't have her around to be teased by, or to impress, not ever. It's the truth I'm telling you. She's gone. It's forever. You might as well hear this from someb——"

There was a fuss. Joel flinched, one electric quiver that seemed to lap down his body like a wave. He shrank from Ben's side. In a hurry about it, he tried to roll himself over the trampoline and in his agitation he brought the whole thing off its balance. The trampoline swayed and tipped, flattening beneath them.

For a moment Ben was dazed and unsure what had happened. There were shouts and Téo was outside again, brought running. He comforted Joel. The kid was hysterical. In these moments of other people's overreaction Ben had learned to stay still, stay where he was, wait for it all to move on somewhere else without him. Half the trampoline remained upright on its legs, forming a sort of pallet that he could lie against. He bit a fresh cigarette out of his packet and got it alight with cross-eyed and cupped-fingered care. He brought his shoulder up to cover one ear. Joel's crying was loud.

As expected, Ben got the telling-off from Téo, who spoke as if they'd all decided something in consultation. "You need to leave."

"Yeah," he said. He stood as gracefully as he could manage in the circumstances. He didn't attempt a defence, not even when Téo said a second time, leave.

FOUR

SIBYL

Enfield was old. Local people said so. Punishment stocks were preserved on neighbourhood greens and certain noble buildings were admired as though they were the rings inside trees, firm proof of endurance. The peaceful dozing branch of a national bank, for instance—that had been a 1930s music hall, a place of music, glamour, bustle, though scarcely anybody alive could attest to the fact. The building next door was erected in the year that the Light Brigade charged, when cholera was still in the streets. A betting shop now, you could see the initials of the building's Victorian architect preserved in its brickwork. On the pavement outside, modern metal arches were ringed with disavowed bicycle locks. Orange fencing had been dragged into the road and weighed down with sandbags, to keep pedestrians away from a mechanical digger that took lumps from the surface asphalt, getting at clay. Construction workers were laying cables. Somebody had found a china pipe, centuries old, broken into pieces by the pressure of all that earth and all that time. The local newspaper printed a photograph. Sibyl Challis, doing her duty as a rabbi in the borough, new enough to want to impress, had studied up on all of this.

It was a Friday.

With an hour to herself, Sibyl walked a mile or so away from the synagogue, revising this part of Enfield, swotting up. She recognised many of the faces of her congregants as she went. She wasn't off-book yet with their names. The sky was striped today like a toothpaste, the colours perverse, bands of blue-seeming cloud obscuring a clotted beige behind.

She passed a shop for karate supplies, its display dummies poised to fight, then crabs, live ones, making slow drugged pleas for clemency against a fishmonger's window. She turned around and went back, this particular road manifestly more Jewish the closer she got to shul. There was a bakery selling the dainties, those hard and sweet biscuits that were tied in knots before they were put in the oven, the loaves of challah that shook off poppy-seeds and left a trail wherever they were carried. She passed a falafel bar where they broadcast Israeli sport, then a bric-à-brac emporium that had brass menorahs on display. The second-hand bookshop had some Jewish-interest titles in the window. One caught her eye, WHAT MAKES A JEW?

Here was the synagogue road. Trees were venturing into colour and one of them had come fully alive before the rest. It bloomed with porky white and pink petals. Sibyl didn't know its name but when she was near enough she stroked the tree's gnarled trunk, glancing up and offering her thanks. In the dis-tance, a shop's waterproof awning (its hem made to ripple in the breeze) shook off a morning's worth of rain, ten or twenty drops at a time. Faith was most palpable to Sibyl when articulated in the form of her gratitude. She retained a playground sense of justice that a compliment, where honestly expressed, ought to be heard and acknowledged. She stood with her hand on the textured trunk of the blossoming tree and she waited. It wasn't a voice she waited for, more an answering twinge. There used to be a sense of some completed and satisfactory exchange. Sibyl felt nothing. Which would have to be okay. As she had often told her congregants in times of their own distress, fortitude, patience.

She said hello, hello, how are you to the congregants who passed on the road. She took care to walk with her shoulders back, part of a rabbinical metamorphosis after many years of slouching. That day, with bands and clips, Sibyl had tamped down the enormity . . . the *project* of her hair. She wasn't ready to surrender to the frumps on the leadership committee who expected her to cut it. Before moving to take the job at Enfield Progressive she bought a wardrobe's worth of shirts in drab, non-frightening colours. Through the winter she wore a robed coat that had no cuffs, no belt, no decorative flourishes whatsoever. When she dressed each morning in her residence behind the synagogue, she stood in front of a mirror and asked herself, would my sisters wear this? Would I have dressed this way myself, fifteen years ago, teaching every day? Any sort of answer in the affirmative and she skulked again to her wardrobe.

The hair, the bloody hair. Sibyl used to think she looked quite good wearing big sunglasses to balance it out. That was not a practical way to live. In those days, her teens and the start of her twenties, she stared into mirrors and rated herself a Nearly. Some time teaching squashed even this moderate amount of vanity. On the staff of a London secondary school, you were best not being noticed, neither above nor below the middle rank. Today, at forty, she was a glancer when it came to mirrors. She did not fancy herself or loathe what she saw, she only cared to be credible out of doors and she hoped that the impression made was neutral, no more likely to attract than repel. She had learned that to go about the neighbourhood as their rabbi asked for impractical blends of qualities, qualities that contradicted each other. Sibyl was meant to have confidence in buckets and also humility, nerve and circumspection. She was to be interested in her congregants' smaller problems while counselling them to think of larger matters. She was supposed to be nosy and confidential. She was supposed to pry just enough but never too far. If she investigated her own faith she could not afford to degrade that faith. Her favourite congregant was dead and there was nobody she could talk to about it, apparently not even God.

<hr>

At the next morning's service she stood on the bimah and she looked out at her congregants. They had embarked on a hymn about the unity of prayer. They belted out its chorus in Hebrew. Behold! they sang. How pleasing! This expression! They sang with most gusto from the front row that stretched the width of the synagogue sanctuary, a dozen chairs, an aisle, then another dozen chairs. This pattern repeated itself many times to the double doors at the back.

People took the same seats every week. There was nothing Sibyl could do about it. She had come to understand a rule, predating her tenure, that the closer a congregant sat to the raised central bimah the more important to Enfield Progressive they imagined themselves to be. Because of this, most members of the leadership committee sat in her line of sight. Hymns were a chance for them to have the louder say.

How pleasing!

This expression!

Prayer book clasped over her stomach, Sibyl closed her eyes. She tried asking, "Are we going to communicate this week at all?" After hymns she delivered a sermon, then there were house-keeping announcements, times agreed for music rehearsals, Torah study, charity gatherings. When Sibyl stepped away and ceded the microphone to a reader from the congregation, she kept watch on the starrier families in row one, the doctors, teachers and law-yers, the broadcasters, ad makers and estate agents. Quite a few were present when she was interviewed for her job. Sibyl had been invited into some of their homes, handed pieces of sugar-dusted stollen and cups of Earl Grey tea. Some members of the leadership committee had made it clear to her that even though they wouldn't dream of missing services they had not made a complete sub-mission to faith. They were proud of their secular hesitations. Sibyl was told in confidence that her selection as rabbi, against a field of more experienced candidates, was the consummation of a war between the reform-minded members of the committee and those who wanted to make the synagogue a more stringent observant place altogether.

The choice of Sibyl was a victory for the reformers. They'd noticed the dwindling numbers at Friday and Saturday services. They hoped a more youthful rabbi would use her probation-ary year to attract a broader membership. Energise us, they told Sibyl. Don't be afraid to shake things up! She'd been on probation for six months. Her ongoing employment would be reassessed in time.

Now she squinted out beyond the front rows to the middle seats, then to those who captured her imagination in particu-lar, the congregants who always hid at the back. Why not come closer, she asked them, whenever she could snag one in conversa-tion; why surrender the front to the grandees? She learned that many of the back-row congregants shared a concern. They did not consider themselves real or proper Jews.

"What is a real Jew?" Sibyl had asked them, one by one. "What *is* a proper Jew?"

They shrugged, helpless. "The mum business. The mum thing."

"Then your mother isn't Jewish. But does that affect how you feel about God?"

"No . . . I don't think so . . . I guess not."

Sibyl asked them all, "Don't you feel Jewish?"

"Yes . . . Sometimes . . . I feel I want to come here."

She was fascinated by these congregants, some of whom had journeyed over universes to get to Enfield Progressive, starting out as members of other faiths, coming in from atheism, some of whom were rediscovering a Jewish heritage presumed lost. She looked to those at the back today and she picked out one empty seat in particular.

How flattered Sibyl had been when Lia sought her out in the residence. This happened late last year. Sibyl was in her study, books in piles around her, computer cables snaking between her mugs and chocolate wrappers. It was to appeal to the Lias of the neighbourhood that she had been appointed; it was the Lias she had in mind when she spent hours in her study, honing scripts. When Lia knocked and entered, Sibyl did some hurried clearing.

They got talking. Sibyl fancied she understood what the matter was. She supposed she was being asked for the normal assurances. And what a relief. She rolled out some standard sentences about religious doubt. "No, not religious doubt," Lia said.

Sibyl suggested it as a starting place. "If we tackle those doubts, we might find we solve other difficulties."

Lia sat in silence for a moment. At first Sibyl interpreted this as her agreement, a willingness to try. In fact, Lia was only disappointed. She let out a sigh and she asked herself, "What am I even doing here?"

"Please. Don't go. If I've said the wrong thing, it's because . . . it's because I'm only guessing. I'm making this up."

Later, when Lia was a regular visitor to the residence, she

quoted back this statement to Sibyl. She said it persuaded her. "That you would admit you were only guessing as well." They started to meet at the same time each week. Lia would come as soon as she'd dropped off her son at nursery. Sibyl did not try to put any more frames around their conversations. She made strong teas. She posed questions that were led by her curiosity. She hoped to understand Lia's unhappiness, figuring they had the time they would need. As though she were a therapist or a person on the radio, Sibyl kept asking: "Can you explain that? Can you tell me how that makes you feel?"

"It makes me feel I'll be a bad example to my son. That maybe I'm already harming him in ways I don't want to."

"You're his mother. You love him. How can that be a harmful example?"

"He copies me. He learns from me. He'll learn this other part of me too."

"Then what? So what if he does?"

"I'm his mum. I'm not supposed to let the bad stuff in, I'm not meant to be passive, not if I can protect him."

"You come here. You discuss your anxieties with me. I don't call that passive."

"I wake up, rabbi, I feel empty about the world. And there are days I let Joel see how empty I am. I can't help it. He shouldn't have to have a parent like that. He should have one like you, a parent who believes in something, who's sure."

"Sure of what?"

"That there's a point to it all."

"We're back at religion."

"Mm."

They smiled at each other. They did sometimes.

"Well done you," said Lia.

"I'm innocent. I promise. The subject found us."

"Bet it did."

Sibyl was at her desk when she learned of Lia's death. The news reached her as an enquiry. The social workers who were assigned to think of Joel's continuing care—they were aware that Lia was a member at Enfield Progressive. She hadn't left any instructions, they said. Would Sibyl advise? Would Sibyl handle the funeral? She decided not to say anything about the weekly meetings. These had been confidential in life. On the day of Lia's funeral Sibyl got out of bed and showered. She contained her hair with clasps, all the while noticing, trying *not* to notice, a flatness of feeling, an absence between her collarbones and her spine. She pleaded with Him, "Don't do this to me, don't go quiet on me today."

The service was over. Sibyl shook hands with everybody who lingered in the sanctuary. She felt herself scrutinised, peered into by some of the members of the leadership committee. She drew her robes closer around her throat and reminded herself it was only their job, they were trying to judge how well she was doing. When the sanctuary was empty, Sibyl walked the thick-carpeted tributaries that led around to the back. She had to cross a court-yard to get to the residence and her study.

Sibyl had amassed quite a collection of left-behind possessions during her six months in charge. Now she brought out this box of lost property, placing it on her desk and picking through the items with care. There was an umbrella in its sleeve. A patterned spectacles case. There was a silk scarf that carried the smell of an intense, stifling perfume. Eventually she found what she was looking for: a paperback novel, one inch thick, that Lia had left behind after a visit. This book must have been a favourite, Sibyl judged, considering the ruin of its spine. The cover was tea-stained front and back. Tucked between its crinkled pages she had found receipts, bus tickets, also photographs, including two of Lia's son. In the first photo he was a baby, round and wet-chinned. In the second (captured earlier in grainy monochrome) he was smaller, only a germ inside Lia's body. She had written on the back of the scan, "20 weeks." Sibyl meant to return the pictures to Joel Woods in time.

He was living with the Erskine family for the moment. Sibyl knew the father, Victor; he attended every Saturday. She had got to know the son a little as well. Asked to sit in on meetings with Joel's social workers, she sometimes felt like an umpire or ombudsman, invited along to make sure that everyone understood what they were agreeing to. Téo Erskine had passed an initial assessment and afterwards been classified as what the social workers called a connected carer, somebody who might look after Joel for a few weeks or even for a few months while a permanent guardian was sought. "This is to get us through to the end of the summer," the social workers had said to Téo.

"All right," he had said, glancing at Sibyl as if to ask, *is* it all right, will I be all right?

She nodded, trying to encourage him. The social workers continued, "Then we'll reassess. The most important person in this is Joel. We have to help him find his feet. We have to make him feel safe."

"Yeah," Téo had said.

"Meanwhile we have to make a reasonable effort to locate his father."

"And if you can't find him?"

"We're exploring every option."

"Like a foster parent? Or someone to adopt?"

"Maybe."

"Here, in Enfield?"

"We're exploring every option."

Now, in the quiet of her study, Sibyl touched her fingers to each of the photographs of Joel, wishing the best for him, wishing him plain pagan good fortune.

Tactfully ignoring the fiat not to pursue too strenuous an activity on the sabbath, her congregants went off to swim in the neighbourhood pool after Saturday services. Or they drove around the North Circular Road to show up and support one of the nearby football teams. Sibyl herself took a practical attitude towards Saturday afternoons: practical meaning, in her case, she allowed herself some honest leisure and she was discreet about it. Her favourite thing was to duck into the darkness and anonymity of a neighbourhood cinema.

When she first moved to Enfield this cinema was a fertile place for her, somewhere to sit and pray and commune. The less plausible the film the better. Blockbusters were excellent: heroes and bangs, the works. She would sit amid the hectic action and mutter about inconsistencies, outrages, shoddy dialogue, relishing the swells and heart-pips and spine-runs that might have been responses to the movie or proof of spiritual rapport. Though part of a chain, her cinema was an uncared-for satellite, the lettering outside bleached and jaded. The plastered front of the building was so discoloured by soot that if not for an employee rotating the film posters on display she might have thought it abandoned. She chose between the silliest films, cross-checking run lengths and programme starts, adjusting for adverts and trailers, trying to keep one step ahead of the benign lie that was cinema timekeeping. She picked through the blackness of the theatre to find her seat.

This afternoon's film had a couple of warring hard men. There wasn't much else in the way of a story, just the main rivals taking interesting liberties with historic landmarks in whichever city they happened to visit next. After laying waste to half a dozen European capitals, they arrived in London. "Oh dear," Sibyl said, watching St. Paul's Cathedral go. The cinema was empty. She could speak out loud. "Dear oh dear."

Does it irk you, as much as it irks me, she thought, when a film fails to establish whether or not its characters have celestial powers? Extra strength? Immunity from wounds? Perfect judgement? It was almost over anyway. Sibyl fidgeted through a clinching kiss then the exaggerations of the music as the surviving characters stared at each other, pleased. When the credits came she put on her coat. She'd no plans.

These silences pass, they do pass, she promised herself. Outside she found comfort in the high street, its sensible clockwork order on a weekend afternoon. Behind a trestle table a fruit-and-veg man took instruction from queueing customers. His produce was neatly grouped into basins of opaque plastic. He ballooned each carrier bag before filling it, like someone trying to catch and keep the air itself. A lorry bringing ice had stopped outside one of the restaurants. Passing the bookshop again, Sibyl noticed that title, WHAT MAKES A JEW? She would say to those who came to see her, "Join me in an experiment, will you? Put aside blood. Put aside belief. Ask yourself: are we your people?" She meant, does the oxygen breathe well in shul, do you have a taste for the humour, do you delight in the meals, the vowels, are you warmed by the songs? Pressed to admit her most extravagant ambitions for Enfield Progressive, she would say that she hoped to make it a place that took in gut Jews, Jews who would not be recognised as Jewish anywhere else, Jews by deed and affinity, those who only felt an inexplicable conviction they belonged.

She had always meant to prioritise the ground-level aspects of this job. During training she saw herself as a pavement rabbi, a teatime rabbi, someone who would be there in a room should people visit. She had mislaid something since Lia's death, a means of fluid communication with God. She would have to wait and hope that returned. Until then, Sibyl decided, she would pour her energies into the parts of the job that were tangible, here, in front of her. She had love to spare. Only fair this surplus should go to her congregants, to her neighbours, to these hundreds of strangers out on the road. One of them, a pub landlord, wheeled around a bottle bin that gobbled and clinked. Dogs were led towards the park by their owners. A group of young men walked by wearing football scarves. Over by the Jewish bakery she thought she saw Téo Erskine. He stepped aside and there beside him—yes—was little Joel.

Both looked frayed.

They looked appalled by each other, perhaps at the middle point of a quarrel which the buying of baked goods was supposed to resolve.

A bus drove by, shuddering and spewing compressed air as its rear doors folded open. Shoppers closed around the scene, blocking the pair from Sibyl's view. She would telephone, she decided. As soon as she got back to the residence she would call them, she would ask, are you there today, can I visit?

FIVE
TÉO

The boy never climbed down from height how Téo begged him to—not if he could drop his weight on to a cushion or a mattress and bounce wherever the shocking physics took him. In rooms, as in playgrounds, as in parks, the most difficult descent was Joel's way. Now he stepped off the arm of the sofa and he crumpled on to the front-room carpet.

"You okay? You hurt?"

"I fine. Stop *ask*ing."

Téo went upstairs to run a bath. As he aimed the liquid bubbles into the water he revised his list, his next moves, how Joel would have to be persuaded out of clothes and into the tub, then fought back out of the tub right when he was comfortable and prepared to linger. He would have to be put in pyjamas. Soon as the bedroom lights were dimmed, Joel would complain, as if privy to a scam, that Téo had not read him the agreed amount of stories. Téo would go back and forth, back and forth, fetching water, tissues. Finally Joel would agree to the lights being lowered until they were nearly off. That was the good part of the evening.

Overnights were terrible. At night, nothing Téo tried made a difference. Hour after hour Joel sat awake, sometimes with his face between his knees and rocking from side to side to register refusals of milk, another story, warmer pyjamas or a cooler pair, some late-night toast, whatever Téo's wearying imagination could think of. And was it that same imagination playing tricks or did Joel smell different at night: even sour? His throat had to be hurting him. His hands. There had been shouting and lashings-out. The detail of what Joel said was sometimes roughed away, except when he aimed at Téo those four same words, spaced for clarity: "I don't want you."

They would be past a reasonable bedtime. Joel would stiffen the muscles of his neck.

"I don't WANT you."

During their long lunar nights together, Téo dwelled on alternative timelines. He parachuted other people into their situation, trialling mates, colleagues, film stars, footballers, anybody who might be managing the scenario better, maybe relishing it as a test. Because. Weren't people supposed to rise to occasions or something? Become their own better versions? Téo wondered when he could expect that transformation, the hero dawn. Joel needed him to be someone with coping in their bones.

"Don't want you," the boy said again. This was on a weekend, a Saturday in the second week of April. Joel had been with the Erskines a fortnight. And here was Victor coming into his bedroom as well, prepared to make matters worse. In his flannel pyjamas, his battered slippers, Victor had started to haunt the landing outside Joel's room, waiting to be asked for his advice. He clomped about and muttered, eager for it to be understood that old Vic Erskine, father-of-one, and a man of some experience, had been through all this before. He fancied he'd held on to some small knowledge about how to deal with a child who would not sleep.

"Go nuts," said Téo at last. He stood aside and let Victor have a turn.

The daydreaming was getting out of control. Téo imagined climbing into his car and gunning it south to his empty flat by the river. He had walls of his own there, modern appliances, he had subscriptions to three expensive magazines. Along the communal corridors, staggered fire doors slurped open like the decompression chambers in underwater-explorer films. Entry was electronic. You were admitted everywhere with the two-tone sound of robotic welcome (*Buh*-BLINK) or else denied with a sceptical *Ner-r-r-r*. Téo's flat was on one of the corners. He could see a part of the Thames, a silvery fragment that meant everything.

Now he listened to Victor and the boy talking in the bedroom. Apparently Victor was going after plain talk—honest, macho stuff. Téo had to wonder what sustained it, this gruff generational confidence that older men carried around with them. They were sure that their attention and some sharp common sense could solve any problem the world had to offer. Téo waited. Before long Victor left the room in a huff, his efforts at persuasion a failure. Victor's feelings were hurt. So that night there would be two wounded boys to comfort.

Sometimes, around 4 a.m., the worst of Joel's dreams brought him up on his knees in bed. He protested. He groaned. Blanket shaken off, his waterlogged nappy sagging towards the mattress like a paunch, he turned his damp head as if in refusal of a bad idea. He said, "No. No." He said, "Is mine." He said, "A tiny *bit*." By getting it wrong, night after night, Téo learned how to help Joel through. It was not a winnable contest, you with your adult pragmatism, your thirty-year-old's smarts—not against the seductive technicolour range of a little boy dreaming, a boy more fluent and more suave in his dreams, allowed to handle truths there that were normally kept out of reach. Kneeling on the bed in the dark, Joel was unreachable. He could not be comforted with logic. You couldn't persuade him away from whatever scene it was that had seemed so real to him a moment ago. He could only be shushed or murmured at with nonsense, met on his own murky terms. He seemed to respond to being hummed to. He relaxed when you rubbed his back or his forehead. Without warning Joel's body would loosen and turn floppy; buckling, he would land down on his mattress for the only escape from a disturbed sleep, which was more sleep.

These broken nights were a part of their routine. Téo accepted them and assumed they would last for however long the boy stayed in the Erskines' care. More disturbing, because rarer, were the moments in the middle of a day when Joel looked around the front room with apparent surprise, as though he was only now aware of where he was, as though he was measuring the dimensions of his situation with fresh eyes. He once asked, "Is dream?"

"No. This is real. You're awake. You're safe."

"Is wake?"

"You're safe."

After a while Joel said, "More some Mama."

"You want another story about her?"

He did. He specified: "More some Mama is small."

"Okay. Let me think of one from school. Er, have I told you about this time, we're young, and your mum's snuck into the teachers' staff room to have it out about a history mark . . . ?"

Joel nodded rapidly. Which in fact meant no, he hadn't been told this story; he had no idea about staff rooms or history marks. He *was* eager to hear about any person who snuck anywhere. And if the story involved his mother all the better.

Téo went through the high points with absent-minded dash, good at the details of this one. He had spent so much of his youth as a Lia fan, his area of expertise the version of her that existed in public view while they were at secondary school. In those days he collected attitudes of hers, expressions, postures. Years of futile hoarding seemed less shameful, even noble, since Joel had started asking for stories. Téo talked about Lia's maturity beyond her years and the thrill whenever that maturity cracked. He talked about how she was the naughtiest out of all of them. How Lia's position in the friendship group was to know more, the most.

Over the years she'd taught Téo so much. That in the scheme of things they were specks. But in small small ways they could matter. Lia showed him the easiest trick, that you only had to imagine yourself into another person's head, that you only had to think of wearing their skin for about thirty seconds . . . and there was empathy, there was insight. She might have taught him more, Téo realised. When he was about fifteen he got bogged down in really loving her. He stopped listening to Lia with care, instead, the appearance of care. Inside it was all burn and impatience. Something precious had been wasted. He said to Joel, "She was good your mum. My favourite. You wanted to be near her as often as possible, maximise exposure, whatever she'd allow. You hoped she would rub off."

Joel considered this. He tried to put what Téo had said in terms he could appreciate. "Mama is winner? Actually?"

"If you like. Yeah."

Sometimes, he felt like a keeper of her legend, a torch-holder type, he could enjoy some of the reflected glory that emboldens any disciple. Over time he became queasier: aware of a lack. He always told stories about Lia as a schoolgirl or a sixth-former or Lia in that swirl of rebellion after she messed up her exams. He realised how little he knew about her in the last years of her life. He had no stories about Lia as a parent. This became a heavier regret, that he'd turned away from her when she became pregnant and started out on a phase that didn't match up to his carefully assembled idea of her, that didn't involve him much at all. After Joel was born, some of their outlier mates tried being funny at Lia's expense; at Téo's expense really. There were muttered cruelties at poker or in the pub. Nothing these idiots would ever have dared try if Lia was present. They made jokes about who Joel resembled. This or that teacher from their old school, some actor off TV, an England footballer, even Ben Mossam. When Téo came back on his weekend visits he never rose to their provocations. He wouldn't be drawn. He was so busy not rising or being drawn, he had his guard up around the whole subject of Joel's parentage; he stopped being curious. Had to be some bloke. Someone who hadn't stuck around. Sad to think of Lia at home on her own with a baby, but Téo was never generous enough to wish her into a tidy family unit with anybody other than himself. Joel was Lia's son. Joel was Lia repeated, he was Lia again. And the thought of that, over time, became a comfort. It always suited him not to wonder about any sort of dad.

"More some Mama," said Joel.

It was a Tuesday in early May. A Thursday. Téo didn't always keep up. "I dunno," he said, "maybe we've done enough stories?"

"More some Mama is small."

"Will you tell me one instead?"

But Joel could only be silent at this request. It didn't track. Joel was the receiver of stories. That was their dynamic. That was Téo's entire point.

"What was she like when it was just you and her?"

Joel remained silent and afterwards, ashamed, Téo told him another story after all. He chose one about Lia in the playground, persuading the whole lot of them that her personal blessing would make them ten per cent better at football. They formed a queue.

"While I've got you," Téo said.

Joel's social workers were visiting. The rabbi was over as well.

"I think—I might be wrong, cos the nights are easier—but I think his nappies might be bugging him."

Joel was appalled by the fuss that followed. Summoned to the kitchen, asked to join in while Téo explained the problem again, Joel hid his face in the tea towels. They managed to tug open the crimped elasticated band of his imitation jeans, trying not to embarrass him. The older of the two social workers, Gil, the one who was on top of things and had the mad teeth—she had a look first. She explained to Téo that Joel only needed slightly larger nappies.

"There are sizes?"

"Yeah."

"I can buy some," said Rabbi Challis. "I'd like to. What size should I get?"

"What's he in now?"

"I don't know," Téo admitted. He went to the bathroom and he came back studying the packet. "How can he have changed sizes though? He's only been here five weeks."

"You'll have to keep an eye on his clothes as well."

"Ah . . . his clothes," said Téo. "I was starting to think I was getting the hang of this. Like a computer game."

"You are getting the hang of this."

"You both are. Baby steps."

And it was true, step by step, Joel was starting to settle. He seemed to submit to what was happening. "Forever" became a big word of his, there in the brain and brought out on every sort of occasion. He would live with Téo forever, he announced. He wanted to be served a forever amount of toast. Upstairs? The bathroom? That was forever away. "How long's that poo going to last," Téo asked him one day. Joel's answer made them all laugh for the first time in ages.

They'd been indoors too much, that was the problem. Rubbishy spring weather made it easy for them to choose to stay in. They ate. They napped. They read from Joel's growing pile of storybooks. Téo did not always have the energy to read aloud, sometimes only turning from picture to picture, waiting to get to the end. When they chatted before bedtime, Joel refused to take proper questions. He would not say how he was feeling. In Téo's mind he had become like one of those famous inscrutable figures in the public eye: an Olympian, caught-up-with on the evening bulletins or a prince on the cover of a newspaper. You wondered about their true minds and what the private motives were.

Téo was learning to speak another language of Joel's instead, the subtler language of his temper. When he threw a tantrum, because some puzzle or plastic brick of his would not cooperate? That normally meant he was hungry. Those sobs that seemed to rise out of his middle, from the stomach area, as though Joel's body had got confused and decided grief was something that could be sent to the gut for the piecing-apart? Téo understood this sort of crying meant that he was remembering his mum.

Two months had passed since she died. The time markers went by them in the flat without ceremony. They kept on with their reading and their games, with meals and telly. Téo kept extending his time off work. "Compassionate leave," he explained to his dad. Together they made it to June.

A whole night! reported Téo. No calling out. No bad dreams. "At least, no dreams that were bad enough to wake him."

Téo had lazed on his makeshift bed in the front room till 8 a.m. Somewhere in the back of his mind, while he dozed, he was aware of an unlikely sensation. He missed Joel. To be out of Joel's company during a clock-round sleep made Téo uneasy. Eventually he got up and took himself to the kitchen where he prepared a pot of strong, tarry coffee. Instead of sitting at the table with it, maximising the peace and space made available to him by Joel's epic conk-out, he took his coffee upstairs. He padded about with it on the landing.

"Tay-OH . . ."

Said with impatience. As if Joel had been majorly neglected in there.

"Yes, mate."

The bedroom had that fug after someone's long legitimate sleep, also a sharper smell—surely urine—that must've seeped out of Joel during the night. His cheeks were tattooed by the creases of a pillow. "I have a show-you thing," he said at once. Then he was out from under his covers and passing Téo at the door. He ran ahead to the stairs, fast-stepping them and gesturing for Téo to do the same. Back in the front room they sat on the floor together. They spent the morning in busy managerial patter as Joel outlined a plan to stage a new and more complicated civil war between his toys. The Viking barbarians: they would be declaring against the American commandos today. It was to be everything or nothing, a battle for the ages. Following Joel's specific instructions, Téo placed figures around the room, on sills, on Vic's mantelpiece, on arm rests, anywhere except the sofa itself. This, it transpired, was to be the scene of a climactic battle.

Joel ran his toy figures on training drills across the carpet. He wanted them scaling up and down the curtain cords. He launched them on grand slo-mo space leaps across the remote controls and Victor's landline phone. It was time for the sofa to be stripped, Joel ordered next. He wanted the cushions piled as high as they would go, this so that certain favoured figures of his could be positioned on top, leaving the rest at a tactical disadvantage. Afterwards, when the commandos had triumphed and the barbarians had sued for peace, Joel took himself to the kitchen to wait for his breakfast to be served.

"You must be hungry after so much playing."

"Thas right."

Said as though: but where's the fucking breakfast then?

Cereal boxes were lined up for his perusal. Joel pointed twice and Téo tipped some parched kernels and some sugary puffs into the same bowl. As the cereal rang and settled, Joel observed this procedure, ensuring the proportions were correct. He waited for the tidal slap of the milk then he ate as if under time-trial conditions, as if he were chasing a personal best.

"Chew. Chew," Téo begged. "You'll bring back that tummy ache, remember?"

Joel said through a mouthful, "Is favourite."

"Which ones, these ones? These were my favourite too . . . Oi, Joel, where you going?"

"More my mens."

Another routine developed. The mornings were for Joel's wars. They overturned the box of his figures as soon as he woke. He liked to arrange the toys into nimble fighting parties of four or five, their talents and weaknesses accounted for, the selections grave affairs. If Téo was going to interfere it had better be for a reason. "I've got a suggestion," he said one day.

It was decent outside. The weather was bright and appealing. Téo cleared his throat. "Why doesn't that strong guy" (he gestured which) "team up with the centaur today?"

Joel kept still.

He breathed through his nose, bringing Téo down a peg.

"No. You're probably right. We'll keep the strong guy with the one you've chosen, what-ja-ma-call-him."

"Leopard-boy," said Joel.

"So what's the thinking? The big toys and the small toys are working together?"

Joel shrugged. He had no time for these enquiries. He was always careful to spread around blatant advantages in size or strength. He had true-felt ideas about which of his figures were most skilled and which underpowered. So a muscle man, dressed pants-only, and with the sculpted body of a pillock at the gym—he had been grouped today with a wiry child wearing leopard clothes. Joel added to this team a pixie type with wings and a polar bear. "This team's for better," Joel said, "see?"

"Hey. I've got a different idea. Why don't we take these toys over to the park and play with them there?"

They were out of practice. The weeks of Joel's keenest knock-down tantrums had coincided with grey skies, with a spittley nuisance-rain that flecked the windows and obeyed none of the usual weather laws, travelling horizontally if it chose. He had reasoned, they weren't missing much. Staying inside seemed to relax Joel as well. Now it was June, fuller-bore summer, and there was no excuse. The trees were green as could be, deluxe; the pavement slabs were starting to waft off that seasonal smell, as though warmed enough by the sun they would surrender all the evidence of dropped drink and dog wee they'd soaked up through the winter and the spring.

In the kitchen, the tumble-dryer stopped churning and beeped, wanting emptying. Téo peeled out warm clothes. Washed, Joel's shorts had shrivelled in on themselves, like small or scared animals that needed coaxing to admit their real shape. Joel shouted through to the kitchen. He'd had an idea. They could go to the park.

"Oh yeah? You up for it?"

Joel said, "Quickly. Don't always be slow."

His jokes were rare. When they came they heaved in from a distance. Today Joel went ahead of Téo and stood by the door. With a frightening concentration that altered the shape of his face, he put his feet inside the wrong rubber sandals. Left for right. Right for left. He waited to be discovered like this, biting his lip.

Téo said, "Oh dear," and Joel laughed so much he had to lean against the wall.

"I wrong."

"We can fix it though."

"I wrong."

It wasn't far to the nearest park. Téo whisked them the cleverest route, showing off his insider knowledge of these Enfield roads. He demonstrated for Joel which of the pelican crossings answered quickest when you pushed the button; which took ages. He pointed out where you had to dodge the wing bones and the gristle on the pavement, this Hansel-and-Gretel trail of dropped chicken a legendary local feature because it was where the schoolboys always gathered after lessons to feast. They took in other sights. People's gym kits. Their haircuts. A supermarket had its auto-doors set to keen mode. Téo waited a while. Finally he had to drag Joel away. "You'll break them."

"Is magic doors."

"No."

"I'm allowed."

"No, you're not. Anyway it's sensors, not magic. It's machines, Joel."

With eerie electric grace one of the newer hybrid buses hummed by them. Two older models came afterwards, buses that sputtered, making pigs of themselves on fuel. By the gates of the park they met a cleaning contractor. The man had a couple of different brooms slung on his cart, and a transistor radio that he'd strapped to the push bar. A muted song played out.

Joel nodded his head to the beat.

"Your son likes music," the man told Téo, turning up the volume.

Téo heard: something nice: drums, a keening voice. He couldn't be sure what genre. A lot of music sounded the same to him. His mouth was dry. He hadn't played Joel one song, he realised, not in all this time—ten weeks.

"Oh yeah?" he croaked.

"Look!" said the man. They watched as Joel swung his body around. He jabbed out stiff hands, as immersed and transported as Téo had ever seen him.

When they got inside the park, Joel sprinted the gravel paths, keen that Téo should time him on these runs. Over and over again he skidded in the same patch of gravel, bringing dust up in clouds. Afterwards they went to inspect the plants on the park's perimeter. They found interesting insects there. They learned that the fat blankets of ivy that lay over the fence-tops were best for spiders. There were bees in the park who appeared to have gorged themselves stupid on flowers already. They met a shambling, drunk-seeming one who needed several heavy attempts before she could lift off and buzz away.

The sun overhead went unchecked. Just the one or two mateless clouds in the sky.

It turned hotter and picnic groups formed in the park. People lay about on rugs, spacing themselves into roomy wagon-circles, their crisp sacks sighing open as the seals gave. There was that sellotape complaint as gummed plastic lids were torn from containers. Bottles of wine sweated liquid beads in the heat. A smell of sun lotion made Téo wonder whether he ought to have slapped some on Joel. He'd learned bits. He'd learned *in* bits. There was so much more. But that, Téo supposed, would be for Joel's next carers to worry about. He wondered how much the boy would remember of these weeks. He wondered, would they meet one day, and would he know?

Joel had brought along some toy figures in the pockets of his shorts.

"Is easy," he said to Téo, showing him how, "is holes."

They unpacked his collection. The choice of terrains in the park was a treat for Joel after so many play sessions indoors. The chalky gravel paths left his hands pale and seasoned-looking. Where the branches of a willow hung low enough for him to reach, he commandeered the branches as vines or ropes, even prison fetters, whatever his narratives required. While Joel played, Téo sat on the ground in the sun. He lay back and he straightened his fingers in the grass, number-fouring the legs and conducting an imaginary band with his toes. He listened off and on to Joel's game. The boy was over by a flowerbed. His toys were not allowed to touch any mud. Which right now was quicksand.

". . . Téo?"

He'd been asleep, he must have been. He came up fast on his elbows and said, "I'm sorry, I don't know what happened, I dropped off. You okay? You safe? What happened? What's the matter?"

Joel held out one of his toys.

"Is died."

"He died? How?"

Joel pointed. Some acted-out scene by the flowerbed.

"Can we save him . . . ? Here. Pass it."

Téo examined Joel's toy, which was heavy, factory-modelled, made out of a few connected plastic chocks. He said, "No, this one's healthy, see? He's a polar bear. He's strong. In fact, he wants to get back in on your game."

Joel frowned. "Is forever."

"Yeah?"

"Is died."

Grass came too, wisps of it clinging to the clammier parts of Téo's arms as he stood. Joel's other toy people, abandoned in the middle of a game, were set out on a wooden sleeper that bordered the flowerbed. Side by side, they had the appearance of waiting mourners. Téo improvised some words of remembrance. He spoke about his qualities, this polar bear, then he showed Joel how to push aside some earth for a burial. "Bit deeper, that's right. Do you want to say anything? How people said things at your mum's funeral, like memories?"

Joel shook his head.

"You sure?"

"I . . . am." He pirouetted.

Together they placed the toy in the hole and they covered it over. They smoothed the earth and chose a couple of interesting stones to mark the spot. "Then tomorrow or the next day," Téo said, "when we come back, we know where to pay our respects."

"No-o-o."

"No what?"

"I want to stay *now*."

"We can stay a few more minutes."

"Tay-OH. I want to stay for long."

"What about your other toys?" He pointed in turn at the muscle man, the pixie, the leopard-boy.

Joel said, "They very sad."

"Ah. They would be."

"They tummy ache."

"Ah. We should probably get them home then, shouldn't we? Come on."

It became a habit. Another tradition for them. They'd be in the flat and piling blocks or squeezing a stuffed toy to activate its interior electronics. They'd be digging around in Téo's drawer of extension leads, disentangling the cords and putting them in neat rows on the floor like subdued snakes. They'd have the mattress off Joel's bed, a miniature football between them, to practise the difficult art of the diving header. Whatever the game Joel would tire of it and groan, offering up some non-specific complaint that didn't quite match the moment. ("I'm not sleepy.") Then he would ask Téo, could they visit the park?

They had the journey down to a minimum. Long as they got lucky with the crossings, as long as they race-walked the distances between, they could reach Joel's flowerbed in ten minutes. He was content to play for hours, often staying close to his buried toy and always hanging on and on till Téo insisted it was home-time, mealtime, bedtime.

"Hey, Joel."

"I'm not sleepy."

"No that's fine, you can stay a minute longer. I only wanted you to know. If it's ever that you want your toy back, your polar bear, he's in there—we can always dig him out."

"Is forever, Téo."

"No, listen, y'see . . ."

"Is never COME."

Joel was furious suddenly. All the walk home the hot slab of his hand squirmed inside Téo's. Joel would be leaving soon. Téo wondered about the next family, the next bunch of carers. Would they think the boy had been set up well?

"You must rethink," Victor announced later. They had a moment to themselves in the front room. Joel was upstairs having a nap. "You're scared, Téo, and you're letting it affect your judgement. I see it clearly."

"Oh yeah? Whatever you reckon, Dad."

Their arguments about Joel were referee-less, occasionally brutal, though not without rules and red lines. Téo was about to complain that Vic had gone too far with that scared comment. But he was curious and he asked, "Scared of what."

Victor crinkled his greying lips. "Loving the child? Being vulnerable because you love him? I understand what I'm talking about here."

"Fucking tired, Dad," said Téo, "is what I am. Barely recognise myself."

Victor peered over, as if to ask, what are you complaining about? I recognise you. He said nothing more. He was shading his eyes with a wavering hand. You could see that Victor's body trembled more and more. The lights in the flat were becoming a problem for him, blinding him even though they weren't that bright. Victor no longer strayed too far from his armchair. Once, Téo offered to drag around some of the furniture to make the routes through the flat more convenient. The offer was refused. Victor made incredible claims that neither the armchair nor the sofa would stand being shifted. Another time he pretended that this arrangement of furniture was the one that Téo's mum had set her heart on. Soon enough, Téo figured out the truth. His dad had learned to negotiate the ground floor by certain paths. He got around by a stealth falling-over, a series of managed slow-motion stumbles that were always interrupted at the last moment by his putting a hand on some well-known surface.

"When are they due today," Victor asked, "the social people?"

"Social workers." Téo looked at the clock. "They told me six p.m."

Joel woke from his nap. He ate a snack. When Gil and Alistair came into the flat they sat on the floor with the boy, joining him in his games, ventriloquising toys. Afterwards, while Joel watched TV, they settled with Téo and Vic at the kitchen table. The biological father had not come forward. There wasn't yet a suitable foster place in the borough, nothing that would cater to Joel's religious needs.

His *what* needs? wondered Téo. His view, you could be Jew on your insides, Jew in your cells, and it didn't matter much what books or what outfits or what rules you swore by or didn't. He tried to recall if he'd once mentioned to Joel their shared distinction, about them both being a thing called Jewish. "Is it a deal breaker, that his next carer be a Jew?"

The social workers said it was something they had to take into consideration. Joel was at a difficult age, aware, unaware, both at once.

"We have to make the effort."

"In the first instance."

"Aren't we past that? If there's no one here, can't we widen the search?"

Gil and Alistair took a moment. They shared a glance. Before Lia died, they said, she enrolled Joel at a nursery nearby. Joel had been going there a few days a week at the start of the year. The nursery was willing to re-enrol him. "And if he was back at nursery during the day," Gil said, "you'd have the opportunity to return to work."

"Oh. Right."

"You could take him to nursery in the mornings, carry on your job as before and pick him up afterwards. Maybe Victor could help. Rabbi Challis has offered to pitch in where she can."

"Keep him longer you mean. Stay here in Enfield."

"If you were able to break your lease in Aldgate, we might be able to secure funding to cover some of the cost. We see you as an excellent candidate for Joel's permanent care."

"Thanks. But."

"You don't need to decide today. Think about it. If you could agree to keep Joel another three months, at least, it would help us."

Téo felt hot. "He'll think about it," Victor said.

"Oh yeah, for sure," Téo agreed.

***

"Well well," said Ben Mossam.

He came to the door wearing shorts. He had on a damp T-shirt and his running shoes, ones with colourful liquorice slugs up the sides. He must have been exercising. Téo felt sure that if he had to argue with Ben tonight he would lose. The relentlessness and the repetitiveness of childcare, it halved you then it quartered you. Always another request, another fall, a second stubbed toe. You answered again and you answered again. Ben's person was intact. He hadn't changed. Ben was led by his interests. He ate, moved, shat whenever he pleased. Téo envied him more than ever.

"You drive here?"

"Yeah."

"Is this going to get expensive for me, like last time?"

Téo sniffed.

"'M I coming in or what?"

They had a stunted way they communicated after a falling-out. They were shy of each other and reluctant to get started on amends.

"What do you think?" came Ben's answer. "Get in here."

And with that they offered each other fists, they were tight again, they grasped each other, slapping and grunting, pleased. Téo followed Ben through to one of the lounges. He found himself explaining about Joel and the music, how he'd never played him as much as one song. "I don't know where I'd start, unless it's radio. And then I'm paralysed, like, which station?"

"On this I can help. What's Joel into?"

"Um."

"Guitars? A beat? The old rockers? Bit of rap? Your disco?"

Ben led them over to shelves which were crammed with records and CDs, the snug spines betraying some careful A-to-Z work. Téo remembered how much of Ben's time was spent curating and adding to his music collection when they were young. As a whatever-year-old he'd trooped along to the same gigs as Ben and Lia, pretending he was equally excited that some next band had announced some next tour. The relief, when he got older. When he could admit it, I'm immune, music doesn't touch me.

"Who's this bloke singing?"

Ben was playing an album. "You're kidding," he said. He stared. "You haven't changed a bit, T, God bless you."

He handed over a stack of albums he'd selected. "Be careful with those. We bought some of those together, me and Lia." He kept running his finger along the album spines, pulling out more and more.

"Says explicit language, this one."

"Best ones do."

"Which do I play him first?"

"Whichever. What does it matter? . . . You feeling okay?"

"You'll have to come round, Benno. You'll have to choose for us."

"Hey: sit a minute."

Ben had this vast modular sofa that curved in a horseshoe shape around one of his lounges. He put Téo on a part of the sofa you could lie on, full stretch if you chose.

"How have you been sleeping?"

"Not great. They want me to keep looking after Joel."

"And that's bad? Or good?"

"It's . . . I don't know. I left Victor alone with the boy and I'm not sure how long he'll cope. Thanks for these albums."

"Few more minutes, surely."

Téo checked his phone. "Few more minutes. Okay."

They relaxed on the sofa. Ben opened out his shoulders, wincing, showing the relief as his bones clicked and some internal discomfort went away. Before sinking into a recline he strummed curled fingers up his chest, a characteristic gesture that meant he was being asked to focus for too long on a subject that didn't involve himself.

"How have you been sleeping?" he asked again, and now it was Téo's turn to stare. These narcissists, he thought, God bless *them*. They gave it away, less in their actions or the frequency of their speeches about themselves, more in the rote and childlike way they had to remind themselves to be curious about realities other than their own.

"How am I sleeping? Like I said, Benno, not great. I've been on Dad's sofa for . . ." Téo counted. "Too long."

"Stay here when you need."

Ben stood up to change the music. They listened to the shrill sweet chime of a disc as it engaged. When Ben sat down he was holding an album case. With care he removed its liner notes. The song had that sound of the north of England, of rebellion, even Téo recognised it. "This was one of the few bands I discovered before she did," Ben said. "Remember those epic bus journeys we used to take?"

Téo did remember. There was a bus out of the neighbourhood that wound a route across Enfield, with many feints and doublebacks, to reach a new concrete shopping centre that was built near the motorway. Be as many as a dozen of them making these journeys, ten, eleven boys—and Lia. They commandeered the upper deck. They jockeyed for position, trying to predict which would be the hilarious seats, which the fight seats, which the seats closest to their one girl. Some of the group brought along music for the journey. Lia and Ben always did. They left off their headphones and allowed the music to play disregarded into their throats and their laps while they chatted instead about top-five songs, top-five hooks, best front men, best drummers. They were the sort of teenagers who showed middle fingers at adult drivers on the road, jealous of their privilege and what they imagined to be a freedom from being told what to do.

"Remember those journeys," said Ben, "when Lia would rest her head on the glass to go to sleep. We worked so hard to keep her attention."

There were trips when Lia might not have liked them at all, when they might've been younger siblings to her, sexless. There was one trip when she asked if she could switch seats and move forward to sit beside Téo. He could picture her gymnastic contortions as she climbed the seat. She was bored. She wanted company. She handed him the earbud for R and kept the L for herself, the two of them yoked together for the rest of the journey. He had counted the stops that had passed. The stops they had left. At the destination there was a dimming of the bulbs, the bus driver's way of telling them, leave me please.

In Ben's lounge, the second track of the album kicked in. The singer, who'd previously sounded upbeat, was of more mixed opinion.

"I should get going."

"Cool."

Ben ejected the album. He replaced the fragile disc in its case, putting back the liner notes, careful to tuck the booklet under the acrylic grooves without any chipping or creasing. "Don't borrow this one too long, okay? I'll miss it."

Téo took the album and he said, "You fancied her too back then."

"Only sometimes. Off and on."

"Ben. He's not yours, is he?"

"Who we talking about?"

"You'd have said. You wouldn't have kept us in the dark."

Ben stared, as if his mind was already on to something else.

"No way," he said.

The child's body was neatening itself, packing tighter. He was taller; Vic insisted on that. They had begun to mark pencil lines on the wall to prove it. Through May and into June, up, up, up Joel went. He hated to stand still for these measurings. "Keep your back straight," Téo was saying to him in the corridor.

Joel sounded hassled. "I straight."

"Be a statue though. Let me measure you without you fidgeting."

Joel must have gritted his teeth. That's right: he was trying to speak without moving his lips. "I . . . hmm . . . a . . . stashoo."

Vic was listening to them both from the kitchen. He'd had an idea he would cook a Sunday roast, his first in years. "Well?" he asked, raising his voice so that they'd hear. "Am I correct?"

Téo answered, "He's taller all right."

"I tall?" said Joel.

"You're getting there. Soon you'll be up with the grown-ups. Soon you'll be taking Vic's hand to help him cross the road."

"Hey!"

"Look rye," Joel recited, "look left. Look rye again."

Oh he was a tiring child, a tedious child. At the same time he was a hero to Vic, every encouragement for an invalid to make more effort. Joel trooped about, devoted to his interests. He drank in a day, slurping it and spilling it, there was a great greedy spend of his vitality. Vic used to be known for stamina too. He stayed later in the office than everyone else, putting colleagues to shame. Having Joel around reminded him what tirelessness looked like and how its example could galvanise. Through the child, Vic was catching glimpses of the world as first met, when novelty triggers the passions and makes sagas of commonplace events. There was that afternoon they endured the tragedy of Joel's first paper cut. And, oh, thought Vic, remembering it, Back-Rash-Day . . .

"Is, no clothes?" asked Joel. He had his snout over the edge of the kitchen counter.

"This chicken here? He's been plucked."

The pale bird had been rubbed over with salt and butter and set in a heavy oven tray. Vic had surrounded it with halved white onions—so much he remembered of his method. He was missing herbs, he thought. Maybe a lemon? Téo had gone to the shop for whatever they had.

Vic's hands were already trembling from the effort of peeling potatoes but he ignored the problem as well as he could. His was a wasting disease. From what he recalled his doctors saying of the symptoms, he could expect an intermittent creep, a slow series of failures. Some days he found that his coordination was off. His tongue or his lips miscued, leaving him stranded and responsible for a slurred utterance that nobody else could decipher. If he laughed too loud or too late he did not always realise this mistake until other people stared back at him with concern. More and more he kept on his coat indoors. He slept in socks.

The kitchen boiler stirred awake and went *er–r–r,* went *um-m-m,* as though trying to remember what to do next as well. Vic looked around, wiping his hands on his trousers. He had used so many utensils already! A bag of cornflour sat before him on the counter, retrieved from a cupboard though for no immediately obvious purpose. Didn't flour go into his homemade gravy? He thought that half a cup was the amount. It would come to him.

He had not taken charge of an ambitious roast in a while.

And what Vic meant by ambitious? He meant real pork stuffing, he meant garlicked greens and teeth-staining beetroot— a choice of jellies. "Téodor," he shouted, sending his son to the shop again, because they had to have jellies for a Sunday roast. "One jar of redcurrant, one of mint. Go now please, I'm working to a strict timetable."

"I know you are," Téo grumbled, "I grew up with this."

During their best years as a family, back when they had infinite time, the Sunday lunch was Vic's to oversee. Once a week, all through Téo's childhood, Vic prepared them a chicken from start to finish. He would rise at dawn to start paring, stuffing, clattering, swearing. He would have their meal on the table at 1 p.m. sharp. Better for his wife (better for everyone) that Vic should have something consuming and definitive to do on Sundays. Without work or shul to distract him he was quick to impatience in those days. By family agreement he would be stationed in the kitchen where Sal found no welcome, none, not if there was a roast to prepare.

Now Vic sat and rested his aching arms.

A brief sit, he told himself, then he must get that bird in the oven. The surface of Sal's kitchen table had been scratched and stained over time, though agreeably, in a way that evidenced decades of honest use. He had a memory of her walking a circle around this table as soon as it was brought in by the deliverymen. She squatted: wanting to see as each family member would, wondering, what sort of view for their son, placed here, and her husband, placed here? It was time for Vic to start cooking the chicken. But now he saw with dismay that he'd forgotten to pre-heat the oven. It wasn't piping in there, hell-hot, how he liked it. The dials were out of reach from where he sat. Vic put his palms on Sal's worn tabletop and began to push himself up.

Coming into the kitchen, Joel asked, "Vic's hurt yourself?"

"Something like that."

"Is bleeding?"

"No."

He had not listened carefully enough to the doctors. It was an English-sounding disease, fancy-sounding . . . Vic ignored the details, the causes, the expectations for his health and his comfort, he couldn't bear it. He scowled at the doctors instead, feigning comprehension, waiting to get the Christ away home. Modern medicine was too complicated. That was Vic's opinion. He was "nae well." That's all that would've been said in the Scottish village where he grew up, nae well. "There are some days worse than others," he told Joel.

"Y'need my help?" came Téo's voice.

He was back from the shop.

Vic grimaced, winking at Joel and muttering, "I wish he'd stop *pestering* me."

The child loved a conspiracy. Now he tapped his finger—all adult savvy, and nearly getting it right—against the side of his chin. Joel was almost three years old. It was his birthday soon. In his own mind, doubtless, he was older than that, almost at school, almost in pubs and driving cars. The child's enthusiasms had become the household's enthusiasms. They watched his favourite cartoons together. They all knew which pair of shoes he was most proud of. It lifted Vic's spirits and made him feel energised, just to watch as Joel charged about the flat, full of ideas and cunning work-arounds. The chaos in Joel's movements was purposeful. Stay with us, Vic thought.

"And where is our guest?" he asked.

This bloody Ben. Vic had no love for him. He walked around their neighbourhood with a preternatural confidence, Ben Mossam, whistling the themes from films, swinging his arms. He'd been arrogant like this since he was small. Wherever Enfield pavements narrowed, with only the space to accommodate one pedestrian at a time, Ben would wave others through first. He directed traffic, you next, now you. Vic had been encouraged through like this himself while Ben stood and smiled his fool's smile. The family was rich.

"He'll be here," Téo said.

"And you bought us jellies? The expensive kind?"

"The only kind they were selling. Take it easy, Dad."

But the time for heavy lifting had arrived. Vic could no longer put this off. When Téo and Joel left the room to play next door, he got himself over to the oven. It was built into the kitchen cabinets at chest height and there was no obligation to bend. Even so, some ingenuity was required. Vic drew in a breath. Using his stronger right arm he took up the tray that held the chicken and with an unstoppable motion that required success, first stab, or else clattering shame, he swung around his weaker arm, landing it on the horizontal bar of the oven door and leaning his weight so that as the door fell open it became a shelf. He was able to slam down the tray in time, before his arm lost strength. He stood panting, pleased though, dumb as a boxer might be in the interval between blows.

Now Vic planted his feet again. He seized the tray with both hands, falling forwards with it this time and ramming it into the oven, pushing off afterwards so that as he backpedalled he was able to close the door with one hand and find the table edge with the other. Patting for a chair, he sagged back seated.

He made a mental note of the time. He turned to face with loathing a second heavy tray that held the veg.

"Téodor . . . Is nobody listening to me out there? . . . *Téo*dor."

His son appeared. He had been bouncing with Joel on the trampoline.

"What is it, what's wrong?"

"And where is your supposed friend?"

Vic aimed a finger at the digital clock on the oven. It was coming up to one and he was furious.

Téo said: "I thought there must've been an accident in here. Way you were shouting."

"This Ben of yours. Is he coming? There'll be too much for us to eat."

"Then make less."

Téo surveyed the kitchen, after which a gentler note entered his voice. "Or we could get a takeaway. Pizza or something. Ben won't be fussed."

Vic was thinking of his ambitions that morning, the meal as laid out in his mind. He'd given up on stuffing and even beetroot. He was going to die from his illness and he wondered again, would he manage it with Sal's poise? He looked around at the mess he'd made of her kitchen. There were ingredients unused and still in their plastic wraps. He was determined to finish at least some of what he'd started. He snapped at Téo: "Takeaway? What for? Your lunch will be ready. I only hope Ben gets here before it spoils."

"I'll message him."

"Please."

"You know you don't need to do all this. If it's making you frustrated. Me and Mum, we always used to wonder, why did you want to make these roasts? If they caused you so much stress? It was almost a relief when you stopped."

Vic opened his eyes much wider. He smiled bitterly.

He'd waited for some attack and here it was.

He said to Téo, "Am I to take that as criticism?"

"Eh?"

"When your mother died I was outmatched. I can admit that. But in the circumstances, those presented to me at the time . . ."

"It wasn't criticism, Dad. If it's criticism you're after I can mention stuff."

Arguments that were stumbled into by accident, brought about because of a carelessly chosen word or a moment's inattention— those were the worst because avoidable. There were arguments perpetuated by the frustration that an argument was even happening at all.

"I know you felt neglected."

Téo considered this. He shrugged. "You stopped coming home."

"I worked hard. I was needed at the office. I didn't do any of it for me."

"Cool."

"Oh! Your generation."

"My generation, is it? What about my generation?"

"The hand-holding. At your job, for instance . . . they've given you *how* long?"

"It's called compassionate leave."

"Well, I had no compassion. Nothing was given to me. Not in my career and not when I was . . . not in my . . ."

Vic had found a seam, his childhood, the disparity between

his own and Téo's. It might once have kept him going. He couldn't get at the words today. Eloquence came and went. "I wasn't shown how," he concluded, lamely. "Never mind."

A flicker on Téo's phone distracted them. They were pulled back from further argument. "It's a message from Ben," Téo said. "Turns out you were right, he'd forgotten about the lunch. Says he's coming as soon as he can."

Here was common ground. "Ben Mossam was never reliable."

"No," Téo agreed.

Vic considered offering up some of the rumours he'd heard, about Ben, about Lia. "I only pity the child," he said vaguely.

"Which child, who?"

"Never *mind*."

When Vic and Sal became parents they were older than their peers. It was true he'd been given no instruction, there was no one from his youth to look to for advice, no model, the few memories he had of his father were so worn as to have the musty hand-me-down feel of goods that were the possession of somebody else. His father was a large man. A man (that's right) who came to visit their cottage in the Highlands wearing leather waders and carrying in with him the smell of fields and the wet. If Vic was brought forward to shake his father's huge rough hand, the man would never bend, as though on principle—as though it was known that the child must reach to the adult. There would have been a voice. His father must be long dead, the big hand fleshless.

At a different point in his life Vic started to look to Sal's father as a surrogate. Téodor Kiryluk used to speak with passion about his personal fortune, even as it fluctuated. He never told Vic how to get rich, instead, how to *be* rich. Old Kiryluk was small and tightly wound. He'd escaped from Poland as a child, a terrible story. As they got to know each other better, Vic explained some of his own story, the household fire, his mother's poverty, how Vic was put in the car of a priest, aged six, and driven to an orphanage in the nearest city, Aberdeen. Later there was a train ticket south to London and a provincial boy's job in the civil service. If Vic was ever sorry for himself he could comfort himself in the language of home. "Me too," Sal's father had said, "for me in Polish, *ja biedny, ja biedny!*" It was the warren-warmth of Jews towards Jews that appealed to Vic. He liked them for their anecdotes and how they carried themselves in conversation, how sons would kiss their fathers on the cheek.

Ben Mossam was wearing one of the flat Jewish skullcaps, a kappel, when he came into the kitchen. He raised his chin at Vic, which was accounted a respectful greeting these days. Among the young men of Téo's generation, handshakes were no longer firm. They sometimes wanted to touch you with their fists instead. Etiquette drilled into Vic as essential, man's pass, was vanishing altogether. "Young man," he said.

"Mister Erskine! It's been a while."

"Yes. Call me Vic please."

"Ben please."

He scratched himself. When Vic declined to continue this unreasonable exchange any longer, Ben wandered off to join Téo and Joel in the other room. Knees wide, they sat in a row on the sofa and argued about football. It was that time of the early summer, the lull between league years, when pre-season friendlies were about to begin. Vic listened as they agonised over their team's personnel. They explained to Joel what their hopes were for the coming season, their fears; they tried to predict the next unknowable months.

Vic returned to his cooking. He had the homemade gravy to prepare. The greens. He decided he would abandon greens. Next door it was Joel's turn to decide what to play. He asked that Téo and Ben pretend they were hot. He asked that they lie down on the floor to have their temperatures taken. "Ah-h-h," he told them, "you're very hot."

"It's arguing about football."

"It's the weather outside."

"Is, you're both hungry."

Later, claiming mass starvation in there, Téo tried to get through to a cupboard and retrieve some snacks. Joel petitioned for entry to the kitchen as well, rubbing his belly and talking to Vic in a slow throaty way that suggested malnourishment. Vic shooed them out. They would eat soon enough.

In truth, he was tired. Both his arms felt looser in the sockets. He could not say for certain when the chicken had started cooking. As for gravy—he was coming to the view that home-made gravy was beyond him. Granules from a packet would have to do. He shouted for Téo, dispatching him again to the corner shop. "And Téo . . . ?"

Vic wanted to tell his son he was grateful, he was proud, he wanted to confirm there was love between them, however rarely it was voiced. Worse than their quarrels, somehow, was this awful diplomacy that had to follow a quarrel, the cold and careful treading, as hurtful between family members as cross words.

"You will rush, won't you?"

"Jesus. Yes, Dad. I'm going right now."

He slammed the door. When Téo was a baby, when Vic was new to being a father, he had seen it clearly: events that must happen in time. He saw their future as though in a painting. He would flourish at the office. Rise there. He would make enough money for the family to be comfortable. He would be admired for this. The feat would be to maintain an even distribution of his efforts so that he advanced steadily into wealth, esteem and love at the same time.

And he had done well in his job. By the end of his career he was writing speeches for statesmen and their aides, who often passed off Vic's drafts as their own. Occasionally his words were read aloud in Parliament. He earned a good wage. Once a week he cooked his wife and son a roast, carving it theatrically, the legs and wings off first, the breasts finely sliced, two firm oysters of flesh pushed out of their housing beneath the carcass and put on Téo's plate, because Téo liked these parts the best. Somehow, all of this, it hadn't amounted to enough. After weeks in Joel's company, Vic was able to see failures of parenting he was blind to at the time. Plain hours, passed together: there hadn't been enough. But he had tried his best, he'd made a decent fist of being a father and, yes, from time to time, Vic allowed himself to say so.

"'A decent fist of it'?" Téo repeated.

He was back from the shop, unpacking what he'd bought. Joel was helping to set the table. Ben sat in one of the kitchen chairs.

"You two hearing," Téo asked them, "how old Victor rates himself as a parent?"

"Leave me out of this," said Ben. He tipped back in his chair, weight on the hindmost legs, and he put his hands over his ears. Joel climbed to sit in one of the kitchen chairs too. He tried to tip backwards but he hadn't the strength.

"Don't do that," Téo warned, "you'll fall and hurt yourself."

"Let him try, let him fall," said Vic. "It's how he'll learn."

"Learn what? No."

"Ben agrees with me."

"What does it matter if Ben agrees? I'm not letting the boy break his neck so you can make a point."

"It's how we men develop. We get hurt and we learn to avoid that hurt the next time."

"And we never mention that hurt again. We tuck it away nice and deep."

"Quite right."

"I'll explain that to Joel's social workers, will I? When I hand him back, injured and repressed, I'll explain it's because I listened to my dad, who's sure he knows better."

Ben had his palms over his ears again and this time Joel copied.

"I don't know what that fool's doing," Vic complained. He waved an arm at Ben. "Pretending he isn't involved in this."

"What d'you mean, involved."

"I can't hear you," Ben shouted.

"Have I ever told you a story," Vic said (and he put his hands on either side of Joel's head, keeping the child's muffling palms in place), "how I grew up having my own father pretend *he* wasn't my father?"

"Dad. Don't bother us with more of your stories."

Vic kept talking though. It was as much his regained eloquence that intoxicated him as his need to show these two, he perceived things still, he hadn't turned stupid.

"My father was a farmer from one village over. He crossed the linn between our houses in his waders. Everybody knew what went on. In those days it was a shame to be a bastard. As though the bastard could choose—as though he'd chosen rashly! When my father visited us I was brought forward to shake his hand. I had to call him mister. Then I was sent outside to play, whatever time of day it was. Big man, big coat, dripping waders, and a bloody painful handshake. From *that* I had to fathom the role."

"Why you telling me this?"

"Because fuck off, Téodor. I tried."

"All right. I know you did. All right."

The clock on the oven chirped to signal the hour. Vic was aware that meant . . . it used to mean the food was ready. But when did the chicken go in? He shut one eye. He would allow it another few minutes, running the risk of drier meat but heading off the possibility of the chicken coming out pink and inedible.

Joel continued setting the table. Reaching as far as he could, he slid jars of jelly and mustard into position between the plates.

Loyal to Vic's instruction he went back and forth from the cutlery drawer, putting out forks, knives, spoons, and (his own flourish) the metal skewers from Vic's old barbecue set. "In case," he explained, "is baddies."

"You used to get me setting the table like this," Téo said. He was trying to be kinder. "D'you remember, Dad? While you prepared the gravy?"

"Gravy!" wailed Vic. He felt the enterprise was lost then. His clarity was gone, the mental cloud had returned. Téo reminded him, they were making gravy from a packet.

"You sent me to the shop for the ready-made stuff. Remember? It's easy, I'll handle it."

Vic sat and rested while Téo stirred boiling water into the wormy gravy granules, bringing samples over for him to taste. Vic said he liked the thickness just this side of glue.

"I know you do . . . Joel. Where's Joel? Drum roll please."

The child rapped his fingers on the side of the table. Téo lifted the steaming chicken out of the oven and set it in front of Vic, who waited till everybody was seated before he tapped the flat blade of his carving knife against the cutting board, as a conjurer might, to satisfy his audience that the blade was real. He started to carve the chicken, making unapologetic use of his fingers as he slid away piece after piece of skin that was crisp on top and sticky beneath with fat. He took his fork and he pinned the chicken to the board, cutting the breast as thin as he could. White meat fell away—turning pinker and more raw the deeper he cut. Before Vic had made it as far as the breastbone he needed to saw with the knife just to part the flesh. His arm hurt. Tears burned the corners of his eyes.

Joel moved closer to whisper, "Is bloody."

He sounded impressed.

"Yes. I don't know what's happened to me."

"I'll get us pizzas, Dad. Rest."

Téo left with Joel, promising he would return with a takeaway as soon as he could. It was late in the afternoon now. Sitting across the kitchen table, Ben was playing with his mobile phone. He had propped this device against his stomach in the manner of an accordionist or an ice-cream seller at the theatre . . . Vic presumed he was communicating with friends, telling them what had happened here, what a mess Mister Erskine had made of his lunch. Vic felt the urge to upset this young man, who was handsome, complacent, with a rich and level life ahead of him. As if a truth had been seduced from him, or as someone surrendering to interrogation, Vic said: "You must be honest with Téo. You must tell him that Joel is yours."

Ben stiffened. He put his phone down on the table.

"We don't know the kid's mine. Not for sure."

Vic clicked his tongue. "Be serious, Ben, you've had time to pretend. You must take sons seriously. You can't waste them. I know this."

Ben sulked. "Nothing's definite."

"Take Téo aside and tell him, or I will."

"When though?"

"As soon as possible."

Ben stared into his phone again, as though a solution might be found there. "What do I say to him? I don't even know what voice to use."

"That's up to you."

Ben seemed to be relishing the dilemma now. "What do I *say*," he repeated, wonderingly.

SUMMER
TO
AUTUMN

SEVEN

BEN

An old brick wall ran along one side of their park, a wall that was high and orange, a little banked, so that it resembled the ramparts of an armoury. There were only more houses on the other side. Only the back yards of shops and the cinema's bins. But because this was where the football pitch had been put, the top of the wall was ridged with broken glass to deter anyone's ambition of climbing over to retrieve a lost ball. The orange brick had been painted on with names and requests and injunctions, all the plump mismatched scripts of your Enfield graffiti artists. At ground level, up to about tit height, Ben would have said, the wall was claimed in another way by a tough green weed that found purchase in the crumbled lines of mortar and climbed along eye-catching perpendicular tracks. A square of weather-resisting turf had been laid in front of the wall. It was fenced in on three sides by wire screens.

The teenagers who'd claimed the pitch first today clung on for ages, long past their allotted hour, shaming themselves. They swore they were only chasing one more goal, a winner; but it wasn't etiquette. When they finally trooped off, they waved their hands at Ben to reject his criticism. "Don't pull a muscle," they advised. "Mind you do your stretches," all this.

Soon as he could, Ben jogged a lap of the pitch. In fact he *was* more patient over his stretches. He paid attention to a trio of traitor muscles, the one beneath his right shoulder blade and the chocks of cartilage under either knee. Although they had relinquished the turf, the teenagers hung around, nothing to do except hold their boots, apparently, and spit. They waited to be entertained. And that, Ben thought, I can do.

He sent around passes. He found his range on goal. He had smoked more, eaten more, stayed up later. But for Ben it was easy to impress behind a football. He learned how at school. A game began and he played with the ease and authority that used to be his when he was the year's football maestro. He barked orders. He started to understand where the inferior players on his team should be putting their bodies. He struck a clean rising shot . . . the geometry loyal . . . his first goal of the day. Two more, he said to himself. If I get the hat trick, I'll do what Vic wants, I'll face Téo and admit the truth.

Some of the watching teenagers nodded approval at the quality of Ben's next goal. "You learning anything yet?" he asked them, jogging by. "Why you lot hanging around if you're not taking notes?"

He was delighted to be so good at this. He concentrated on his level, curious as to the upper limits of his talent these days. Indicating where he wanted a pass with a slack sweep of his fingers or a clipped and unemotional command, Ben started to govern the game. Out of patience conducting these shoddier friends of his, done educating, he dashed at distant opponents himself. He tackled them solo. A couple of times he even thieved the ball off the toes of his own teammates. He refused to delegate or to share, sending in shots that went all over, some very wild indeed. The teenagers wandered away. As for Ben, when his body started to tire he did not ease off. He harried and bullied. He was clever in his exploitation of his height and his momentum, feeling a mounting permission to do as he pleased. He wished that little Joel was around to witness this. And letting fall one shoulder (no!) the other shoulder, Ben feinted, escaping his marker, almost scoring a third.

Hands on his hips he stretched, breathing at the sky for the ten count. Then he jogged then he sprinted, timing a lunge to intercept someone's pass and chasing the loosened ball along its altered trajectory. He toed the ball to slow it. Toed it again to situate it. And he curled it . . . curled it . . . curled it . . . a goal, his hat trick after all.

An hour later Ben was off to reward himself with a sundown coffee at his favourite Enfield café. Regular doses of caffeine and nicotine, that was his preference these days. *Then,* around 8 p.m., the first real drink. It was all part of a routine, along with the five-a-side football and his hot, hot showers, two per day, showers so hot that Ben expected to be scooping a passage through bathroom mist. He paid for his clothes to be laundered. He liked his T-shirts pressed so firm they took a moment after readmitting him to cede to his torso's true shape. Ben knew how to treat himself well was what he meant.

His hands made rocks. His hands made paper then scissors, warding off the numbness of inactivity as he idled along the high street. He started to run, carrying on for most of the length of the road, pushing himself. He ran past a chemist and a pub and a shop with a pushed-forward carousel for sunglasses. He stopped at his café where they served him shots of coffee in a thin-lipped glass that was Ben's and kept aside special. The café had that barkish smell of obliterated beans, a sweet note as well from people's sugary drinks. He took his first shot of caffeine standing up, impatient for the kick, the instant mental brilliance. He ordered another. His shot glass was weighted in the base so that it tocked any time he set it down. Chart music played. The staff banged their funnels and their filters, DJing the competing sounds of grinder and pressure machine. Ben took his next one outside. Despite the hour, it was still warm.

He laid some possessions on a table: his phone, his keys, a vintage album on CD that he'd taken to carrying around in his pocket. He unpinned his kappel and he added this to the pile in front of him, a preferred arrangement for deep thought. People were coming out of the café holding coffees of their own, sensational coffees, comedy coffees, too heavy to lift one-handed, some of these drinks capped with spirals of cream or placed-on sweeties. The air tasted faintly of salt as the chip shop got into its stride for a Saturday night. It was almost dark and the streetlights showed their orange, the sky above a varying colour, graded blues and purples. Day backed away from night with its hands raised: your turn. Soon enough the whole of Enfield would have that lamplit Victorian vibe that Ben treasured.

Caffeine sat high in his chest. Both his eyeballs were heavier. The universe came into better view. He knew how to rinse joy from things; that was his secret. Big things and small things. Expensive things and free things. Ben loved to eat cubes of strong and aching blue-veined cheese, taking these giant bites how someone else would eat a choc ice. He loved his spliffs, his internet sex vids, his roomy no-rush dumps, his pills. There were flirtations. The rare steaks. Music on vinyl and CD. He liked meals and between meals, the tide-overs. Tireless ingestion was a strong suit of Ben's and he was capable of eating two substantial dinners in one night. Because he gambled, because he was often in his casino till late, new windows for eating had opened. It was a life of organised doses, nothing to excess, the main pleasure being the constant chaining-between.

He was not precious about sleep. However late Ben got his head down he tended to wake again early, to participate in joys that were uniquely the morning's. Intro yawns. A phase of scratching in the bed as he tried to restage how much money had been won or lost the night before. Who had been met? Who befriended? Who fallen for? First thing in the mornings he liked to pose himself two questions, are you well, friend? Are you up for another twenty-four hours of this? He couldn't understand Lia's thinking at all, that was the sad truth. He couldn't understand how anybody's answer to such questions might be no.

He called up a photo of her on his phone. In old pictures, your dead friend looks like someone with a plan in motion, he thought. They look ready to astonish. Ben struggled to be all that interested in Lia when they were growing up. As a fellow ninja-savant of making an impression on people, he understood it was one of Lia's cultivated traits, a source of sly pride to her—that she inspired fascination. For years he watched Téo squirm and pine. He let Téo praise her, be silly about her, overselling Lia's guts and her good taste, the cut of her, Lia's shadow, Lia's spine, whatever-the-fuck Téo could think of to admire next, the programmes she watched and when. He spent so long listening to Téo rhapso-dise he started to understand in theory what it might be like to obsess over Lia himself—and it was this feeling he tried to tap into when they had their brief affair. Dispiriting for everybody involved, that.

When it was over . . . a couple of weekends, three? When it was over, Ben swore the others in the group to secrecy. He took their word of honour around the table. He knew they sometimes baited Téo. Dropped hints. They did it to amuse each other and maybe to enjoy one of the rewards of hanging around Enfield for longer than him. Ben knew that none of them would break a promise. Theirs was an iron discretion, sworn in front of mates and policed by mates. It was a discretion that had passed over naturally to everyone's dealings with the social workers. Asked who might be Joel's father they all shrugged, they all tutted as if out of ideas, damn.

Ben's favourite casino was near the retail parks, in earshot of the roaring North Circular Road. Run down, never teeming, it was staffed by men and women who gave him a cheerful welcome, everybody from the bartenders to the croupiers to the overnight chaplain. Ben decided he would square away a piss on arrival so that nothing interfered with his poker flow later. He drank a vodka, appreciating the clevering high that came with the night's first take of alcohol.

"You all right, Ben?"

"Yessir."

"Evening, Ben."

"Good to be back."

He inhaled it, the smell of spoiling leather, the fried food, lesser gamblers' anguish. Hello, the one shabby roulette wheel. Hello, the tables for blackjack. Underneath his feet, the carpet was a livid red, the colour of a tongue that was not healthy. Ceramic tokens clicked like teeth. They had the volume up on the propulsive spectral music that always played here. Around the edge of every half-moon table curved a cushioned buffer, there to afford the happier players somewhere to rest both forearms while they gambled; and there no doubt to stop the losers from stoving in their heads after another intolerable hand.

It seemed natural the atmosphere would turn more electric as Ben sauntered through. He said his hellos, he pointed with-

out menace, he touched people on the shoulder or the arm—
and in fact he felt as the sun, moving across a field in shadow,
he was luminous tonight and exactly what they needed. Nods
were issued back at him from far-off tables. Chins lifted. Ben was
admired here. He was feared as well he thought, really a sort of
sheriff to them, in to collect what was owed. Ben stopped for a
few minutes' chat with a blackjack regular he recognised, asking,
"Is your luck in tonight?" No winner would freely jinx himself.
And no loser confess. The regular said something non-committal
and Ben touched fists with him, mentioning he was gathering a
poker game. Usual table. "See you over there."

"Might join you, yeah."

"See you over there."

He identified other possible entrants. "Yo," he told each of
them, "you're a sight for sore eyes." And, "Haven't seen you
around much. I'll be getting up a game in a minute. Usual table."
Soon they were ready to begin. Ben made any newcomers feel
welcome. It was automatic work, he was vibing already with the
cards, concerned by the cards alone. "About time to call over a
croupier I reckon," he said, once they'd sorted their orders for
more drinks. He was feigning a ridiculous warm-up with his
wrists . . . a bit of bullshit to leave his opponents wondering. The
croupier took a position at the flat head of the table. Soon as
the game began, an hour vanished.

It was a mystery! Time had been carefully neutered inside the
casino, that was true. Windows were covered over and the walls
gave no clue whether it was night or day outside. But something
about the rhythmic stress of gambling seemed to hurry forward
the normal churn of minutes and when Ben looked again it was
10 p.m. Some of his poker acquaintances had wives and kids. They
showed up on weeknights and weekends all the same, hanging on
like this towards midnight then the morning. Maybe, thought
Ben, it would be all right to be a parent as well. Maybe he would

master the dad bit, how he had mastered many skills. Maybe he would find the high in it, a good deed being its own kind of stimulant. Or maybe he would bend some version of dadhood to his established high-chasing routines.

The casino got emptier as midnight came and went. There was a different energy about, with only the most devoted gamblers left. Ben tipped the croupier again: a large amount. He was known here. His preferences were accounted for. She wandered away for an unscheduled break and while he had the other players to himself Ben made a suggestion. They ought to add in side bets, he said. Enhance whatever was already on the table by raising the emotional stakes. Money? That was represented by the chips they had in their tidy piles. The side bet had to be of sentimental value. A piece of the heart.

"Winner takes all of course. No slope-homes," Ben said.

This was mere formality. The players at his table were a self-selecting crew; the most reckless; the ones who sought out Ben's games precisely because of these opportunities for amplified risk. Somebody wagered a pair of tickets for the pre-season. Somebody else staked four excellent pills they'd been saving. Gambled as well were photographs, rings, favourite coats. This was better, thought Ben, as his pulse quickened. This was the point.

He pulled his kappel off his head, laying it in front of them on the table so that they could see the date from seventeen years earlier stitched inside. The kappel contained an embroidered message from his parents, wishing him well in English and in Hebrew. "My mum and dad gave me this. Their little bar-mitzvah Benjamin . . . We done? We agreed on our side bets?"

It wasn't enough, they complained. One skullcap? Ben would have to boost the value. Smiling slightly, he listened to their objections, a teacher impressed by the developing nerve of the students. Very well. He took from his pocket that vintage album on CD. He rotated the case from its corners in the manner of an auctioneer, letting the acrylic flash under the casino spotlights. "Treasured possession," he admitted. His throat was dry. "I'd hate to lose this. It means a lot to me."

The croupier returned. They were dealt new pairs of cards from the deck. It got later and later and one by one the losers walked away from the table, wandering out on to the casino floor to fritter helplessly or else arrange a taxi home. Ben played for everybody's quick extermination. He had committed to another side bet, this one in private, a personal wager with himself.

Win tonight, Ben swore, and tomorrow I'll tell Téo the truth.

More and more losers stood up and left. When they did they uncoloured in Ben's eyes, like spent matches that had flared once and been interesting and now were beside the point. Invulnerable to superstition as a rule, he had discovered that it brought him the slightly more favourable cards if he touched this CD that he'd once bought with Lia. He beat his last rival in the minutes after 3 a.m., pocketing all the money and the tickets and the pills as well as some hastily scribbled promissory notes. Congratulations, however muted the actual words, were never denied a winner. At Ben's table you always said "well played."

A tired cashier swapped his chips for money. He tipped: enormously, everyone. He said his goodnights. Before he left the casino, Ben put his head in at the chaplaincy door, meaning to say a few words to the religious figure on duty too. They sat in here for hours, the vicars and imams and rabbis. They left their door ajar, a dish of mints out and a welcoming chair turned at an angle for any gamblers who might need to sit a while, decompress. Some of your casino customers became despairing in a moment, a danger to themselves. The management let in faith leaders of all stripes and they staffed this chaplaincy as volunteers on rotation.

Normally, when Ben looked in, the chaplain was reading or even dozing. They were not often visited. The heavy gamblers of Ben's acquaintance had their eccentric theories about luck, especially luck's provenances. You saw them stacking their chips in fiddly denominations or avoiding specific patches of carpet, drinking specific brands of beer to specific schedules. Walking around the casino, they chose routes that avoided the chaplaincy door. The little room was felt to be bad luck. It was where you might end up yourself one night.

Ben said as usual, "You okay in here? You need anything before I go?"

It was the new rabbi from Enfield Progressive. He'd never seen her on duty till now.

"No thanks," she said, showing Ben a polite smile, then returning to her book.

She had brought along a stack to read, he saw. Not being much of a book person himself he often fancied them. He hesitated at her door. "I recognise you actually. You're my rabbi. That is, I'm local, I'm technically a congregant."

She considered this. "Technically?"

"Yeah: apologies, rabbi, I haven't been acing my attendance of late."

She gave the impression she didn't give two fucks whether Ben found her attractive or not. That was *his* lookout, for him to worry about. Of course he was entranced. His legs were limp, maybe from his exertions on the football pitch earlier. He had to sit. "Er, you mind?"

"Go ahead."

The rabbi marked her page in the book and put it down. She was maybe a decade older than him. She wore a dude's dark coat, a jumper, three sprays of gold: a hoop in either ear and a thin chain across her throat. Ben had a rule. Try not to fall in love with them immediately because of their interesting outfits. What else? Cool fingers, cool wrists. So much of the rest of her was hidden by the coat. He would like to take another long look at her face, that puzzle! With its elements. With its beauty and ungainliness sort of mashed together. She seemed unbothered by Ben's presence, not at all moved to curiosity about his own interesting face. He believed he detected an arrogance in there, of a flavour well known to Ben, though in the rabbi's case it was an arrogance that had maybe been disavowed or suppressed. Ex-bitch, he was thinking. Someone all high and mighty at school before she reformed. He liked her. He resolved to be charming for however long she'd have him in the room.

"Can I ask you an interesting question? How come you're not wearing the gear tonight, the robes? Are you keeping a lid on your powers or something? Are you assuming a civilian identity?"

"If you like," she said. "But we encourage first names in here. I'm Sibyl."

"Ben."

"One of my lost sheep then."

"Suppose so. I keep meaning to stop by one Saturday. My parents . . . they paid for that bimah of yours."

"The Mossams? Oh, we're all grateful to the Mossams."

Wide opinion, the bow was over. It had had its day the bow, it had fallen out of fashion ages ago. Just sometimes? Personally? Ben liked to bow. What he did, he touched where his heart was meant to be, he didn't smile, he tipped forward maybe twenty degrees—*in silence*. Women bought into this, they really did.

Ben bowed at Sibyl and she stared back at him.

"You'll tell your parents I sent my regards?"

"Definitely."

He didn't get out of the chair just yet. Instead he turned his head to read the titles on the spines of her books. They were about faith, or misplaced faith, he couldn't quite tell. "I don't have any problems myself. If that's why people're meant to sit here."

"We're visited for different reasons," said Sibyl, turning her palms over. "People knock. They sit. They talk or they don't. That's it."

"If someone knocks I'll leave."

"Okay. Is there anything you'd like to talk about while you are here?"

"Honestly? I should probably bounce soon, rabbi. I should probably vacate the seat. I've seen a few desperados out there who might need you soon."

She said, "Sibyl."

"Sibyl."

"You cover your head yet you don't come to shul. Explain that to me."

"Ah," he said, adjusting his kappel with a hand, "thing is, I'm Jew. I don't mind people knowing I'm Jew. I *like* people knowing it. Jew being normal to me, a mode, what I am in my bones."

"You wear the kappel as a statement of this?"

"If you like. Yeah."

"And let me guess—to antagonise people as well."

"I don't shy away from fights, if that's what you're asking. This." Ben touched the skullcap. "It's my show of no surrender."

"But."

"Hm?"

"There's a but?"

"How I think of it. And I've never spelled this out before, so bear with me. I'm Jew. But I'm not *a* Jew."

"What's the difference?"

"I'll take the part I'm born with. Family part. Genetics. The organic matter and the blood. But I can't be dealing with someone telling me what choices to make. I won't be bossed. Y'know, keeping kosher when nobody's watching. Turning down parties on a Friday night. Boo, gambling, boo, drugs. That part of being a Jew where you get told: here are your rules for living! They come from boss-height, the boardroom, they can't be refused."

"God as CEO. That's a new one to me."

"I don't mean God. I mean old men stroking their chins. Me and God are on okay terms."

"So you do believe."

"If you plant it in anyone young enough, it's difficult to uproot."

"I'm still not sure I understand why you wear the kappel."

"For another thing, it reminds me I have parents."

Sibyl nodded. "How long ago did they move abroad?"

Ben loved how carefully she was paying attention. His whole life he'd been a talker. He had a hypothetical question for any-body who wandered across his path. Would you rather one packet of your favourite crisps? Or a hundred of your worst? Lia was a talker as well. She expected her words to land, to decide matters, she cut Ben and Téo into pastry shapes with her sentences that had the serrated edges. Ben loved talk; he was Jew in that. Even so he appreciated the space that someone like Sibyl left around the sides of a conversation. Easy to forget people like her, the Téos, the listeners, how valuable they were too.

"Ages. I was eighteen."

"Young."

"I didn't think so at the time. Were you always a believer from the get-go? You always went in for religion I mean, as a kid and that?"

"My parents weren't religious," said Sibyl. "They were secular Jews and I was raised like them. I used to live in a different way. I taught for a while."

"Ah-h-h: party animal."

Sibyl conceded this may have been true.

"We probably saw each other out," Ben suggested, "back in the day, without us realising. In the clubs I mean."

"I doubt that. How old can you have been? Unless you got started young."

Now it was Ben's turn to concede, yes, so much was true.

She pointed to the CD he had in his hand. "Don't see many of those any more."

"I collect them. It was Lia who got me into them actual-fact. You spoke at her funeral back in the spring. Lia Woods?"

"My goodness. I think about Lia a lot, a lot. How is Joel? I must visit the Erskines again. I promised them I would do more to help."

"Joel's good. Joel's decent. Joel's his own . . . uh." Ben contorted in his chair to glance at the door. He kept thinking he was about to hear somebody knock. Surely there must be people out there in more of a state. "If I'm in this chair, I suppose I might as well say—I do have a small difficulty. Like a dilemma. Do you accept dilemmas?"

Sibyl gestured: I will look at your CDs, I will look at your dilemmas.

Ben said, "I think he might be my son. Joel."

For some reason he laughed again. It was hearing himself say this out loud for the first time. "I expected them to track down somebody else. I was waiting to hear about some random unreliable bloke from Lia's past."

"And here you are."

"The timing does make sense. And the more I see Joel, if I let myself *see* him, the more I recognise my mum's features. Dad's. Laid over the top of Lia's."

"Did you have a long relationship?"

"Me and Lia?" Ben blinked. "No. It was one of those."

"One of those?"

"My relationships run a particular course. I'm . . . a lot. Another thing, we had this friend, me and Lia. He loomed: even from a distance."

"Téodor."

"Mm. Téo always loved her. Still does I think."

"Have you told him your suspicions about Joel?"

"His dad's figured something out. Maybe there's been more gossip than I realised . . . He wants me to tell Téo soon."

"What's stopping you?"

Ben was almost drunk or high off this honesty. He followed the rush. "Guilt's there. Guilt's a factor. What it is though? Being truthful? I don't want to look after Joel. I like my life. It works."

Sibyl nodded. They were coming to the end of her shift. The casino would soon close, to be cleaned in a rush before it reopened. Ben was on his feet as well. He held the door open, timing the in-breath for hair smell, fabric smell, what perfume she wore. "I think you should arrange to come and see me at shul," she said. "We should finish this conversation."

Ben said, "Deffo." She had written her number on a piece of paper. They walked together to where two or three taxis were parked. Ben let her talk, stuff about the synagogue, her employers, she sounded troubled, he wasn't really listening. In his kitchen, soon as the taxi dropped him home, he would pour himself a drink. He would float to his computer and find out as much as the internet had on Sibyl Challis. He would think over moments, this dialogue of theirs, arranging the visuals, the sense-impressions, archiving them.

In the morning he came awake on a bare mattress. His sheets were off him, twisted into opposite corners of the bed. He went to one of the bathrooms and sounded some phlegm into the sink. Here it came, a small hangover, a curling wave that moved through his body, that crested and broke. He remembered those football tickets he'd won and he sent Téo a message. "Fancy the match today? I've come by a couple of seats. Long story how." Ben could always persuade Téo to do his bidding. He wondered, would they even get high at the game? Téo would refuse at first. Ben would harry him. These were the terms of the friendship.

Téo replied, "It's amazing to me."

"What is?"

"That you've still got idiots who'll bet you this kind of stuff."

"Short story then."

Phone in hand, Ben was doing a morning run on the machine. "I'll pick you up at midday," he wrote.

"What about Joel?"

"Ask your dad to mind him."

"Not sure Dad's up to that."

"Find a babysitter then."

"Who?"

"I'll find you a babysitter."

"I can't leave him with a stranger."

"Won't be a stranger."

"And not one of your girlfriends."

Ben stopped running. He wiped his forehead. "She's a pillar of the community. Leave all this with me."

Out on the doorstep he stretched. The hangover was in retreat already. Cats lay on the pavement and they watched him, recognising kin. Some delivery driver, low-gearing along the road, on the lookout for an address, wound down his near-side window. Without any obvious malice he spat an inch of spittle through the aperture. Ben nodded. He said yo to a jogger who passed, then someone swinging a plastic two-pinter of milk. People wore shorts, T-shirts, summer wear, same as Ben.

Going past his old school he ran his fingers along the wall where the bricks were engraved with the names of notorious pupils from the past. An immortal pair were observed kissing on this spot, as far back as the 1980s. He put his fingers around the iron bars of the gate and he pulled, testing the strength, this gate elaborately locked with chains as though the current load of students might want to escape one day; as though the former load of students might want to get back *in*. The playground was painted over with the same tennis-court tram lines in yellow, the basketball dashes in red, those long white strokes to mark out a football pitch. These were boundaries rejected by Ben and his friends when their games ranged as far and as wide as they needed to, overlapping and countermanding others.

At the Erskines' flat he found Téo flustered and still not sure about the plan. "You asked *who* to babysit?"

"It's cool," Ben replied, "she's trustworthy."

"I'm not questioning the trustworthiness of the rabbi. I'm wondering how you had the fucking nerve."

"She knows we've been through a hard time."

"We."

"You. Joel. Everyone."

Téo was bent over the kid in the kitchen, trying to persuade him to have his face wiped. There were relics of breakfast under Joel's nose and around his chin, an imitation beard made of crumbs and jam smears. Ben said, "She offered to help. And these seats. They're bang on the halfway line."

Téo clicked his fingers: show me.

He checked which stand they would be sitting in. He checked the price. Téo was always checking prices. They let Joel handle the tickets. Supervising him, they showed him how to angle each one in the light to make the holographic panels glow.

"Is my birthday," Joel told Ben.

"Tomorrow, mate," corrected Téo, "not today . . . What time did you say the rabbi was getting here?" Not long later they heard the garden gate scrape open. They waved Sibyl inside.

At first Téo was bashful, muttering, she could still say no to this.

"I'm glad to help," Sibyl said. She knelt and greeted Joel as a friend. Téo was explaining to her the latest routine. This account was so full of anticipated needs, habits and treats, it occurred to Ben that Joel's average day involved about as many crammed-in distractions and luxuries as his own. He went to smoke on the front step, warding off a growing impatience. After a couple more cigs Joel came panting outside to find him. He grabbed hold of Ben's hand. There was a message from Téo, apparently—an important message, some instruction that Joel alone had been entrusted to carry.

"What Ben remember *is*."

They got it out of him eventually. Ben must not throw any more of his cigarette stubs on the lawn. "Oops," he said. "Listen, birthday boy, you have fun this afternoon. Show your games to the rabbi. *All* your games. And your toys. All of them: don't stint."

Mention of the toys stirred some memory in Joel. He recounted for Ben the different ones he'd lost over time. Ben nodded and nodded. He said, "Oh a polar bear, was he?" Joel had his T-shirt up to reveal that he was wearing a utility belt. Ben got a comprehensive demo of its workings, how the belt was fitted with an imitation hammer, a saw, it was meant to have a drill, but who knew where the drill had got to. Joel showed Ben the empty housing: "Lost."

"Happens. Why don't you scour around and find it?"

"You come."

"Go by yourself."

"You come, Ben. Please, Ben."

"Nah."

"Found it," said Joel.

"The drill? You're kidding me. Can't have been very lost. I call that a false alarm," he complained.

"You see," Joel was saying, waving the recovered toy as if to draw a line under a long and unseemly argument. He stared at Ben a while. He whispered, "Is your birthday."

"Not mine—yours. Tomorrow apparently. What presents you getting?"

"Big ones."

"Ah. Best kind."

Téo had joined them on the step. They were ready to leave but, it was annoying, Joel wanted reassurance that Téo would return. "Come back in a minute" was how he put it.

"We'll only be gone a few hours," said Téo. "The time'll fly by."

Joel seemed to expect something more, a cuddle or what-have-you. Ben left them to it. He waited on the pavement. "Freedom," he said later, "am I right?" He punched Téo's kidney as they went. Téo punched him back in the rough-same spot. They rubbed themselves better. They ran when they saw the bus.

Theirs was a middling football team. No use denying it. They'd been middling so long you barely heard the heartfelt complaints any more. Fans filled the concrete stadium each week, regardless of whether the team looked likely to win or be humiliated. Loyal and doomed, they bought the latest replica kits. They walked around (grown men and grown women) with the names of bang average players across their shoulder blades. Ben appreciated many things about live football, mostly that for hours it was legitimate and even encouraged to behave badly in public. Before kick-off, when there were thousands of people converging on the stadium, you were allowed to walk in the middle of a road, any road. Respectful people spat. They swore and they laughed at volume, this to confirm that it was not your average afternoon.

Whenever a shout rose out of the mass of people—some provocation, a lyric half sung, one of those ritual plaintive questions, who are we, who do we love?—everybody knew what to answer. Ben and Téo were queuing on a driveway beside someone's trampled lawn. Retailers paid off local residents to set up their stalls. Ben studied a burger menu. He heard the shouted question from the road and he muttered on cue: who he was, who he loved. After the match was over and thirty thousand fans had trooped away home, these roads would be left stunned-seeming, in recovery mode, carpeted with food scraps and napkins and dropped plastic cutlery. Sanctioned littering! Again Ben marvelled. At the football, breaking rules was near enough a rule in itself.

"Hey," he muttered. He back-handed Téo on the arm: be cool. He brought out the pills he'd won at poker.

"Nah," said Téo quickly.

There was an aspect of priggishness to it. High holy Téo, who never used to want to cheat in their computer games because it denied you the experience. Ben managed his annoyance. "You've had a difficult summer," he cajoled, "the kid as well. By my calculations you're both owed some leeway."

"How does me getting off my head help Joel?"

There was debate. Ben wore away at resistance he'd been expecting. "Let's have a look at them at least," said Téo, and Ben brought up the four pills in his palm. They were square-shaped; a garish factory yellow. For a moment even Ben baulked at swallowing two of these things. But he tugged at the pocket of Téo's shorts. He pushed and he pulled his friend around on the road. "Careful," Téo complained, "you'll drop mine."

So they were doing this. First they ate the burgers they'd ordered, flat floury baps, wide as saucers, that needed eating with both hands. They chased the burgers down with watery beers. After the last swallow of his, Ben said, "Pudding?"

Téo looked at the pills again, peering at them as if wondering what they brimmed with, what hours they wanted him to have next. "What did you say these were?"

Ben decided to be honest. His poker acquaintance was vague on details.

"But what did he tell you?"

"He told me they were 'good.'"

Téo exhaled. He lowered his hand, refusing to participate after all. "Can't do it, Benno," he said. "I'm on story duty later. I've got to be in a fit state for Joel's birthday. You go ahead."

A challenge had been put to Téo and he'd failed it. Now his only option was to recover some pride through sanctimony. Ben felt the old hatred stir.

He put his palm to his mouth, same as old people do, or young children, when something is a shame. He swallowed down a pill then he said:

"Me and Lia. We had an affair."

"What?"

"A few years ago. After you left."

Ben waved a hand to demonstrate how small a deal it had been.

"What," Téo repeated, "what?"

He took a pill from Ben's hand and he swallowed it. Then

he took another pill and he swallowed that too. He swallowed a third—startling gestures.

"Jesus, T," said Ben, "what you doing?"

"I don't know. What affair? What?"

"It was something short. It didn't last."

"You went after her even though you knew how I felt?"

Ben said, "You weren't around."

"You went after her *because* you knew how I felt."

"This is a couple of weekends we're talking about, this is some cold November weather and nothing to do. There's already more analysis gone into it, the two of us stood here, than in the whole time me and Lia were together."

"Together! I can't believe this."

"It was a neighbourhood thing, a boredom thing, it was someone to get excited about for a minute. Being honest? I don't think Lia even liked me."

"No. She didn't."

Ben waited a moment. "That'll sting all the more for you then. Why didn't you make a move when you had the chance?"

"I did. Summer after school. She said no."

"Why didn't you hang around and try again?"

"Cos I'm not you. Because she said no."

"Once? You gave up after one attempt?"

"And then . . . I wasn't expecting the relief in it, when I went off to college, when I got some time away from you all."

"You swore you'd come back."

"I did come. Once a month."

"With a time limit: like you couldn't wait to get away to your place again. The group always noticed."

"Oh, the group always noticed."

"I noticed. Lia noticed."

"I'm sorry then."

"I'm sorry too."

They walked to the gates of the stadium where it was all cram, all bodies in crazy number. Their team was not the favourite today and some of the fans who passed them were debating the odds of a humiliation. They coloured in details; they scripted disappointments. It was cooler inside. When the familiar shout went up—who are we?—the question echoed off the lacquered walls. It wormed inside Ben's ear, demanding an answer more honest than before. He racked his brains. He tried to figure out who he was. So many of the bodies in the stadium moved against them now. Fans in different sections shuffled clockwise towards their seats while Ben and Téo tried to go the opposite way. There were collisions, clipped elbows, sorry-mates. Ben's body was powerful and easy to manoeuvre. Then he seemed to carry no weight.

"Does that make sense?" he asked Téo.

"Slow down."

Téo had him by the sleeve. They climbed a numbered staircase and journeyed over knees and feet, none of these fans on their row seeming to understand, it was imperative they got to their seats in time, because they had to let the referee know he was permitted to blow his whistle and begin. The noise of the home crowd built till the moment the players emerged and there was that fast and thuggish clouding-over of sound. Ben and Téo stood. They shouted the encouragement along with everybody else. These pills had maybe done them a favour. The timing was right. If they rode the high well, if the game fell favourably, they might expel months' worth of checked emotion. It would be nice to get an early goal. "Nice to get an early goal," Ben said.

Téo couldn't speak.

The referee blew his whistle and again Ben roared his belief.

There was a free kick. A promising position. It was a chance. "Wouldn't it be good?" Ben prayed, as thirty thousand fans did the same. When the goal came, Ben and Téo turned towards each other, breathless and gaping. On the pitch the players hurried to attack again. They went piling into the opposition as soon as they could, which was correct. "They've got the scent," Ben observed. His legs were trembling and he had to sit. Téo was already there. Flushed and nauseous they kept their movements to a minimum. Ben concentrated on a flag that whipped around its pole, high up in the ramparts of the stadium. At half-time they stayed in their seats.

That it was daylight above the opposite stand was intriguing to Ben. He realised: none of this could last, their electric arrival at the stadium was a memory, the match was almost over, their walk home getting closer. He was part present, part ahead, at the house and in his bed and ruminating on a difficult day. He was hot. Could be, his skin was made out of one unbroken piece. He could feel every part of it and every part was damp.

Ben suggested they get some water.

Téo shook his head, not possible.

Instead they stared out over the pitch. With care, Ben tracked Lia Woods on her walk between spectators in the opposite stand. He watched Lia as she climbed over knees and feet herself. He was struggling to breathe again; he had to be stern with Téo in asking for a turn on the air around them.

"What do you mean? What turns? What have we taken?"

"As to that," said Ben. He did not finish the sentence.

Half-time was nearly over. Ben could tell because the stadium seemed to gird itself and brace for the weight and trouble of more hopes, of hearts that had got like stomachs too full from an early goal. When the time was right Ben let the referee know he was permitted to blow his whistle. The match resumed.

With one knee on the pavement, Téo lowered his head, as though for the solemn amen at the end of a prayer. He vomited out a colourful liquid gust. Ben stood beside him, facing the emptying stadium for them both, having brought up his burger already. He told any passersby who asked, "We're fine, we're pleased with the result that's all." One more heave brought everything out of Téo in a rush, like an inspired sentence. He groaned. That part was done.

He moved cagily at first, as though he was old and ill like Vic, as though he could not risk another fall. The game had been finished an hour. With disorientating thoroughness the roads were empty, there was hardly anybody left around, only the animal police and the genuine elderly who had waited for a clear run at their departure. Clusters of kids and their parents lingered in the club shop. Ben smoked, wanting the better taste in his mouth. He lit one for Téo. They spat into drains, purging. Ben had those sharpened senses, the upgraded awareness that came in reward for a sobering vomit.

"So."

"So."

They were overtaken by buses heading in the general direction of home. They seemed to be in agreement that they needed time and privacy, they needed a practical reason not to look at one another. They carried on on foot.

"Why didn't either of you tell me?"

Ben wanted to know, "Am I meant to troop down to your flat in Aldgate, knock on the door, tell you I'm the prick again? What I figured was, you and me would find a time to talk about it. I'd tell you when the time was right."

Téo complained, the time's not right, this time is not right. "I've already got to cope with her being gone. I've got to last another few months with Joel. You ever tried to get a little boy under a blanket when it's coming up to midnight? You ever tried to keep one of their million hungers satisfied? I'm already a decade older since March. I don't know where to put this, what you're telling me."

They edged towards the side of the pavement, weak. They leaned for support against a betting shop's big window. There were posters behind the glass that boasted the chances of more events happening, tomorrow, next week. "You told me this to get a reaction," Téo said, "because I wouldn't join you on a pill. I feel awful."

"Me too."

"Let me say no like an adult next time."

"All right."

"What happened?"

Ben drew a breath. He said, "We had an affair."

"Like what," Téo asked, "like hold hands, send cards?"

"No."

"How long?"

"A fortnight . . ."

"You said November."

". . . maybe three weeks."

"Oh my God. So he *is* yours? Joel?"

"Look at him."

"Look at him. Fucking hell. What are we gonna do?"

"I don't know."

They got home on legs that worked for themselves, lungs too. The sun was hunched behind rooftops, hidden but not yet ready to say good night and go. They were caught and passed by more buses on the road. They latched on to each other by the

elbow. They held each other's necks, affectionate and exasper-
ated in equal measure, how they were as schoolboys, shoulder to
shoulder at their desk, the classroom's scaly carpet beneath their
feet. There were paired white lights from every car that came
towards them; and two beady reds that contracted to angry dots
behind every car that drove away. Soon they passed a pub that
was showing the football highlights on TV. Ben pointed out a
replay of their team's early goal, decisive in the end, a goal that
felt days ago. The bars of reception on their phones kept mounting and mounting and disappearing. Both of them tried to text
Sibyl. Finally one of Ben's messages pushed through the conges-
tion. He got a reply from her, we're fine, how are you?

As it got darker the neighbourhood was coloured by that
changing telly glow out of front-room windows. There were
smells of spiced food. It was the hour for deliverymen on scoot-
ers. They hairdryered around the neighbourhood carrying paper
bags patched with grease. People were seeing to their evening
pleasures. Ben was jealous. As soon as he could he got away home
himself.

Morning again. Another day of his habits, his treats. Ben was
capable of playing football to a decent level despite the sore head.
There was something about a comedown that made him more
decisive and lethal on the pitch. But he clapped his teammates
to show that it wasn't all about him, this was a group effort. He
reminded himself that the opening goal was not so important. It
only set the table. As he ran around he was thinking of the loss he
represented to professional sport, he was thinking, what a shame
he'd never had a job that paid. Comedowns from pills would do
that as well, they would make you question yourself. Ben ran it

off. He plotted in detail the next two or three text messages he would send to the hot rabbi. He scored another goal and he registered two assists.

At the end of the match, he found Téo and Joel waiting for him in Téo's car.

Ben could only imagine what sort of three-ply hangover Téo was undergoing himself. It was a surprise to see him driving so soon. "Morning," Ben said. "What you both doing here?"

Téo reminded him it was Joel's birthday.

"Ah yeah. Happy birthday, kid . . . So you were passing?"

"I figured, it's his birthday treat, you should come with us."

"Me?"

"Is a *birth*day, Ben."

"Yeah. Happy birthday. Thing is—I've got plans today is the thing." Ben thought of the schedule he had in mind, a massage, pints of sugary tea, a replay of yesterday's grand prix watched in full, no fast-forwarding. He'd anticipated an early-evening action movie. Casino no doubt. Now he looked at Joel in the back of the car. "Where's this outing to?"

"Zoo," Joel yelled.

"Safari park," Téo corrected, "the one off the motorway."

"You're gonna drive on the motorway?"

Téo shrugged. "I promised him ages ago. I try to keep my promises."

"D'you want me to drive instead? Is that why you're here?"

"You're not insured. I've had this argument with Victor already."

"I dunno, T—old Victor might've had a point."

"You won't be in any better shape than me. And I'm not taking notes on responsibility from Ben Mossam. Get in the car if you're coming."

"Park up here. I'll pay for a taxi. All three of us."

"To drive around a safari park? I made the boy a promise,

Benno, and I'm not letting him down, that's not my game. 'Is that why you're here?' Fucking here cos I thought you might want to fucking see him on his birthday."

"Is bad word."

"Sorry, Joel."

"Sorry, little man."

Ben watched Joel fidget in his seat. It looked as if he was caught between a desire to impress them both (these bigger boys) with his strictest attention, and a competing need to be wherever he wanted to be. "Grown-ups," he complained at last. There was no more restraining him. "Is always take a long time."

Ben got in. Safari park then. His son's birthday. It was all new.

"Thas better," Joel said, trying to console them both in their sulks. They drove north past a golf course then Enfield's oldest pub. They were on an A-road that cut through stubbly dry fields towards the motorway. Ben saw grass lying in heaps that marked a mower's progress. Daffodils bowed their heads as if suffering from comedowns as well. In this sort of state, the colours of a day were harsher, more angry at you. On the other side of Téo's windscreen Ben saw fiery pinks in the sky, explosion-oranges, grey-blue clouds that hung beneath this colour, accompanied by such an impression of a blaze that the clouds resembled the burning spaceships in a sci-fi film. "Hit the de-e-e-ck," quoted Ben.

"Hah?" said Téo.

"Nothing. You sure you don't want me to drive?"

"No."

"Just cos. I know how *I'm* feeling."

Soon enough they found themselves in a jam. They'd been twenty minutes in the car and they weren't yet out of the borough. Ben in his weakness was feeling the summer pollen behind his eyes. Spores of cotton floated in pairs off the mowed fields as though they'd been ordered to hold hands for a journey. After a while, a breeze moved across the road. Some of the clouds in the distance were rearranged. They were stuck in traffic still. Téo had his phone against the steering wheel so that he could write somebody a message. Ben wondered who. Then his own phone buzzed.

"I shouldn't be driving," came Téo's note.

Ben wrote back, "Probably not no. Three pills, man!!! You legend."

"What am I doing, Benno?"

"You maniac."

"This isn't me. Driving intoxicated."

Ben tried writing: "You didn't want to let Joel down. It's fair enough. I'm impressed honestly." He was winging this. It looked good spelled out. He pressed send.

"Okay, I'm turning us around," Téo replied. "I'll have to think of something else to do with Joel. And some fib to explain why the safari's off. Can you help?"

"With a fib, are you kidding me?"

Ben turned around in his seat and he said out loud, "Oi Joel, do you know what's actually better than one zoo?" The boy weighed some answers. He decided on two zoos.

"And do you know what's better than that? *Three* cheese-burgers."

"Actually?"

"Uh-huh," said Ben. "Téo Téo Téo. You best turn this car around. Joel's changing his mind. We're getting three cheese-burgers instead of two zoos. That right, Joel?"

"You sure, Joel?"

"I sure."

Later, on the drive back, Ben's phone buzzed again. "Thanks."

EIGHT

SIBYL

There were green privet hedges that bordered so many of the gardens in their neighbourhood. Loyally if not skilfully pruned with shears or electric saws, the hedges were often misshapen and wildest at the top where the fronds were hard to reach. Some looked as though they would topple if given a sharp tug. Their leaves were discoloured by bird droppings, old cobwebs, smears of pollen, other wind-borne gunk. On closer inspection (Joel taught Sibyl this), the hedges were also repositories of loose sticks. The sticks, which must have fallen from the branches of the over-hanging trees during autumn, had been hardened and shined by the winter and the spring, ready to be drawn out and brandished as weapons now that it was summer.

Strangers in the community had started to recognise Joel. They knew his story, his bowl of dark hair; they were aware of his love of sword-sticks. Builders, waitresses, teachers, suits . . . they picked up sticks of their own and they engaged Joel in brief and gentle thwack-thwack duels. There was one stately middle-aged woman who ran a Turkish food shop. She knelt in silence near a zebra crossing and let herself be knighted by Joel. There were teenaged twin sisters who sometimes passed on their way home from school, sharing chicken nuggets from a takeaway box. Somehow, Joel knew just which expression to make to get them laughing, crouching, gifting him one nugget for free.

Sibyl took Joel for walks whenever she could, whenever her duties at the synagogue allowed. She was trying to do a better job at Enfield Progressive, or anyway a more obviously proactive job. She organised bring-and-buy sales, a new youth choir, membership drives; she doubled the number of study groups. Sibyl had in her residence a typewritten note from the chair of the synagogue's leadership committee—the dread Hilda. Hilda was a popular and even-tempered barrister in her middle sixties who Sibyl (at the start of her probation) mistook for an ally. According to recent shul gossip, Hilda was on track to become a judge, something in the commercial courts. It was questioned whether Enfield Progressive could keep a judge. "You'll have noticed the empty seats," Hilda wrote, in what was advertised as "a friendly note" . . . It was true, on Friday nights especially there were whole rows that stayed empty now. Some of her front-seat reliables had gone missing. Perhaps they were trying out other synagogues.

So Sibyl was waking early again, the old problem. She was brought out of sleep by the question of what would happen next in her life. Seasons of insomnia had come and gone before. It was distressing. Then, because it was routine, the insomnia took on some qualities of a comfort. Up and dressed, usually when it was still dark, Sibyl cleaned the residence or read books, beginning to think of ideas for jazzier sermons, scheming to enlarge the congregation. She encouraged those who had trouble sleeping themselves to try contacting her during these hours. "It is always worth the speculative text," she insisted.

Sometimes, if he was up early with Joel, Téo Erskine called. He didn't like to discuss his own feelings and for the moment

Sibyl was letting him get away with this. They discussed child-care instead. She had no idea how to raise a small boy; but she was a quick and shrewd reader, blessed with a filter for writerly infe-licities and a useful sense of what to discard or retain from self-help books. By letting Téo explain his concerns over the phone, then by taking herself off for immersion in Enfield Library, she was able to help him answer questions he was reluctant to take to Joel's social workers. How much TV was enough, how much corrosive? Was Joel's fascination with adult penises undue? Téo worried about the boy's fingernails, all ten, which seemed to accumulate new commas of dirt the moment he touched any-thing. He worried about the additives in frozen food. There was worry in the worry—whether Joel might absorb or imitate his anxiety and because of this lose his easy artless way with the world. "I wanna know, but I can't ask the social workers, how much am I allowed to mess up before they intervene? Like, is there a number? When do I go from doing an acceptable job to a bad job? And from a bad job to a disgrace?"

"You're not doing a bad job," she assured him.

Reading through leaflets and online documents, even poring over transcripts of family court hearings, Sibyl learned that there were high tests to meet before a council would remove a child from its parent; and although that test was not so high for an interim carer such as Téo, concerns would have to be profound before he was ever forcibly separated from Joel. Social workers were trained to watch for signs of deliberate maltreatment. Alco-holism or drug use in the home. Neglect.

"Not too much freezer food?"

"No, Téo."

"Not too much TV?"

"No."

Sibyl was in her study one day in July when he came to visit in person. She was eating a sandwich, large bites, and leafing through a stack of news magazines she kept to hand in case a visiting congregant should be made to wait. There were to be more cuts to local services, she read. Councils all over the map were shrinking and merging vital departments, trying to carry on as before only without the proper sustenance, like animals in an experiment. Over three months had gone by since Joel moved in with the Erskines. They were due to meet with his social workers soon to decide something more about his future.

"How are you both?"

"Yeah," Téo said.

It had rained that morning and the light outdoors was enriched, clarifying surfaces, exaggerating the drama of quotidian colours. Sibyl led Téo through the synagogue to the residence and her study. They crossed the damp courtyard where the green of her pot plants was exceptional, nature making the most of what remained of its season to display. "I was passing," Téo explained.

"You don't need a reason. I'm glad to see you."

"I wanted to tell you about Joel."

"How is he this week?"

"It's the nappies, rabbi—I think we've beaten nappies. We used the last one in the pack. Since then we've sort of done without. Joel's in pants, nappy-free, he uses a potty if he needs to go. Or the floor. It's been a mix."

"But this is enormous."

"Think so, yeah."

"Come and sit. Tell me how you feel."

"Me? I feel all right I guess."

"You have to push and pull your feelings—just a bit. Try letting those feelings take the shape of sentences, Téo."

"It feels like . . . I've managed to get Joel through one more level of the game."

"And?"

"And I wanted to stop by and tell you."

"Soon as he's off the potty I want several sentences out of you. A paragraph."

Téo laughed uncertainly. "Don't think he'll be with me long enough for that." With a hand he made a visor over his eyes and looked around her study as if made shy, as if seeing something private or even obscene. "This is weird for me," he admitted, "I haven't been back here since Torah practice. I was twelve or thirteen. This was with the old rabbi. This was back when I was getting ready to have my Big Mac."

"Your . . . ?"

"Bar mitzvah. Somehow we got from there to BM to Big Mac. It would have been a bit of sarcasm that stuck. Lia's most likely."

Sibyl went to her shelves. "Here," she said. "I found these inside a book of hers."

Téo sat and he rubbed the back of his head. He leafed quickly through the photos.

"I kept meaning to bring them to your flat."

"No, this is better. Thing is, with a dad like mine, whenever I say the rabbi's gonna come over again he's nagging me about cupboard supplies. He's worried about the functionality of the doorbell. It's easier if I sort as much as I can without consulting him."

"How is Vic?"

"I think we're all tired. You seen him lately? The way he moves? Everything takes him ages. Brewing tea: that's twenty minutes. Getting to bed: it's a whole event. But he won't accept my help. He's secretive about his medication. He insists he can make his own snacks. I watch him, right, and he's trying to time his trips to the kitchen around his favourite programmes. There's been more falls." Téo pinched his nostrils together. "It's like Dad knows he's marked for something. He has these tremors, which are almost like confusion or fear, on *top* of the illness. But I'm not describing it right."

"How does this work with Joel there?"

"Oh Dad adores him. Dad can't get enough of him. He waits for Joel to wake up from his naps. He says to me, he says: Joel is the only thing that makes the days worthwhile. He tries to guilt me. When the social workers come again he wants me to offer to take Joel long-term."

"Is that something you want?"

"No. No."

Téo flicked again through the photographs in hand. There was one of Joel as a baby. There was a pregnancy scan. There was also a third photo that showed Lia and Téo and Ben. It looked as though they were at a teenagers' party. Somebody's sixteenth, Téo confirmed, examining it. "Lia was rushing us when this one was taken. She always wanted to leave a place. She never liked to stay, not at that age either."

"Do you find yourself thinking about her?"

"Course."

"I do as well."

Sibyl had wondered, during bleaker moments in this study, whether her disappearing congregants could *tell* that her faith had been wavering since Lia's death. Sometimes she needed to pool all she had, come a Wednesday or a Thursday, just to face another weekend. In those moments she felt a shameful indignation towards Lia, for destroying so much without warning or explanation. It flared and went quickly; afterwards Sibyl wanted to cry out or kick things. Guiltily, she turned to her books. She went to her shelves and picked off volumes, scattershot fashion, reading a chapter here, a page there, religious books and secular books, histories and novels, comforted as ever by strangers' anxieties well voiced.

Téo flapped Lia's photographs under his chin as if to cool himself. He glanced at the topmost picture and said, "Now that I look at Ben as a kid it seems so obvious."

Sibyl waited. She took a risk: "You think Joel's his son."

"I know he is. Ben admitted it. The day we went to the football."

"No wonder you looked so pale when you returned."

"Mm."

"Will you tell the social workers? Do you think I should?"

"It's for Ben to do, isn't it?"

"I'm not sure. I can see the argument both ways."

"Me too. Like . . . it's for Ben to *want* to do."

"Maybe we can encourage it though. Point the way. Let me think about this, Téo."

Her clock chimed, surprising them both. Outside the day had begun to dwindle, putting aside its twitch and potential. Téo brought out his wristwatch with a quick movement of his forearm. "I need to pick him up from nursery soon."

"Tell me something. How would you feel about letting Ben have a turn?"

"A turn at looking after Joel? I'd have one or two reservations, rabbi."

"Tell me."

"Oh, it's just Ben. He's a walking, talking reservation. You'll have reservations about Ben yourself—now that you're getting to know him better."

Sibyl nearly blushed. She nearly gave herself away. It was as though Téo had brought up for frank discussion one of her innermost feelings, a feeling she carefully, professionally suppressed whenever she was in shul or this study and playing the role of their rabbi. She'd had *one* improper dream about Ben. That couldn't be helped. There were other symptoms surfacing, though. When Sibyl visited the cinema now, her appetites were different. She shied away from the brash and violent action films that crackled like silver foil and instead she chose dramas, the grounded and the real, she wanted interiors, conversation, weather. She paid money to watch romantic comedies, a genre she always dismissed as smug and offensive and that suddenly seemed to pay her subtle compliments, offering up intermittent highs of recognition.

You're falling for a *congregant*?

That was her sisters' response when Sibyl tentatively admitted it. They were fascinated, eager for particulars of this new and enormous piece of Challis goss. But she could see they were both troubled by the confession as well. Her sisters were secular Jews, proud of Sibyl's devoutness and drawing from it a vicarious privilege, because at least someone in the family had God's number to call in a pinch.

He's not exactly a congregant, Sibyl told her sisters, and I'm not exactly falling for him.

She went on to admit that she was too old to pretend that something wasn't happening when it was. She talked through the signs. She knew herself. We've started to find ways to be in rooms together, she admitted. We linger for no other reason. I've been around long enough to recognise that tilting of the world for what it is, she told her sisters, who replied: oh, Sib.

In the study, Téo held his hands apart. He was maybe deciding to be more diplomatic about his friend. "Ben doesn't like being predictable," Téo said, "he doesn't like being boring. And because of that he isn't always reliable when I need him to be."

"With age, sometimes . . ."

"No. If anything with age he's stretching out his capacities. Yeah: Ben's been trying new methods of letting us down. He's already missed a bunch of play-dates with Joel. He came once. And even then I caught him with that wide-awake look, a look he sometimes had when we were at school, whenever he felt cornered . . . No one tells you how total it is, looking after a kid. Or if they do, you can't imagine it."

Sibyl said, "Have you tried telling Ben 'I trust you'? Responsibility can bring on outsized effects. I was a different person before I started as a rabbi. I've become many different people since." She glanced at the letter from Hilda on her desk, with its tacit warning about her future. "I will be different people again, I expect."

"There is a part of me that reckons . . . let Ben have a try, if only to give Joel another example."

"Go on," Sibyl encouraged, "say more."

Téo stared at his hands. He still hadn't taken off his coat.

"So Lia dies on a random weekend, same as my mum. And the world, both times, does a sort of handstand. And I'm rolled over by it. But the second time, with Lia, it was like it proved something. Something I had started to guess at when I was a teenager, spending evenings in a hospice and holding Mum's hand. There are no safe paths—are there, rabbi? On either side of us it's quicksand, spikes, a drop . . . Joel's too young to have to know about this. But when I'm with him it's all I can think about. He wants the world in three dimensions. He wants to take knocks and have them rubbed better. As he should! I'm the one who's messed up, being scared for him, and it seems like I *have* to be holding him back."

Téo's sentences, offered shyly at first, kept spilling out of him, as though permission for this honesty might be revoked. He looked at Sibyl and he said, "Until you spoke at Lia's funeral, I didn't even know she came to services here. I didn't know she was that religious."

"She started attending last year," Sibyl said. "She always sat as far away from me as possible."

"Funny. That was Lia's style at school as well. Let me guess. She wore her expression. The one that was all, 'Impress me if you can. And by the way . . .'"

"'And by the way you won't impress me.'"

"You saw it then."

"Have you wondered why she chose you to look after Joel?"

"I don't think she did choose me. I happened to be around that weekend." Téo didn't sound convinced. He turned sideways on his chair and he folded his limbs, addressing the wall. "It was chance."

"I would suggest, either way, that you've been a good friend to her. You've done your friendship justice."

"Did she ever come and sit back here as well—one-on-one, how I am now?"

Sibyl remembered the clutter of cups and saucers and their left-behind discussions as they raced between subjects. She remembered a few arguments and the one surprising time that Lia wept. They would sit opposite each other saying incredible things: you must be strong for your son; I can't be strong enough. Depression was not an adversary to be talked into a corner though. It wouldn't be bested by clever reasoning. Sibyl took too long to grasp this. When she finally realised she was not the person to be having such discussions with Lia, that they might even be sinking together, it was too late. One morning towards the end of March they sat down in Sibyl's study. There was tea in the pot as usual. Lia lifted the lid to smell it, she seemed content.

"A lot of congregants visit me here."

"She, uh . . . did she ever talk about me?"

Sibyl saw Lia sitting in that same chair. Occasionally she spoke about a friend. He grew up in Enfield. He came home for visits to see his dad and Lia looked forward to it, she said, because he was stable, he was somebody she could trust. "I choose to think, Téo, that people's private confessions should remain private in death."

He nodded at this and he said, "I'll take that as a no. I used to think about her all the time, all the time. The night before she died . . . we hadn't hung out properly in ages. But I'm back, we're in our pub, we're talking. And it's like we're closer than we've been since we left school. It's like it's starting over again, the obsession, and I'm undoing the effort of years to put some distance between us. In my head it's: we'll get together now, because she's seen how much I've changed. In my head I'm actually annoyed with myself for not doing this sooner. When she asks if I'll look after Joel I don't think twice, I'm thinking of course I will, of course—for practice! I'm thinking that by putting in a few good hours with Joel I'll prove to her how right we would have been together. She says, will you look after my son? And I don't hear any second question in it. Now I do. But now I don't want there to have been a second question. Because that would mean Lia planned this. It would mean I helped set this in motion by holding on to these feelings."

He had pocketed the photographs. He stood. "I should never've got back involved."

"I don't think that's true."

Outside, the sun had started its blinding afternoon dive. Téo explained the errands he had to run, beans in cans, more bread, a new marg, some extra pants for Joel if he could find them. When he'd gone, Sibyl wrote a sermon for the weekend. Once, with Téo, she had felt the fuller stirrings of faith: when it seemed to her that two people, one living and one dead, were able to communicate through her, speak to unfinished things and confront an opportunity missed. Sibyl's muscles were tense. She noticed she was listening with all she had. She said, "You're around in this. I know you are."

She looked out into the courtyard. That morning, lonely pellets of rain had slapped hard against its tarred floor. As though sent on dead straight trajectories from above, each raindrop threw up a stiff bar of spray that flared white against the surrounding tar before collapsing, drinking itself, barely observed by Sibyl before it vanished, like those dust spots or blemishes that wink through old celluloid films. The rain fell more thickly after that. Because of some trick of the light, this rain could not be seen from inside the study, the only proof of it the small rivers that began to course around the edges of the courtyard, the racket of the gutters, those short-lived flarings of white against the tar, little asterisks that rose off the floor and flickered for attention, phantom beds of flowers that came and went and came and went.

It was time to start locking down for the evening. Sibyl settled rooms. She turned off lights and bolted doors. The synagogue had a fiddly alarm system, its workings demonstrated to her by the old rabbi—but only demonstrated once. There was a box on the wall with many buttons. She tried pressing combinations of them, listening for a particular rising melody of notes that meant run, hurry, you've got five seconds, four, three.

"That was close," said Ben Mossam.

He was waiting for her outside. Some nights, if it occurred to him, he helped her drag shut the synagogue gates. He helped her secure the gates with chains, difficult alone.

"I was wondering about that meal. Or a trip to the cinema."

"Not tonight, Ben."

"Band then. Comedian. Bowling. Biking."

"Biking . . . !"

"Party then. A rave somewhere."

"I don't think so."

"Lecture? Recital?"

She smiled with genuine gratitude. This was costing him. "No."

They had the gates closed and locked. "I'll try asking again tomorrow. I'm guessing you're upset just now. You're worried about that letter the synagogue sent around."

"What do you mean, what letter?" Her tone was harsher than she intended. "I didn't know about a letter."

Ben seemed caught out: as if he had tried being interested in someone else's problems, and look where that adventure had landed him. "The leadership committee sent a letter to my house," he explained. "It was addressed to mum and dad. They've still got a vote, what with the money they've spent."

"I wasn't told that a letter was going out. A vote on what?"

"Whether you're made permanent or not. Personally, I'd vote permanent."

"That's kind of you. But don't do that."

Sibyl's hand was on her forehead. Well.

Ben said, "Didn't you know this was coming? As a rule I try to tell myself: chaos next."

She was thinking about his question. "I knew I was a gamble for them. The reformers on the committee were behind my appointment, the traditionalists, not so much. It's been almost a year. I should have known, you're right."

She was giddy. The sting would come. For the moment it was only absurd to hear the news in such a way. When they sacked her she would have to find somewhere to live. She would be put back at the start. "Was it bowling? One of your offers." Some of the old recklessness was in her, a reluctance to miss too many more opportunities of her own.

"Yeah. You up for it?"

"I haven't bowled in years, Ben."

The alley he chose was dark and cool; peaceful enough, once Sibyl surrendered to the rumble of rolling balls and the higher hollow rattle of thrown-about pins. "Honest lanes, these," Ben said without elaborating. He pestered Sibyl to play against him. He struggled to believe she would refuse to borrow and wear the loaned leather shoes, his favourite part of the enterprise. But he seemed happy enough to challenge himself to a game, twice inputting his own name on the terminal at the top of their lane, so that BENNO was pitted against THE MOSS-MAN tonight.

The walls bore fading frescos of bowlers in motion. Lasers cast shapes of blue and pink on top of these figures. Ben stood with his back to Sibyl, a marbled pink ball propped on the heel of his right hand. His left palm steadied it. All the finger holes were worn smooth by years of use, Ben promised her. "So they're comfy as mittens." Having said this he murmured something that was only for his ball, lips almost kissing its polish, then he marched forward, negligent, as though without a care, twisting off a preposterous curling shot that almost fell into the gutter right away but instead cleared the danger and turned inward in time to scatter all ten pins. He folded out his bottom lip, shamming humility. He muttered, "This Moss-Man. He's under pressure already."

Plain enough to her that Ben took pleasure in being watched. Sibyl fidgeted, disturbed all over again to find that she took so much pleasure in the watching. She put a hand to her hair and her stomach, shaking her head, met by an impression of a younger Sibyl Challis who'd been stirred awake, who wanted it noted for the record, she used to be lighter on her feet, she used to be capable of negligent brilliance, she used to be worth watching too.

"Have a go," said Ben. He was standing in front of her. "Take one of my turns."

"I'm fine. Very happy sitting here."

Coaxing. "You'll like it if you try it."

"I've tried ten-pin bowling, Ben. I'm a rabbi, not Neolithic Man."

Seated at the terminal, punching keys with two fingers, Ben was editing one of the player names, changing BENNO to COOL RABBI. "You're getting a head start," he promised, "a free strike. What's not to love?"

"I won't swap my shoes."

"Who cares? I'll square it with the shoe police."

She was thinking of birthday parties at school, the shouting and the too much sugar. She was thinking of early crushes on boys, rivalries with other girls, hardly identifiable in the classroom or the playground and suddenly made glaring by sporting competition. She dragged her ball to the line and flung it, watching it go, impressed by its trajectory and the promise of a high score. She found herself whispering a prayer of thanks. She said to Ben, "Beginner's luck."

"When did you say you last bowled?"

"I would have been eight or nine years old."

"Cool kid as well I bet."

Sibyl wondered. It was when she was eight or nine that she first determined to be a rabbi. She was spoiled, already occupying as the eldest Challis girl the second-best bedroom in the house. She gathered the nerve to ask her parents why couldn't she have the better bedroom, their bedroom . . . then it was something that came and went quickly, a little slackening of Dad's love, only sensed; Mum's flinch of disappointment. Her ridiculous request about the bedrooms was turned down (and afterwards repeated as amusing family legend), but from that moment Sibyl knew more, what a crushing betrayal it was, to be fortunate *and* greedy, to know it of oneself and to let others see it. She swore to fight the instinct. As children will, she made a fetish of a pledge.

At the time, the Challises were members of a synagogue in northwest London. They attended whenever the major festivals rolled around, big-ticketers, her dad called them, the Yom Kippur service, the Passover one. Sibyl was sitting with her family at Passover when it struck her that Judaism wasn't only a mysterious prize-giving machine, two or three times a year dispensing a free day off school, it was a system, it was explanation; by adhering to the rules of this religion she could live with other people foremost in mind and always know why. It was as easy as putting down one book and picking up another. She would be a rabbi.

There were fraught conversations about this. Years! However much her parents admired the principle and the constancy of her ambition, they were appalled in their hearts and they got worse at hiding it. They were in no hurry for any member of the Challis family to *de*-assimilate, undoing generations of work to fit in with England. In desperation they bargained with Sibyl, suggesting she try medicine, law, they would pay for whatever training she wanted, therapy, teaching.

"Oh yeah," said Ben, "you used to be a teacher. You mentioned that, first time we met. How old were you when you gave it up?"

They were sitting together in the polished slippery seats at the top of their lane. Ben had bought them both colas.

"I stopped teaching at about the age you are now," she said. Adding: "You're trying to figure out if we overlapped. Teacher and student. But my school was a few boroughs away. You wouldn't know it—Greenhills."

"Greenhills," he said, frowning. "Three-nil. Or maybe three-one."

"Excuse me?"

"I know for definite I scored a hat trick. Even though the referee was biased against us. North London Intramural . . . quarter finals this would've been. We got knocked out next round. Same ref!"

"I'm going to guess that your parents weren't around a lot back then."

Ben writhed, pleased, spilling drink. "Keep going," he said. "I like hearing myself explained to myself."

Sibyl considered him. "It comforts you to be seen in action. The bigger the action the better, because the more seen."

"This is good stuff. When's it my turn?"

Sibyl waited. She did not expect Ben to have any flair for this kind of analysis and she was impressed when he said, "If you're hanging around with me then something's wrong. Something's missing."

"Why do you say that?"

"That's the pattern. Women are most attracted to me when they're trying to blow up their lives . . . I don't mind. I'm half flattered. It's like I'm a dangerous weapon. Rare. They don't make many like me. It's the only reason Lia was ever interested. And then not for long."

"Before she died, I used to brim with belief," Sibyl admitted. She held up her drink, sloshing the liquid to demonstrate. "I'm still so angry at myself for not hearing what Lia had to tell me."

"I reckon if I was you, I'd be angry with God as well. For sitting on his hands."

"In fact, that was start of the trouble. I *wanted* to be angry at Him. I expected to be. I would have preferred it. But as soon as I formed the thought I knew I was forcing something. A connection had been lost, some resonance, and I couldn't be angry at God any more than I could be angry at, at, at those bowling balls. We had stopped being of the same stuff. We had stopped sharing a language."

"Shit."

"Uh-huh."

"So what next, you faking this? Or you quitting?"

Sibyl couldn't help laughing. "That's actually a very helpful question."

Boxy square screens, suspended over every lane, rotated through adverts for local businesses. There was nobody bowling. The din of a computery pop song echoed off the polished pine lanes. They had finished their drinks. They started to talk about their families, their ancestors. Ben asked her, "So were your lot . . . ?"

He let the query hang where it was, unfinished but comprehensible enough. That pause. That slight wince. That apologetic widening of the eyes, to acknowledge the size and the cumbersomeness of the subject. Among the English Jews of Sibyl and Ben's generation, miles and decades removed from Hitler's Europe, there wasn't much left to feel but a dull, woozy bafflement at the dispersal and death of millions of their babcias and nagyapas, their onkels and tetyas and kazans. "Yes. On my father's side," she said. "How about yours?"

Ben tutted, no, the Mossams were lucky as usual. "It's been a bigger deal for Téo."

"On his mother's side."

"Yeah. Though I'm wondering now."

"Go on."

"T's pangs. His handwringing. How he measures risk and gets his numbers wrong. I'm wondering, is that something to do with what's in his blood? He always looks so culpable, so nervous. Have you noticed? It's sad to me. Infuriating. I wish he could relax for one minute. I wish he could do something purely for himself."

Sibyl stayed quiet.

"What? What're you shying from saying?"

"I'm wondering what Téo would reply to you if he were here. If he had the courage to!"

"Didn't realise you and him were talking."

"We talk."

"Gimme your best Téo then."

"I think he would say . . . what I'd *like* him to say to you is, 'Ben. Do something purely for someone else.' "

Ben sulked at that. Sibyl let him. "It's a crap impression," he complained.

Soon there would be another meeting with Joel's social workers, Sibyl explained. "We're deciding about the next stages of his care. Who can do what. I've said I'll be there. I think you should be there as well."

"No chance."

"Ben. Do something purely for someone else."

"This you talking? Or you-as-Téo?"

"It shouldn't matter."

"Is this why you came out tonight, to waylay me?"

"I don't know why I agreed to come. Something told me I should."

"As in . . . God did?"

Sibyl shook her head, no. She sat in contemplation for a moment. She'd always wondered about faith's staying power, perhaps intuiting how entirely and with what speed it might one day desert her. She had prepared contingencies, she had sketched out a post-faith plan. What she would do (she decided) was take away the remembered best of faith, for instance that overspill of confidence that made it easy to offer out compassionate counsel, that tolerance for other people's enormous flaws. Now a new question occurred to her. What if the loss of faith she felt after Lia's death was less a crumbling of something, instead a deliberate reorientation, a small act of God in itself? This new silence: it left room for another voice. To be faithless did not have to mean to be aimless. She had learned so much in her work that would be useful to someone. Joel was someone.

"I want you to come to the meeting," she said to Ben. "This is me asking, not as Téo, not as your rabbi, this is me."

She had taught herself to live as though under an adjudicator's eye, practising courtesy when it was not called for, forcing herself to be hospitable and generous without hesitation, always quieting that childish voice inside her that whinnied and complained, me first, me instead. She watched Ben as he pouted and tipped about on his seat, as though on board a rocking boat. She thought, he's pondering the novelty of a new idea: me second.

"It might be all right," Ben agreed. "When's the meeting?"

Apparently Joel had already *been* through the ordeal of a splinter. The flat was in a spin about it, Téo was, Vic was, Joel of course. The garden fence was the culprit. The boy kept brushing his hand against the rough surface of the timber while he played. In the front room, Joel came over to Sibyl and Ben with the gravest face, cradling his hand like something impossibly precious they must want to see, explaining that he'd had two splinters in two days. He was taken away to the kitchen freezer where Téo, having numbed Joel's finger with a bag of sweetcorn, nipped at the reddening skin with tweezers. This shard of wood was lodged at an awkward angle. Joel's composure soon broke and he sobbed. They had to try a few different methods of removal, including one that Sibyl dreamed up involving a piece of thread cleverly knotted and used as a miniature lasso to yank the splinter free.

"Do sweetcorn again," Joel wailed.

"I'm doing it," Téo said. "You're okay, mate, we've been through this before."

"Tay-OH. Is hurts."

"Keep still. We've got through worse."

When the social worker arrived she apologised for coming alone. It was Gil. She was perhaps in her early fifties, Sibyl judged. She had a kind voice, kind eyes, her teeth were . . . not bad but definitely memorable, they were fissured and irregular, like the monoliths Sibyl once learned about in school. They sat around Gil at the Erskines' table. "As a department we're always a tad stretched," she said, "and sometimes not a tad. That in mind, I'd like to start by thanking . . . Ben, is it?" Gil opened her notebook. Yes. "I'd like to thank Ben for joining us. The more people on Joel's side the better."

"Cheers, ta," Ben said. He spoke as someone receiving an expected compliment.

Across the table, Victor snorted. Téo stared at his hands.

Gil continued, "As the rest of you know we've spent the last few months trying to find a legal guardian for Joel, someone who'll take him on for the remainder of his minority."

"His . . . ?"

"Till he's eighteen," said Téo.

Ben whistled.

"Téo passed our viability test back in the spring. His willingness to look after Joel as an interim measure has allowed us to keep our heads above water. I want to say again, how grateful we all are." There was a stir at the table, unmistakable as an elderly man's discontent. Gil corrected herself. She would have sat around many such tables, Sibyl presumed, trying to keep the attention and goodwill of cross and combustible people. "Victor's assistance has also been important. And we're grateful to you as well, rabbi."

"Trampoline," Ben coughed.

"I'm sorry?"

Gil checked this, there was nothing in her notes.

"It's hardly worth mentioning. Small fry. Only, I bought Joel this big trampoline. Probably not important. Tell 'em, T—about the massive trampoline."

When everybody was looking in Téo's direction he pushed out his lips and he tucked his chin against his chest, the mildest affirmative.

"A-ha," said Gil, "the trampoline outside. Thank you, Ben.

Thanks as well for agreeing to join these other three as a part of Joel's network."

"His . . . ?"

"The people who look out for the boy," said Téo. He circled his head. "Me, my dad, the rabbi. Now you as well."

"As I understand it," said Gil, running the tip of her biro down a page, "you've offered to look after Joel for one or two days a week when Téo goes back to work."

Ben looked at Téo then at Sibyl in wordless appeal: Have I offered that?

"That's right," said Téo.

Victor made a series of low noises.

"Cool, it's cool," Ben rasped.

"Good." Gil wrote something down. "And Rabbi Challis has offered to make herself more available. She has said she'll keep taking Joel for walks in the park. Sunday cinema trips. She regrets she can't do more for the time being."

Sibyl said in her defence: "The synagogue. My congregants," exculpations that sounded sturdier a week ago, when she had written them in an email to Gil.

"It's July now," Gil said. "Come the autumn we'll need to make a court application. Téo has agreed to continue as Joel's carer in the short term. But he has told me that he doesn't want to apply for permanent guardianship himself."

Téo kept looking at his hands. Victor shuffled. Gil explained: "If nobody comes forward by the time we need to file the application, it's possible a judge will order that Joel is moved over to state care. If we *do* find him a family, they may not be in London. It is unlikely the family will be Jewish. There aren't perfect solutions."

"How long do we have?" Sibyl asked.

"Two months? Three at a push? September. October. Services are overburdened. Nothing moves quickly. But in Joel's case some extra time might be useful. We might hear from the father, still, or somebody else might step up."

"It is time for *me* to speak," said Vic.

"Dad—"

Vic talked over this objection. "I nominate Téo and myself. We will continue to work together as we have been doing. We'll raise the child ourselves."

"Till Joel's a man? Tall as me? No," said Téo.

"Then I'll do it by myself if I have to."

"You can hardly get around. How would you reach things for him, chase him? You can't lift things. You can't bend, Dad."

"Not true." Vic appealed to Gil: "That is simply not accurate. I want that stricken."

Gil had closed her notebook. "There's no record here. We have time. Not a lot of time but some. Please keep thinking about this—all of you."

She looked at them one by one. "We'll sit together like this in the autumn. Meanwhile, I'll see some of you when I come to visit Joel. You can also find us in the children's services department at the council, whenever you need. I'll write down the address," Gil said. "I'll write it down four times."

NINE

TÉO

A finger in the bathwater to test its temperature. A last rush of hot from the tap. When Téo returned downstairs, Joel was no longer being a knight: he was being an architect. The sofa cushions had been pulled loose for the hundredth time and Joel was trying to stack them, cleverly, in due course telling Téo he did not need help.

"Mate, you must be so excited about next week."

"No-o-o."

"You nervous?"

"No-o-o."

"It'll be a change is all. Fun for you I reckon."

"Téo's go work?"

"That's right."

He sat beside Joel on the floor. They did discuss his structural problems, these cushions that tonight would not behave. It was almost the end of summer. Joel had the power to startle Téo with his statements. "I want to keep you for all my day," he complained.

"Oh—thanks. You'll have fun with Ben though."

His bath. His teeth. His potty. The job was repetition inter-
spersed with the remarkable. They agreed it was just excellent,
how the bean of toothpaste emerged with its coloured stripes
intact. "Is magic?" asked Joel.

"Nah. Only a factory trick. Machines."

They tried to predict coming temperatures for the night.
They talked about what combo of blankets and duvets Joel might
want to try. Téo wondered if the boy wasn't coming to the limits
of his patience with that potty. "Would you like to try using the
big toilet tonight?"

"Your toilet?"

"Belongs to all of us. The toilet in the bathroom."

"Téo? Pretend that . . ."

A lot of Joel's notions started with this suggestion.

"Yeah? Pretend what?"

"Pretend is *my* big toilet."

He wanted to be left alone with it. He made Téo wait outside while he exerted himself, the huffs, the heaves . . . three distinct pebble-drops . . . then a flush. The cistern made a din as it
sluiced clear. Téo was tempted to fly in there and celebrate. He
told Joel, "I'm proud of you," as he wiped. They washed their
hands together. "First ever toilet by yourself."

There was so much she was missing.

"I did three poos."

"I heard. I heard."

"Bit messy my fingers."

"We're cleaning you up."

In the bedroom Joel said, "Téo's go sleep as well. Is time. Téo's
tired."

"Is he? Am I?"

It was only another evening of TV downstairs. Only another
of Victor's sulks that awaited him. And some nights Joel wanted
an escort—he wanted to be joined on his journey to sleep, which

meant that Téo had to climb in the bed as well and fake his own wind-down routines, the main lights swapped for bedside, the bedsides extinguished as well. After that they lay together in the dark, Joel determined to stay awake for as long as he could, turned edgewise on the mattress like a balanced coin. When it seemed that he was asleep, Téo reached for his phone. He brought up a page of sports analysis. He frowned over a word puzzle. And he sent another reminder to Ben, fixing their arrangements for the following week, the when and the where, what supplies Ben would need, what mindset.

From the darkness Joel said, "Téo's a bit sleepy!"

"Thought you'd drifted off. Téo's not sleepy. Téo has his mind doing a hundred miles an hour. Téo's wondering what his work will be like after so much time away. Téo's got you"—he tickled Joel's stomach—"gabbing away when it's late. Téo's got you farting under the covers."

"Is true. Is fart."

Folding a pillow, Téo lay on his side as well. They faced each other. "To be honest I might let one off myself," he admitted. At this Joel shivered, delighted by the admission as much as anything. Afterwards, at Joel's request, they lifted the blankets to evaluate the smell. He wanted Téo to joke about which flavour. "Please. Tay-oh."

"Uh, cheese sandwiches. Hint of slugs."

Joel laughed. "Téo's a bit joking."

"No, I've got a real joke for you."

Joel scratched himself. He nodded with impatience when the joke did not begin at once.

"Knock knock."

"What's there?"

"You got to say who. Who's there. It's the main rule of jokes. The only rule. Try again. Knock knock."

". . . Who's there?"

"Boo."

"Boo what?"

Best case it was an improvised sleep. A diet version. It was semi-skimmed sleep: those nights you tried to get some kip beside a little boy. Joel ground his teeth. He made incoherent announcements that came punctuated with stylish laughter, as if in his dreams he could parley with visitors and be informed and suave. He exercised his limbs and because of this he kept spiriting away the blankets that then needed retrieval. After a while Téo snuck another glance at his phone. There was a reply from Ben, who asked, "Are we sure about next week?"

"No choice," Téo wrote. "Joel's expecting it. And the social workers have been told."

"Cool. Only wanted to check."

"Joel's looking forward to it," Téo lied.

"Cool, cool, me too."

Quiet as he could, Téo rolled off the mattress. On the landing he stopped to listen to the sound of Victor's quiz, a staple. They would watch news together, panel shows, for definite they would argue. When Téo got downstairs, Victor was standing with his thighs and his bottom against the grille of the front-room radiator. Never a promising sign when Victor loomed like this, his expression pinched, the TV watched from height. Likely he'd spent the day folding over his grievances and strengthening them.

When Téo first agreed to go back to work, Victor was pleased. He presumed it meant he'd spend more time with Joel. He asked Téo and the social workers, could he walk the boy to nursery, could he collect him after? They had to explain that the rabbi had offered to help as well. Ben had agreed to do something. They had to explain, Victor was an important part of Joel's network. But he was too frail to be left alone with the boy for long. If Joel made Victor feel strong, he only made him feel that way. Victor took offence. Tonight he said, "You would never have taken Joel in the first place. Not without my influence."

"We calling it influence? You lied to his social workers."

"Lied!"

"You let them think I was still close to Lia, perfect mates. You let them think our families were near-enough next of kin. There was nobody around to contradict it."

"Well and what's been the harm? Joel's happy here."

"I know he is."

"Then what's the problem? Tell the social workers we'll keep him."

"This isn't my life, Dad. It's her life. I'm getting closer and closer to Joel. Joel's getting closer and closer to me. And only *I* know, out the two of us, that it can't last. I keep thinking it would've been better if a stranger had taken him at the start."

"No."

"It would have been cleaner."

"There was a reason Joel was left with us."

"There were no reasons in this. Lia was out of reasons."

"I mean a *reason*." Victor took a quick and shifty glance at the ceiling—heavenwards.

Téo was picking up sofa cushions that had been left scattered around the floor. He could only mutter, "Fuck sake."

Victor closed his eyes and said, "These have been the most meaningful days of my life. At least, since your mother died."

"Sweet. No, that's lovely that. Which God, out of interest? Which God has been taking an interest in your meaningful days? Your God or Mum's God? Catholic or Jewish?"

"I was dead, Téo. Now I'm alive. Let me care for him."

"You're not strong enough."

"I'm strong enough for this."

Téo didn't pause to consider it—he was holding a cushion and he threw it at Victor, an underarm chuck, nothing violent. Victor's reactions were too slow. The cushion hit him in the chest and fell to the floor. They waited, both too angry to speak.

"That was cruel."

"I'm sorry."

Later, when they were eating dinner off their laps, Victor returned to the subject.

"You think I'm useless," he said.

The front room smelled of breadcrumbed oven products and open beers. They had shared maybe a hundred dinners like this since Téo came home and still they were not in alignment. They could not make each other understand. Téo imagined his own relationship with Joel mouldering the same, given time.

"I know you're ill," he said. "I know it's an unkind disease and I'm gutted for you. But Joel would only wreck you with his asking, all the finding and the fetching. I swear, Dad, one day alone with him and you'd be hospitalised."

"I'll speak to the social workers myself."

"Good luck with that. Write a stern letter to the prime minister while you're at it."

"Ben will only let you down."

"Maybe. Maybe not."

"The state of you both! That night you came back from the football."

"That was once. I told you, it was a one-off."

Téo squirmed even so. He was ashamed of it. The comedown from the pills lasted days and he notched some of his worst parenting hours during that time. "The colour of your face," Victor said. "You tell me I can't be trusted. But I was the one who did the looking-after that night. I put Joel to bed. I read him stories."

"You did."

"It should be me not Ben."

"And I've told you it can't be you cos then it's me, really, and I don't want to be stuck here till Joel's eighteen."

"Stuck here."

"Yeah—I have another life. Or I had one. I made plans to go out. I stayed in. I didn't have to tell anybody why, what, where. I was allowed to make my own messes and clear them up in my own time. I want that back."

And I want away from Joel, Téo thought, while I'm fond, before we turn into this. Ben was the route . . . if Ben could be persuaded to feel something for Joel then Téo figured he could return to that old life without guilt.

Victor said, "When he lets you down you'll turn to me."

"Don't jinx it, don't *do* that. We owe it to Joel to try with Ben. I've got one or two ideas about how to bring him around."

Because Téo understood his friend. He knew it was not realistic to expect Ben to mature overnight and throw over years of self-indulgence, not unless certain weaknesses of his were singled out and exploited. Ben craved intensity of experience. He expected each day to contain its portion of luxury and its portion of risk. These were pieces of intelligence that Téo could make use of. Trust me (he had said), your appetite for extremes will be well sated by looking after Joel. There's nothing so scary as minding a confident and curious child, keeping them out of a tantrum, keeping them out of an *ambulance*, where all their instincts seem to want to lead them. As for the luxury aspect, as for trying to appeal to Ben's taste for pleasure . . . there were certain things that could not be explained in words. Joel was heaven and he was hell. He was a treat and he was a many-pronged torture. The luxury part of the equation would be for Ben to fathom himself. Téo had said to his friend, in the end it's up to you, mate, your capacity. And that was enough, the grace note, Ben's ego was engaged. He agreed to try.

Meanwhile, Joel was briefed. He was talked in towards a change of routine, his ear bent with encouraging accounts of a land called Ben's House. There were handpicked books at bedtime, stories about children who had to overcome their doubts about a sleepover or starting at a new school. Joel was encouraged into question-and-answer spells during meals or while walking home from the park. He was told, you must be nervous, you must be excited though.

In the middle of August, during days of unpredictable weather and topsy-turvy hot and cold, a neighbourhood foolish without its sleeves one day and everybody sweating in their coats the next, they set off for Ben's. The oaks of Enfield scattered treasure. Téo went ahead of Joel on the road, hoping to show him what to look for on the pavement, what was rare and worth collecting, for instance a mutant acorn that was more cup than fruit. Joel wasn't interested. He knocked Téo's hand aside. Overhead there was that whipping sound, audible only once per year, of falling acorns as they cut through canopies of leaves. Joel didn't want to know.

"The riches you're missing," Téo said, having found an acorn in a class of its own, not green and not brown and instead the same lemon yellow as the parking lines on the road.

He quickened their pace. The route to Ben's was a habit, manageable blind. He used to walk these roads several times a day. When they reached Ben's drive, Joel claimed a crooked stick from the ground. He dragged its end in the shrubs, loosing out leaves; then he dropped the stick and he reached for Téo's hand. "I don't want it," he said.

They rang Ben's doorbell together. Joel held on to Téo's leg. There was an appreciation on Téo's side that this easy physical contact of theirs could not last much longer. Already it didn't feel fully cool for him to kiss Joel anywhere but on the flat summit of his head.

Téo bent and buried into the hair now, a snouty move, his nose as much as his chin as much as his lips making contact.

Ben had opened the door and he watched them kiss goodbye wearing an expression of blatant dread. Téo hustled Joel over the threshold. He thrust on Ben a bag of equipment. He didn't dare linger in case one of them lost their nerve.

Free, unmolested, perhaps for the first time in six months, Téo sat at his desk. His colleagues took an interest in their computers. Sensitive to staring at him or mobbing him, they approached in ones and pairs, grasping his shoulder, repeating that they were delighted to see him and so sorry for his troubles. A few people had this idea he'd been ill. "I was looking after a friend," he explained. It needed more. "The son of a friend of mine. She died quite suddenly, back in the spring."

"Téo," his colleagues said.

"Yeah," he answered. The faces they made. The faces he found himself making. He told his story several times. "One minute I'm here, working as usual. Then I go back to my neighbourhood on a visit and . . . stuff just . . ."

He blinked. Joel: making them chase after a frisbee, the indoor one, manufactured out of foam so that it wouldn't hurt the furniture. Joel: wanting to be lifted up to press a light switch. Téo could carry him easily at first. Lately he had to set his feet. He had to tell himself, Téodor! Consider your spine.

"You've been through a difficult time," his colleagues said.

"Yeah."

"You're back though. You've been through the hardest part."

"Yeah maybe."

The office he worked in was part of a niced-up warehouse. A developer had hollowed out the building, which used to store tea, making it presentable and surgically white. Téo sat nearest the printer, where they kept their piles of accident statistics, pages and pages of them in unjust heaps. He had a preferred mug with the tarry residue of a thousand coffees inside. Their computers were believed to be slower, he heard, since he was last in. A technician had blown through and fussed with the software. Téo drank a coffee and he started to read emails that had accumulated in his absence. There were hundreds, the first dozen from his colleagues, sent that morning and welcoming his return. There was junk mail, every flavour. As he scrolled further backwards in time it was like uncovering changes in rock; he identified eras. People from their school had used Téo's work email to write their memories about Lia. He archived a few of these messages, meaning to pass them on to Joel one day. He kept scrolling back, coming to a seam of emails from his colleagues, queries that were sent in the day or two after her death. Nobody would have known yet that Téo was off on leave. He deleted most of these and kept going, his eye on the dates, wary for the weekend that would always be freighted. There were adverts. Enquiries. Nonsense messages that Téo deleted with a click. He swayed in his chair, half expecting to see he had an email from Lia herself, explaining why she'd done what she'd done, listing the steps she hoped he would take next. But there were only more deals, more bulletins.

Téo scrolled back to the top and saw he had a new one. It was from Gil, the social worker, writing to wish him luck at work and to pass on news. There had been a development regarding Joel's care, she said. They had found a short-term placement in a foster home that could start as soon as the autumn. The family was Jewish. They lived quite far away in the north of England. It was an option, Gil said. Unless the situation in Enfield changed soon, unless somebody made an application to be Joel's guardian, they would move him north. Téo wasn't sure what to do with this. Eventually he clicked delete. His head was blank.

The special treatment, the exceptions made for him, all that fell away as the working day progressed. When Téo first came here he was the youngest in the office, something like a pet or a nephew to the others, condescended to and spoiled. He had a computer-programming degree and trying to impress them he sat down one afternoon to write some software, simple, ugly work, a tool to help their visiting students revise the highway code. Huddled at his desk by the printer, caning caffeine, Téo added more features to the software until almost all of the teaching sessions they ran here made some use of his kit. When he was twenty-five and again when he was twenty-eight he tried to leave, never in sulks, unresentful, only curious about what other jobs were out there. They kept raising his salary. They let him teach.

At 2 p.m. today he led a batch of arriving students into the instruction room. Téo thought of them as students, as if their appearance here was voluntary. The office did get the occasional driver sent in at an employer's expense, to be reminded of the shades and secrets of respectful driving. But his main group, the majority of the people he taught, showed up smarting. Caught speeding on the roads, they would have been sent a letter from the traffic police, insisting they complete a safety course or else take punishment points on their licences. They walked in with open outraged mouths, furious for being cost hours and for having to listen to a mediocre man like Téodor Erskine explain rules they were sure they already knew.

"Afternoon," he told them.

He had a couple of dozen in today.

"Mobile phones should be—?"

He fell back on the old routine. It was expected that students would hesitate and be shy at the start of a session. None of them wanted to be the first to collaborate. "Mobile phones should be off," Téo said. A couple of people glared at him with contempt and this was expected too. He used to be admired around the office for his way with the feet-draggers. He was good at talking down rebels and trouble-makers, having done so all his childhood. Again, he wished that Lia had called him that weekend, admitted, this is where I've got to, these reaches, this is what I need you to do to help. Téo didn't know what he would have said to dissuade her. He just believed he would have dissuaded her.

"We're here to learn about driving—?"

"Better," the students muttered at him.

They were warming up.

"Safely. We're here to learn how to drive safely. Because you've been caught driving—?"

"Fast," they said.

"Unsafely. We'll be refreshing the rules for you today. Rules that are there to keep you and everyone around you safe. Follow the rules and you'll be—?"

The instruction room was the largest space they had, a tall white box with nothing-special windows, no posters or pictures on the walls, the idea being to make it rubbish for distraction. Téo revealed to his students the latest numbers on road accidents. He had a screen he stood in front of and on to this he projected images of disaster, nothing too graphic, more . . . suggestive.

"As we see. This driver's had a—?"

"Nightmare," they said.

"Speak up. This driver has—?"

"Crashed."

Téo nodded. "Misjudged the corner . . . No," he said, stern. Someone's mobile phone was ringing. "I'm normally clear on this. Did I not say about switching off?"

It was like a character he played. He felt he could continue the lesson without fainting, but only if he stayed hidden in the performance. He moved between their tables. Clarifications were asked for, complaints lodged, as well as the smaller ironic remarks. Rebellious students had three habits. They would moan these lessons were all a con to make the government (or the police, or Téo) rich. They would be catty about the highway code, which they were sure was too prescriptive. Sometimes they would offer their world-wise and personal takes on a better code, one that punished the cautious, rewarding rebels for their daring instead.

"From what we're seeing in this next series of images," Téo began.

He held up a remote control and he used it to move through images of disaster.

"This car has driven into a—?"

The students were quiet. From the ruin on display it wasn't easy to tell what had happened.

"Central reservation," Téo croaked. For a moment he couldn't tell which hand held the remote. Whenever a student said they felt ill he was supposed to send them outside for air. "Excuse me," Téo told the class, "this hasn't ever happened to me before."

On the road, bringing London into his lungs, he stood with his back to the building. He let the city swill by. Families were walking in their teams, loners as well. He watched a group of teenagers emerge from a bakery, peeling paper off their after-school snacks. A few times Téo wondered: is that her, turned to face the other direction? Women had aspects of Lia, they shared her walk or her outline. He sensed her around corners or behind curtained windows. One idea made him weak, that by going home he had provoked all this.

He rushed out a text on his phone. "You both okay?" he asked Ben. "Has Joel eaten any fruit?"

He watched his screen for an instant answer, but this was hard on the nerves and he thumbed through his digital photos instead, wanting every picture he could find of Joel. For a moment Téo couldn't remember his smile or how he scolded you. He made some rapid selections so that a photo of Joel would swim on to his phone whenever he woke it from a sleep. Changing his mind, Téo swapped the image back for his football club's crest.

"Seems fine to me," Ben answered. "He's watched a few of his programmes."

There was another message coming. Téo waited.

"What is fruit?" Ben wrote.

"Nice, funny, good."

Okay: he could still spot a joke. He could smile. Téo stood straighter. He shook out his limbs. Leaden arms today, like he was carrying them for someone else.

It was quarter to five, that part of the working day when colleagues began to look for a final distraction, the one-more-thing to get them over the line. Typically, they managed their love lives at their desks or they wrote to friends, squaring evening plans, the office computers absorbing their impatience with a slow-turning fifteen minutes. Téo was applying himself to the last clicks and cross references of some clerical work. After a discussion with his colleagues in human resources, he had agreed he would not teach another class for the time being. He was asked instead to sift through attendance lists, confirming who had been in and completed a session, clearing their debt to the road. At ten minutes to, he slid sideways on his chair and visited the one colleague he'd avoided all day.

Her name was Sabine. She had German parents and the interesting diction of someone who moved to London as a teenager. They'd been out for drinks a few times. He'd even mentioned her to the group at poker. Téo's usual problem loomed over the affair, that she was similar to Lia in ways that freaked him out and different in ways that dismayed him. Sabine's habit as the 5 p.m. finish approached was to look at pictures of available men on her phone.

"What's wrong with that one?" Téo asked, leaning over. "Looks friendly to me."

She browsed on. "I have friends."

"I should have left you a message. I wasn't thinking straight. I didn't mean to go home for so long. And what it was, soon as I got there, everything turned on its head."

"I heard," she said. "From them."

Around the office their colleagues pitched back in their chairs. Arms aloft, they heaved out stretching sounds. Computers were deactivated and there were grumbles at how long this took.

Sabine said, "Was it the same girl? Who died?"

When he didn't answer she said, "I'm sorry for you, Téo."

He rolled his torso inside the straps of his bag. "Maybe we could get lunch tomorrow?"

"I don't know," she said.

"I get that."

Do I get that? Téo thought. Joel never hedges. He never says perhaps. Joel is always present in the room. He sees only what's in front of him. "My head's in two places at once," Téo admitted. "It won't always be."

Sabine looked at him. "Do you want the truth? Before you left, it felt to me your head was in *no* places, zero places. I didn't even know your father was ill."

Out in Whitechapel, the buses and vans paraded by. Walkers skipped past walkers, everyone in that ferreting hurry to be home. Téo was the style of pedestrian who put a destination in mind and accepted a degree of slow movement with the herd. Never a useful overtaker, he let zigzaggers and dawdlers take the city at their own pace. Hijabs went by. High-visibility waist-coats. Underground, his train rocked and roared, a frightening sound when you hadn't ridden one in a while, when you were out of your London habits. Up again, returned to Enfield, he stepped over flat circles of chewing gum, he bisected a cluster of schoolchildren who were shouting at each other their opinions on episodes, plot twists, what it was to fancy and be fancied, the correct words, the gaits, how they should carry a bag this term. Téo and Lia used to explore these roads together, poor to rich and back, the distinctions so obvious to Lia they might as well've been coloured on a map. The richer roads had the runs of mani-cured bushes, the lampposts more like those in films, with an old-days look as though they were modelled on drooping flowers. The richer houses were twice or three times the size that anybody could need. They had spectacular giant's steps and porches tiled in bathroom white. Bankers lived in these houses. The done-well. Business people like Ben's dad, people who'd won in their sectors.

At the end of Ben's drive there were terracotta pots and inside each pot a small tree. Joel would have a good life as a Mossam, anyway a richer life. The front door was ajar. "Hello?"

"In here," shouted Ben, from one room.

"Is here," shouted Joel, from somewhere else.

Téo went through to the kitchen which was stuffy and un-aired. There were empty foil trays on the counter. Ben was on a stool watching sport on his laptop. Joel sat in the lounge in front of the TV. Téo recognised his cartoon. It was about police inves-tigators of no certain age. They had to use their numbers as well as their alphabet to solve crimes.

"Is brilliant," Joel reminded him when an advert interruption came. A voiceover insisted, this yoghurt? You should try it for the gut health. Joel must have seen the advert several times today because he could recite parts of the script. Impatient for the cartoon to resume, he climbed and bounced on the sofa. Teetering, on tiptoes, Joel was able to reach some toy of his that was perched on Ben's mantelpiece.

"Careful," Téo warned, "you're too high."

Ben kept watching whatever was on his computer. It would be tennis, athletics, bicycles, nothing worth paying attention to.

Téo checked: the tennis. "Keeping a careful eye then," he said.

"It's semi-finals."

"Joel. Come down off there. I told you you're too high, it's dangerous."

"He's fine. I gave my permission."

"Your permission?"

"If anything breaks I'll just get it fixed."

Téo closed Ben's laptop. He put a hand on Ben's shoulder. His T-shirt had the starchy suspect freshness of a laundering service. "Not a child." He turned to Joel: "Climb down, mate."

"Doan worry," said Joel.

"Climb down."

"Doan worry."

So this was a phrase he'd learned.

"We don't want you hurt is why. Ben doesn't either, do you, Ben?"

"Uh-uh. Nope."

"You two gonna say goodbye to each other before we leave?"

It had been a failure. Ben opened the laptop again, gesturing at the tennis: "Don't worry, this is nearly done."

"Doan worry," repeated Joel.

They raced each other home. At Victor's front door, Joel stretched to reach the lock, certain that he should be allowed to turn the key himself. He big-chewed his dinner. He had a careful think about which cartoons he would watch at Ben's house tomorrow. After his bath they completed a puzzle together. They sat on his bed, entwined, and read stories. Téo had questions. He was fact-finding about Joel's day and he wanted the boy to stay awake for a few minutes more, then a few minutes more. Joel called time on the evening. He swept up his shoulder and he turned his body to the wall, putting a thumb in his mouth. "Enough bedtime."

"How did it go today," Victor asked downstairs.

"Okay I reckon. Room for improvement."

"Has he let Joel down yet?"

"Not yet."

Téo slumped and held up his hands, surrendering this one before it could start. It was as though the whole flat was rigged with hidden grooves and chutes: they could slip into the same arguments without friction. And Ben did get in touch that night, while Téo sat watching television. Ben wrote a message to say, in actual fact? Something had come up. "I can't do Joel tomorrow after all!"

Téo did not reply. Instead he stepped outside the flat and he phoned the office, leaving word for his colleagues that he would need more time. He wrote a quick email for the social workers. Walking laps of the garden, he tried to contrive another way to fill another day—with story CDs, he thought, with moulded miniature bricks, there was that plastic tortoiseshell comb, Joel liked to press it against his ear as if it were a phone of his own. They would rearrange the cereal cupboard. They would test their aim on Joel's wooden skittles. Téo would observe the boy more carefully this time, revising him and collecting better memories for their next time apart.

TEN
VIC

There were trees on the road that seemed impatient for autumn, browning early, browning first. On the ground (nestled in with the first fallen leaves) were tossed paper receipts and stray crisp packets, this rubbish blowing up Vic's road against a gradient as though busied on and encouraged by invisible hands. "In fact, I have interesting dreams myself," Vic was telling Joel. "In one dream, have you experienced this too? I'm at home. It's the same walls, same chair, everything's comfortable and familiar. Only now there's a door I don't recognise. And on the other side of this door—"

"Is secret base."

"In my dream it's Scotland. A village in the mountains. I don't have to open the door to know."

"Leopard-boy's *base*," Joel persisted.

They were walking to nursery again. It was a job that Vic had campaigned for. At 8 a.m., as soon as Téo left for work in the city, Vic was allowed one hour and during that hour it was his responsibility to get Joel through a final kitting-out, his shoes, his warmer coat, a snack for the journey, his book bag. Vic was sworn in each day like a court official. His obligations ended at nine when he handed over Joel at nursery. He was often at a loss what to do next. Today he had a meeting in the children's services department at Enfield Council. Vic had put on his best suit for the occasion, his funeral suit. Clamped beneath his arm he held his old leather valise, stuffed at present with packets of ibuprofen, four biros and pages and pages of loose paper that were written over with his close inky scribbles. As he waited to hand over Joel, he expected the nursery staff to notice. He thought that one of them might ask, what's different about you this morning, Mister Erskine? What are you plotting? He was sure it must be obvious, that nerves and excitement were plain on his face.

He made an effort to bend and bid the child goodbye. Pulling away, Joel said: "Smells."

Vic was offended. "It's aftershave. And perfectly respectable for a serious meeting. Téo will pick you up as normal. I'll see you at home."

Joel nodded. He was not so interested in the details. That grown men would surround him and await him he took as his due. He lurched away, swerving on second thoughts to surprise Vic with a final embrace. "That's better. That's nice of you . . . I'll see you later, Joel."

It was chillier, yes. September meant awake-again radiators. September meant trees that waved about barer branches. A sieved and jittery light fell on to the pavement, disorientating Vic. He had to stop by the side of the road, waiting for a dizzy spell to pass. When he saw the approaching amber light of a taxi he waved at it and it stopped. By the time Vic was halfway over the road to meet it, getting as far as a raised concrete island in the middle of traffic, the taxi had driven away. Vic struck his cane against the ground in frustration. There did not seem to be enough of a gap between the cars for him to cross forwards or turn back. He might have stayed stranded on that island for some time had Rabbi Challis not seen him and come to help.

She stepped into the road and with an imperious finger she commanded that the cars in the nearside lanes should stop. Somehow she was able to suggest with this same one finger that the drivers ought to feel ashamed of themselves. "It deserves its reputation, this road . . . Are you all right, Vic? Can you catch your breath?"

They made it across together.

"Where to?" she asked.

"Council building. Thank you. I have a meeting in the—they call it the children's services department. But you'll be busy. If only my taxi . . . That bloody cruel driver!"

Sibyl moved an imaginary steering wheel and she struck an imaginary horn.

"I can play taxi for a favourite congregant. Council building it is."

Hand beneath his elbow, she led him through a crowd of morning commuters. He was beyond shame at being handled with care. He liked it a little, her attention, the parting people. Because he was concentrating, trying not to stumble in a rabbi's company, she had to speak for them both. She told him stories about her late grandfather, a man who'd been unsteady on his feet as well. He was an immigrant, Sibyl explained, a dressmaker. There were tools of her grandfather's that were holy as any religious equipment. He kept a tape measure and steel scissors on his person at all times and the weight of these objects made his jackets hang queerly, pendulously, Sibyl said, "As though his world was forever uphill."

Vic listened to her and he found that his panic was easing.

Confidence came back in steady draughts. Joel's presence could have the same effect. Some people had an excess of spirit and it was in their power to share it around. Vic tilted his head at Sibyl not to miss a word. Her grandparents had fled from Russia, she was saying, and as new arrivals they learned to speak their English in London's East End. When Sibyl's mother was a girl she decided she wanted to fit in better—assimilate—and she taught herself a different way to speak, the secretarial way. She listened with care in theatres and in train carriages. She bought records and pamphlets. She ended up marrying a secular Jewish doctor, Sibyl's father, who had a similar basic ambition to blend with England. Both were amazed when a daughter of theirs chose to become a rabbi. Vic was amazed for a different reason, that there could be Jews who wanted to step away and assimilate, who wanted *out* of their Jewishness. He had spent so long petitioning for inclusion.

Passersby greeted Sibyl as they walked. Others who recognised her as the local rabbi went by without speaking; instead they made room and they nodded their heads. The middle of the pavement belonged to Sibyl and Vic without contest; and he took heart from this as they got closer and closer to the council building. His meeting with Joel's social workers had to be a success, Vic thought. After all, he had God's surrogate escorting him in.

Sibyl had finished telling another story, this one about her father, his practice in the suburbs, how hard he worked there. Vic listened for a while then said, "Nobody should become a parent before they're middle-aged." Having voiced this opinion (in fact, a remembered crib from his notes in the valise), he wanted to say some more. He handed off his stick to Sibyl and he took out all of his papers, turning through them one by one. "Because unlike those younger parents," Vic read aloud, "we older ones have learned what the traps are. Because for such a job as being a father it is only possible to succeed at a second attempt."

Vic had reasoned it out to his own satisfaction in three types of ink, black for certainties, blue for imprecisions, a lot of red commentary in the margins. This was how he composed his speeches in the civil service, his office jotters covered in colourful sentences and many a biro ruined for being chewed in contemplation. This week he had tried to catch and transcribe an epiphany, that what counted as a parent was gaze, your attention, nothing else was so important. He hoped to persuade the social workers that whatever his physical limitations, he was a better candidate in this regard than both Téo and Ben put together.

Sibyl had led him as far as the council building. "Shouldn't I come in with you?" she said. "I could help make sure you're . . . understood."

"No need, no need."

"I think I'll wait out here for you then."

"Suit yourself."

The building's interior was old and modern at once. Expansions and renovations, undertaken at different times, had left an incoherent whole. Beyond the tiled and vaulted lobby, Vic was directed to follow a corridor that was patchworked with grey ceiling tiles and greyer carpet squares. Children's services was in a part of the building where more cheerful colours abounded. But this was all worn-out real estate, diminished by constant use. Visitors grated their feet on the floor, reconfirming troughs in front of the waiting-room benches. Vic was early. He sat on one of the benches mouthing phrases, reminding himself which were the most important points to make and which parts of his proposal would require most tact. Téo had done his best. He had brought them all this far. Soon, Vic was led inside a conference room that smelled of whatever cleaning product had been used to freshen the surface of its centrepiece table. A chair fitted with sledge-like runners was pulled out for him. He had met the two social workers on several occasions.

"Hello. Hello."

Still . . . it was hard for Vic to remember every name and face, hardest when he was tired like this and somewhat anxious. *Gil.* One of them was called Gil. He addressed the other one as "young man." It seemed to strike the right note. They were both patient with him. They listened to what he had to say. Vic proceeded with growing confidence. Having hugged his valise coming in, Vic undid the buckle and removed his papers. He coughed, intending to clear his throat, better if he hadn't coughed . . . Gil and her colleague waited for Vic to finish. He had to try not to be discouraged by the fact that they were wearing such casual clothes to this meeting. He put Joel in mind, that blur of industry, Joel's dauntlessness.

He wished the child were here. Joel made Vic feel so much more capable. Joel viewed anybody older, taller, as expert. If you knew where to find the sticking plasters (this was how Joel gauged the world) then you knew everything, the answers, such as which way around to put batteries inside toys or whether pushing or pulling was required to open a door. You knew the worthwhile buttons in lifts. Joel was the only person in Vic's life who did not hold his age or his illness against him. Pensioners or prime-of-lifers were as one to Joel and Vic was convinced, if he could only be left alone to care for the child he could be himself again, master of objects, a confident hummer, snappier in his responses to quiz questions on TV. His brain wouldn't dart, so. He'd be able to hold on to more threads and more thoughts.

"I have come to make a difficult proposal," Vic found himself saying.

They heard him out: the whole argument. They let Vic read from his notes without objection or interruption. There was a time in his career when he'd hoped to become a Member of Parliament. Magpie-like, during his speechwriting years, he put away sentences, imagining he was saving these for himself. He cherished the idea that he would one day rise to his feet, a thumb in his belt, a sheaf of pages in hand, and persuade his fellow MPs to take . . . some course or another. THE PERSUADER, that's what they'd call him in the next day's papers. Vic never had the luck. For all the energy he put into his work, for all the time he spent away from home, he was spat out into retirement and left unsatisfied. Joel arrived in time, Joel was the reprieve, Vic's chance. And Joel deserved someone's fullest attention. He deserved to be first choice.

"You said we could afford to wait until September to resolve the question of his permanent guardian," Vic reminded the social workers. "You said that if Joel's father had not come forward by then, the rest of us would be asked yes or no, would we apply ourselves. Well, here I am. It's September. I've come on the first of the month. I'm at the front of the queue. I want you to help me make my application, speak up on my behalf, I want us to remove these awful doubts about Joel's future. I want him taken out of Téo's temporary care—Téo's reluctant care—and I want this done as a matter of urgency, yes, urgency. I want Joel given over to me instead."

It was the end of Vic's pitch.

The social workers waited as though he would carry on.

"No, that's all," he said. "I've made the points I wanted to make."

The younger one spoke first. He asked about Vic's mention of urgency.

"Yes," said Gil, "what has happened to make this urgent, what's changed?"

He had not anticipated any confusion on this point. He couldn't recall whether there'd been any mention of urgency in his notes. "The situation is urgent to me. And to Joel I expect. Yes."

Sitting straighter in their chairs, the social workers started to write some notes themselves. Gil glanced at a clock on the wall and scribbled down the time. Vic had raised the notion of urgency and perhaps, because of this, they were obliged to pay him closer attention. "Urgent why?" he was asked. "Urgent how?"

Vic's own notes were no longer much help. Even so, he found himself scanning the top page for answers. Then he tried to sort backwards through his grievances, thinking of Téo, not appreciating his fortune in having Joel to care for, thinking of Téo, running out of patience with the child almost every day. There had once been an accident on the trampoline—hadn't there? Certainly there had been a day when Téo and Ben went out to watch football. They returned in a dreadful state. At the time, Vic assumed they were drunk, Téo especially. In the aftermath he went through his son's mobile phone, curious, and learned the truth.

"Drugs," Vic found himself saying, "drug use."

The social workers stared.

"This is, drug use in the same residence as Joel?"

"Mm-hm," Vic said. And then more forcefully: "Yes."

He wasn't sure how the young went about it. Three pills, he'd read in Téo's messages. Vic hoped the rabbi was waiting outside because he would need absolution next. He would need somebody to guide him to the pub for a drink. "I've told you all I know. Téo took Joel in his car while he was under the influence of drugs. There's proof of that. Yes."

"I'm afraid we have more questions."

"It's right that you came."

One glance, and Sibyl seemed to know that something was wrong.

She asked if Vic was unwell. He had to wonder what his face was up to. His legs hurt. He was beyond speaking any more and he hobbled beside her in silence, only wanting to be put somewhere out of harm's way before the consequences of what he'd done were felt.

They walked along the high street together, retracing their steps from earlier. When they arrived at a junction, a turnoff for the synagogue in one direction, Vic's pub in the other, he assured her he could carry on by himself.

Sibyl said, "I'll take you to your pub if that's what you want. But I'm reluctant to leave you in there alone." He might have answered, I'm alone wherever I happen to be, loneliness has me by the other arm. Now I wish to toast my loneliness and get drunk with it. Vic was close to tears. They had reached the pub's doors. "I can't leave you by yourself. Let me call somebody for you. Téo."

"Not Téo."

"Let me call Ben."

Endangered, such pubs, people said. Vic's was a dusty boozer where they kept an old-fashioned till behind the bar, long out of use, its buttons big as teaspoons. There were crisping health-service posters on the wall, tacked up years ago, warning customers not to smoke or drive drunk. Vic carried his pint to a table in the corner. He sat beneath an aged mirror, its glass time-stained. He borrowed parts of a newspaper from a gentleman at the next table and while he read it he listened to the groans of pub furniture and the chunter of daytime drinkers. They were elderly men for the most part, humbled, diminished, same as Vic. The landlady here claimed she could sense it whenever one of her regulars was about to approach the bar to order.

"Need crisps, my love?"

"Another beer for me."

"Another? It's not like you to have two."

"It's been a morning."

"Take this one slower, my love."

He settled again. He had inherited more of the unwanted newspaper and now he read up on scandals, testimony of other people's mistakes, a fall from grace and (next page) a record-breaking drugs bust. Those incautious things he'd said . . . he wondered what the repercussions would be. Then he made himself stop thinking. The second beer helped and he drank quickly. When Ben found him at his table, Vic was about ready for a third beer and asking himself, could he really make it as far as the what-do-you-call-it, the place to order, Mrs. Psychic over there. Trialling his knees up and down, Vic realised he was powerfully drunk.

"Young man," he said to Ben, "funnily enough, you may have to help me."

"What's happened? Can't you stand?"

"This illness," he began . . . he wanted to say, this illness, my grip on everything, don't waste what you have.

Ben wasn't curious. "We all get ourselves in a pickle on the beers from time to time. Let's get you home."

Vic said no, not home. He couldn't face Téo.

Ben was hardly listening. "If we get you outside I can order us a taxi."

Vic found himself being gripped by both forearms. He made himself heavy. He protested, "I won't go home, d'you hear?"

"Stalemate," said Ben, releasing the hold. He sat down.

Vic watched Ben watch himself in the pub's big mirror. There were adjustments made by anyone catching sight of themselves like this, the drawn-in cheeks, the bitten-together molars, preferred lines found . . . Ben though. He tried out nostril flares. He widened and he narrowed his eyes. Vic had to guess he was imagining telling Téo about this. Ben was imagining asking, was he such a bad friend? If he'd shown up to help old Victor as soon as he was asked?

"New plan. We'll hide out at mine till the evening. You can sober up there and as soon as you're in a fit state I'll send you back to Téo. I'll drive you myself."

Vic tried for dignity: "That will be fine."

There was a page of TV listings between them and Ben took it, running a finger over the print. "Golf's on," he said, "a few decent films. We should be all right. We should make it through. What happened here?"

"I made a mistake."

"Yeah?" Ben pushed out his lips. "As it happens, I've made one or two myself."

"You were wicked," Vic agreed, "letting down Joel like that. He'd been told to expect you."

"Had he?"

"He was upset."

"*Was* he?"

They stared around the pub, speechless with their own dissatisfactions.

Ben asked, "Can you get yourself upright?"

"Not on my own."

The next stage of transit was miserable for everybody. Vic had to be carried out of the pub, not only by Ben but by the landlady herself. He pretended to sleep on the taxi journey, then he did sleep, which helped him sober a bit by the time he was led through the Mossams' front door. Vic was stunned by what he saw. He had trained himself not to speak the phrase, but the inner monologue was harder to police—and Jesus fucking Christ, thought Vic, the house was enormous, a fortress. Ben paused them at a panel of switches in the hallway. For Vic's benefit he fanned golden light up one of the walls. He trained spots on certain paintings. Every

step of the staircase could be made to glow, quite uselessly. There
was a passenger lift and using this Vic could be taken on a tour
of the upstairs rooms. They were in the lift and coming down
before he regained any cynicism.

"It's all well and good," Vic grumbled.

He was being led into a downstairs lounge. He was put in the
middle of a large sofa.

"What's well and good, Vic?"

"I only mean. There are one or two luxuries in life that money
can't buy."

"Wa-a-a-y more than that," Ben said. "But I'm working my
way through what can be bought first." He turned on his TV and
he started to skim the channels, sometimes lingering just long
enough for Vic to read the programme descriptions that appeared.
Hopefuls were tasked with cooking a perfect breakfast. Cameras
followed pods of dolphins. Teams of experts battled it out in a
castle. "How old could you have been, when you got the run of
this place?"

Ben explained that his parents had bought property abroad
when he was a teenager. "It used to be, we flew out together in
the summer. Then it was winter and Easter too. Time me and
Téo were in our last year at school, Mum and Dad were only
coming back for a few months in the year. I could tell, this neighbourhood, it was too small for them. It had stopped feeling like
home. Dad gave a load of money to the synagogue. That was to
boss the guilt, I think. Then they left for good when I was eighteen. They don't visit much."

"And you don't visit them?"

"Not lately."

They watched part of a travel programme. The presenter,
who used to be talented at javelin, enjoyed a view. She relished a
sandy beach. "I wouldn't mind going on holiday," Vic admitted.

"Why don't you?"

Vic scoffed. He was sober again. "In my condition? I doubt I'll leave Enfield."

Ben was changing channels. They watched a golfer tee off.

"But I do think of them, the trips I won't take. Scotland."

"Why Scotland?"

Vic hesitated. "You live where you were born. You wouldn't understand."

Ben had his arms folded behind his head. He turned to look at Vic as though not having heard. "Take a *train* to Scotland if you want. Book a taxi to get to Scotland. What's stopping you?"

"Expensive taxi."

"If it's money you're after just ask."

Vic said, "It's too long a journey. I've considered it I admit. But I could never manage alone. I've sometimes wondered if Téodor might . . . he has never been to Scotland, you see. Not to the village in the mountains where I was born. It's on a river." Falling in, Vic remembered! He was only a little older than Joel. Their village was often visited by day-trippers, city people fond of the river where it was shallowest and wound prettily between gouged rock. Invaded all summer, the buses coming in from more prosperous Scottish cities on the coast, the children of Vic's village resorted to tricks to hold their own. Friends were made then quickly betrayed. Children were shoved over in the water on somebody's signal, even after they'd been promised they'd only get their ankles wet.

"I haven't been back in decades. It's where my mother and I suppose my father must be buried. A part of me would like to find them. Their graves I mean."

The golf had finished. Vic couldn't tell if he was being listened to or not. That was a risk with the young, their vanishing interest. The TV showed adverts, one for bottled water that tasted of fruits of the forest. They watched a part of a programme about a mother who had to diet on a doctor's orders. Vic found he had dozed and missed the resolution. When he looked again, the time for afternoon programming was over. The start of the evening was marked by a quiz, a difficult one in which serial champions were pitted against each other.

Vic often watched this quiz at home.

"No," he said, "leave it on please."

"Thought you were sleeping . . . Can I change the channel yet?"

"Let's find out who wins."

Afterwards they watched the news. A government minister, teacher-voiced, was interviewed about young people and their preparation for adulthood. This minister projected the confidence of someone who believed there were only so many certainties in the world and that he had them pat, he could name them. Vic thought again about Joel's social workers. They had asked him to wait in the conference room, then to repeat his allegations in front of one superior and another. Vic was told, this is serious I'm afraid. He thought, I know what's serious, I can see it's serious, I've been waiting to be taken seriously my whole life.

"I have a question for you. I remember Téo saying that you grew up an orphan. But the other week, when I was over for lunch, you said you had an absent dad."

Vic explained, "I grew up in an orphanage after we lost our home in a fire." The colour, he was thinking, before the smell, because the colour made a sunrise where there shouldn't have been one. The men of the village formed a chain to bring water. Vic's future was decided in the smoke. "My mother couldn't afford to keep looking after me. My father was alive but he wasn't involved. When I was put in an orphanage it was some hours away on the coast, in Aberdeen. He never came. My mother I saw a few more times. Then at eighteen I earned my ticket to London. When the day came to leave I went to look for her at the only address I had. But they told me no, she'd moved on."

"What did you do?"

"I caught my train. I didn't see her."

"You think it's what you want," said Ben, "that freedom. On your own in a big house, big world, till you realise: I'm not ready! I'm not cooked."

"We are both a funny kind of orphan," Vic said, "made so by money."

Aware of something too late Vic flinched in his chair.

Ben said, "What is it, what's the matter?"

The muscles around Vic's groin must have been strained by his daytime drinking. Suddenly he wasn't sure of his commands, the crisis was quick and it brought a hot roar of shame to his ears. At the orphanage, bed wetting was punishable. Your competing impulses hadn't changed. You moved at once or you surrendered in place, accepting every outcome. There were two, three stabs of pain in Vic's abdomen. He recalled the words of a doctor, that not only would his motor functions go, there were muscles and organs he had relied on all his life without knowledge or thanks and these things would fail him as well by the end.

"It's not my fault," he said. There was so much piss. Like an animal, like a child, he thought. Ben had muted the news on TV. He didn't know where to look at first, so he directed his gaze at the ceiling. Vic's suit had done nothing to contain the mess. There were pools of liquid underneath him, on the sofa and the floor.

Finally Ben said, "To be honest, it's not the first time that seat's taken a drenching. Had to get it steam cleaned. Uh, can you get to the bathroom?"

"I'm not sure."

"Remind me of the method to move you?"

"Téo normally stands in front of me. He takes my hands and we do a count."

Ben came over. He rolled up his sleeves.

"One . . . Two . . ."

"I won't make it, Ben."

"Have to . . . Three."

"I need to borrow some clothes."

"I'll get you some of Dad's."

Vic was upright at least. The mess was worse to look back on. Vic's shoes and socks were wet and squelching to the lift, he left footprints. The Mossams had a bathroom on each floor. Ben chose the middle one because the shower there was the biggest and easiest to access, he said. The floor tiles pitched cleverly so that shower-water ran down a central plughole. Ben got the water going while Vic tried to remove his sodden trousers.

"I'll fetch you another pair. Have you got a favourite colour? Or should I . . . oh . . . oh, man . . ."

Embarrassment paralysed them both. Steam filled the bathroom.

It was clear the trousers were not coming off without assistance.

"I'm sorry."

"These apologies," Ben said.

He kept his head turned to one side. He knelt in front of Vic and as quick as he could he shimmied off the trousers, then the underwear, working the material down each of Vic's legs, one side then the other, like somebody operating stiff pulleys. He pinned the clothes to the floor so that Vic could step clear of them. To do this Vic had to put both hands on Ben's shoulders. They performed the actions robotically, mortified into machine parts. When Vic was finally under the shower he held on to the thermostat and lifted his face into the rasping water. He spat and he puffed. When he staggered backwards, disorientated again, Ben took him by the arm. He handed Vic a clean towel.

Later, they watched a hospital drama together.

They watched more sport.

Though the lounge smelled bad there was a sense of happy aftermath in the room, a feeling the worst had come and gone. They watched part of a film in which a gangster murdered his friend. They watched the gangster turn remorseful. Ads.

"Is it a worse-and-worse situation?" Ben asked. There was something different between them, a frankness. "This illness you've got. How does it progress?"

"Worse-and-worse, yes. Not reversible. I use a walking stick to get around. Soon it will be a wheelchair. Then bed. Then . . ."

Vic found that he could talk about this and sound casual, dismissive even, except that he was not entertaining the real thoughts. Those thoughts came in the early mornings or late at night. Those thoughts fell on Vic like bullies and only when he was alone.

"How much of this does Téo know?"

"Some. He knows I've been struggling. But chair, bed, dead—not that."

"How long have you got? Years?"

"No no."

It was like having a wife again, somebody you'd let ask anything. Honesty lived behind shame. Was that it? Humiliated and wearing another man's trousers, Vic found that there was not a lot left to make him cringe.

"The sooner you travel to Scotland the better," Ben said.

"Excuse me?"

"If you're gonna get there, it's best you're taken soon."

"Téo would never agree."

"Maybe your rabbi girlfriend escorts you instead."

Vic said: "There's Joel to consider. It's not possible."

"Ask around," said Ben, "you might find someone who can help make it happen."

"Even if someone agreed to take me . . . they might change their mind."

"You'll find there's someone who has regrets about that," said Ben. "Someone who wants to make amends. And Joel could come with us. Téo's always persuadable. It would be a Scottish adventure. Lads on the road!"

"You aren't being serious."

"Like a stag trip. Like a famous holiday."

"Perhaps. Perhaps."

Vic was flattered. Already he wanted this.

"You'll forget."

Ben had his nose over his mobile phone. "There are sleeper trains to the mountains. They leave from Euston every evening. I'm looking at pictures of the cabins right now—they have bunk beds. Tartan wallpaper. Hear that? Tartan."

Leave Enfield, Vic was thinking. Escape the repercussions: at least for a while.

"How soon could we go?"

"Up to us. We'll do a weekend."

"Or longer than that."

"Sure. Sure. A few extra days."

"I have money."

"*I* have money. We can talk about that later."

"When would we go?"

"We'll need to get Téo on side."

"Can you do that, do you think? I used to be something of a persuader myself."

"Let me try first."

"Yes. All right."

"Then if we need a heavy hitter we'll trot you out."

"You're patronising me."

"Yeah."

"I only hope you don't forget, Ben, I only hope you don't change your mind."

But Ben was scouring channels again. "Tartan wallpaper," he muttered, "fucking hell."

ELEVEN

BEN

A Mossam in a bakery! They could not be trusted. They'd be picking for ages, far longer than their rightful turn.

"Four of those," Ben said to the server. He watched as four scorched bagels were dropped into a bag for him.

"And four of those please."

Narrow rolls, white and springy inside, the sort his mum used to halve and top with herring or with egg mayonnaise—they went in as well.

"Four of those, and those, and those. Oh, massively, four of THOSE . . . I've got a long journey today," Ben explained. "Scotland by train. Four of those."

Squares of strudel were added to the bag, also bow-tied kichelach, also those miniature Danishes that held in their pastry guts a dab of rich cream cheese and a dab of sharp cherry jam, a collision of flavours that Ben knew to be superb.

"What else? Four cinnamon snails. That should do us. Oh and one rusk," he said, stepping back from the display. He counted off some money and he ate the rusk as he paid. An hour yet; then their train would sway out of London on its overnight procession north. Ben had jostled through the crowd to get his bakery order in on time. Complaints were made—"But I've got a kid, I've got a kid," Ben explained. He blew out his cheeks, shamming parental helplessness. "You know how it goes. Young mouth to feed. Excuse me, make room, thanks."

Téo had refused on principle to take a taxi to Euston station. *Ben* took a taxi, wondering all that way, would Téo be chill on this trip? Or vexed? Ben planned to pass his friend a piece of excellent strudel. Remind the man. They were yoked by a shared history. Their friendship was meant to be elastic and durable as only friendships begun at school could be. A decade ago, when Téo first moved on from Enfield, it was possible for Ben to tell himself that the distance between them legitimised a cooling of relations. Recently? Aware that his closest and oldest friend lived a few hundred metres away and even so ignored Ben's texts? It weighed on him. He had started to view their coming trip to Scotland as a form of apology, more candidly, as a bribe. "Pack for a week," Ben had told them, "I'm organising this, I'm Papa, I'm handling this from start to finish."

So he booked them cabins on a sleeper train. He arranged a hire car at the other end and a suite of rooms in an expensive remote hotel. Ben even did some shallow research on his phone, to get a sense of the lakes up there, the nicest views and such, scenery they might as well stop and smoke a cigarette in front of while they were driving through.

Now he whistled, turning heads on Euston concourse. Téo, Vic and Joel were waiting where the platforms started to jut and form promontories. Ben raised his arms, weight-lifter fashion, to prove that he was laden with treats.

"You came," said Téo: a grump about it. Evidently he'd been expecting Ben to cry off again. He had both hands in his pockets and he frowned at the clock above the platform as though he was some chilly and sceptical football manager on the sidelines of a match. "Have to owe you that tenner," Téo muttered at his dad, who waved the comment away.

"Do you have our tickets?" asked Vic. "Can we board yet?"

"Plenty of time," Ben assured him.

"I don't want to miss it."

Vic had lobbied hard for this trip. The sooner they left Enfield the better, according to Vic Erskine, who'd been bothering the Mossam landline on a daily basis. Part of Ben—maybe as much as a quarter—wished he hadn't ever mentioned this fucking trip. But then, he reasoned, what else was he going to do with an empty September week on his docket? He had never been further north than Hertfordshire and that time by accident. Scotland might be all right. Ben had engaged his optimism; he was dipping into vast reserves.

Téo grabbed up the luggage. Making to help, Ben followed him on board with the rest of the bags. The carriage was narrow, most of the space given over to cabins. Ben and Téo were standing almost tum to tum. "Kiss me."

"Stop playing. Help me lift these."

"Listen, I get it," Ben said, "you're not persuaded by all this. By me organising this. But don't sink the trip before we've started."

"Sweet talk my dad," Téo replied. "Sweet talk Joel." He was moving away to help the other two get on board. "It's an insult when you try the charm on me."

Ben followed after, complaining, "Harsh." He wanted back in Téo's graces. He couldn't say exactly why, only sensing he'd stretched the friendship to its limit. "I should have done more to help," Ben admitted, "I should have shown up more, sat on your carpet and played with him, I should have minded him when I said I would."

"Yes."

"But give me a chance, T, I'm trying to make things square."

Soon the four of them were exploring the cabins. Instead of

wallpaper there was textured beige plastic on the walls. Crossed through with coloured ridges of orange and green, it formed the promised tartan. They had buttons to call a steward. Sockets to charge their phones. Kettles! These were only crap hotel rooms put on rails but everyone was impressed, Vic especially. He hobbled between the adjoining cabins as if it had all been made with him in mind. He kept asking when the train would leave. Soon Joel was asking the same question, the pair of them only satisfied when the last-chance announcements were speakered through to the cabin. The train quivered.

"Is moving?"

"Look."

London's suburbs, known or unknown to them, passed by out the cabin window. Later, when they got into their beds, they would be rocked to sleep, they would feel the train's unseen workings and become a part of its locomotion . . . Ben was charmed by one idea in particular, that they'd wake up tomorrow and have hundreds of easy unearned miles behind them.

A period of bunk-bed arbitration took them as far north as Watford. It was agreed Vic would take one of the cabins for himself, leaving Ben and the others to share. They folded down bunks that were concealed inside the cabin's walls. They made a berth for Joel on the floor, fitting together cushions and stacking pillows per his orders. It got blacker outside. They were in England somewhere, the middle. When Téo produced pyjamas for Joel, a change of outfit seemed to revive the kid and he undertook a new game, lapping the cabin with his arms spread, making noises that Ben recognised as standard to violent cartoons, *per-KUSH, per-SHAR* . . . Ben tried a few battle noises himself; but Joel, who wanted no adult involvement in this game, glared at him till he was quiet. Somehow you were supposed to know.

"What a busy day," Téo announced. "You gotta be so tired, Joel."

A minute later he tried the same phrase. Téo had a singsong way of repeating it, like an amateur hypnotist, that made Ben shiver. It had the desired effect however and soon enough Joel was slumped on his makeshift bed. He *was* tired, he agreed. He started to cry. He was furious that he hadn't been tucked in already, furious as well that he hadn't been offered any of those biscuits that were tempting him from a sideboard by the window.

Téo and Ben looked. The biscuits he had in mind were Scottish shortbreads, individually wrapped and left out by the train people as a gift.

Joel made an impassioned pitch. One biscuit. Please.

Téo said no. "Your teeth."

And Joel made a solemn promise that he would not use his teeth.

Later there were stories read aloud. There were muttered jokes, additional to the stories, that Téo and Joel shared between themselves, jokes beyond Ben's comprehension. He spread his body on the upper bunk. He put in headphones and when he emerged out the other side of a loud album, Joel was almost asleep. You could tell because the lack of his clamour was itself a disturbance in the cabin, same as how the silence of home rang in your ears after a night out dancing.

Suddenly Joel sat up in bed: "Is a desperate thing."

"What's left?" Téo whispered. "We've done toilet already. Done your drink."

Ben hung over the edge of his bunk. "Yeah, what's your desperate thing?"

Joel was prepared to negotiate. "You my say no."

Téo did indeed say no. Enough biscuits had been eaten already. As a punishment, Joel refused to lie down again. He demanded to swap his bed on the floor for Ben's top bunk. He said he had to run up and down the carriage, nothing else would do.

"But I promise," he said, starting to cry again.

Now Ben (thought Ben, as he hid away) knew how to be self-less on occasion. He bought conspicuous gifts for people without expecting anything back. He made the effort to help out mates who were down on their luck, money-wise. He shone his light in ways big and small—but crucially, whenever Ben had done a good deed for someone, he liked to be thanked. He liked analysis and ongoing mention of his kindnesses. What shocked Ben here was Joel's ingratitude. It was a revelation that the maximum level of thanks any parent or carer could expect from a small child was their submission, their going-the-fuck-to-sleep. Thanks formed no part of it.

Quiet as he could, Ben climbed down. He opened Téo a beer from his bag of supplies and another for himself. The night needed an epilogue, some cap to it before they both went to bed. Ben suggested poker. Vic's lights were off next door. Joel was asleep.

Together they piled cups and saucers to one side, moving around the complimentary shortbreads and teabags on strings. They pushed aside sugars in their wraps and miniature tubs of long-life milk, clearing room on the sideboard. Ben shuffled a deck of cards he'd brought along, a practised cutting and interlacing. They had the idea they could use the free biscuits and such as tokens for their betting. They agreed a set of values, the sugars worth one, the teabags worth two, every shortbread a whopping five.

Téo suggested they stake £20 each and Ben waved him quiet, as if he was somebody dangerous and raving.

"A hundred pounds each."

"No, Ben."

"Eighty."

"Thirty."

"Seventy . . . sixty? Sweet. Cut the deck."

At first they traded cautious wins, pushing low-value sugars between themselves. Ben won a couple of teabags and a biscuit, riches eradicated when he went in overconfident on a mediocre hand. From the next-door cabin they heard Vic clump around. A lav flushed. Ben won three hands in a row then Téo drew level again. The lights were down because of Joel. They could see the dark countryside walloping by outside, right to left, right to left.

"Beautifully played that."

"Yeah yeah. Deal already."

"If playing like a coward excites you, that was beautifully done."

"Deal, Ben."

The main sounds in the cabin were Joel's. He took hungry mouthfuls while he slept. He chewed and he slurped; once, he laughed. His mum slept noisily as well. Ben remembered that Lia used to sleep as if she was unconvinced of sleep as a concept, only forced to try it every night. He thought back to an evening out in the only neighbourhood pub she would tolerate. It went unspoken in their group, whenever they were missing her company or anyway the company of women in general, they drifted to that one same pub and they sent her a message: "Come join?" Most of the time she ignored these invitations. This one night (Ben could probably do the maths . . . nearly four years ago now) Lia showed up. She smoked with them and took part in their retellings of school stories. She joined a noisy game of who could remember Téo saying what. There was a recklessness about her that night and for once she and Ben were in harmony, they'd decided to be fond, some agreement was made with the eyes.

Ben went back to hers. The mum had died, he remembered that. Lia was left with the place to herself. It gave them something to talk about, a shared sophistication. Her flat became the base for the affair, a secret scenario that lasted through a few week-ends, till afterwards Ben put it out of mind. He added another item to his bill for future defray and hardly thought about the consequences. With practice this was possible. Over time, denial became a stimulant, addictive on its own, the bigger the denial the better. His habit was so ingrained that even now, when Ben had come to understand, rationally, that Joel was his responsibility, he kept slipping back into refusal. Let Téo handle it. Let someone.

He lost a big three-biscuit hand while thinking about this.

In his annoyance, Ben brought out his phone, choosing a track that would rasp the miniature speakers, improving the un-poker-like atmospherics in the cabin. "That's better," he sighed.

"No chance. Turn it down," Téo ordered.

"Why? Kid's asleep."

"Turn it down. You don't know what'll wake him."

Ben switched off the music altogether. He was out of sorts, a temper up, and he said quickly, "Lia used to make a racket when she slept as well."

They played another hand.

"Must be where Joel gets it I mean."

Ben didn't know what sort of response he wanted here. Téo was upset. "What are you trying?" he said. "D'you want me to feel bad, feel jealous?"

"Feel *something* anyway."

"Do, Benno. I feel many things. Often."

They both shook their heads.

"In silence," Ben complained, "you do your feeling in silence, and what's the point of that? I wanna shake you sometimes."

Téo said nothing.

"Out of this passivity," Ben explained.

"It fascinates me," Téo said, "that you think of me shutting up as being passive. When you can't know what me shutting up protects you from."

"This," Ben said, "this is more like it!"

"Deal."

Sugars and teabags moved around the table. The cards had that fertile, gummy feel from an hour's constant use.

"What don't I know?" Ben asked. "What you protecting me from with your samurai silences?" He was genuinely curious and also trying for advantageous distraction. The minute they started bickering, Ben started winning more hands. They were risking larger sums, barely glancing at their cards before pushing in bets or folding. Téo folded again.

"Maybe you'll figure it out for yourself when you're ready."

"Two pair. I win again."

"Fucking hell."

Téo was almost finished off by that loss. Only a few sugars remained to him. He could be dangerous in the endgame, Ben knew; but there was hardly anything for him to work with.

Joel snorted awake on his cushions, rearing, turning . . . he'd disturbed himself out of his covers and Téo went over to settle him. When he came back to the sideboard he considered his cards and his remaining funds and said, "Call this a draw I reckon."

It was an old joke of theirs. Ben had to admire the cheek. He smiled, agreeing.

"We'll play properly next time. Meaningful stakes."

He had that new dream about a rabbi. They were exploring their casino together, they weren't being waited for, there weren't any games worth Ben's investment. Instead they walked circuits, no rush, nodding their hellos to the other gamblers but never stopping to join in and play. They considered each other's problems, offering unorthodox advice the other would never've conceived of. His fingertips kept brushing against hers. He was delighted by the warmth under the whites of her nails. He took only one sort of risk in the whole dream: when he shortened her name without encouragement, trying his luck and calling her Sib.

When he woke it was to the clatter of a breakfast trolley. A steward was singing to himself in the corridor outside. Téo and Joel were up already and sat in silence by the window. They had their blankets over their shoulders and they watched the sky, waiting for the sun to rise. Somewhere on the train another lav coughed clear. Doors squeaked and snapped. Ben hung off the bunk for a better view and he was treated to the emergence of an incredible show-off sky, Scottish mountain variety, unlike any sky he'd seen before. It was ribboned with colour, pinks and purples that reminded him of Saturday-morning cartoons, those ones that used to blast them awake with renderings of a brighter spikier world. Well played, Scotland, thought Ben, as he retreated under his covers.

He lay and he listened.

Elsewhere in the carriage a harried dad, out of patience, was arguing with his family for not being dressed yet. Brakes singing, the train slowed and halted. After a trembling wait it moved on. "Wow," said Téo of the changing scenery outside and Ben climbed down to stare at it as well. Really he wanted nicotine to accompany this rolling view, or strong coffee at least. It was the vastness. The spread. He wondered how long it took to form these mountains in their heaps. He liked the mottled patterns up the slopes, how some of the mountains were green, others brown or blotched with white scree. Téo pointed out a gleaming silver streak, a river. The train got closer and closer to this river, their routes matching for a while. Widening and narrowing, the river divided itself around an island and reknit.

When Vic hobbled through from his cabin he was red in the face; he seemed pleased, even relieved to be back here. He had remembered that these were birchwoods, he said . . . the mountains bristled with birchwoods. When they reached the next station it would only take an hour to drive to his village.

"Our wheels," Ben announced.

They were in the train-station car park. Téo was lifting their bags into the back of a hire car. Ben had paid extra to have it prepped and waiting like this and he was the only one permitted to drive. Like an international agent, Ben was thinking, like someone trained. His whole approach to tourism, he decided then, would borrow aspects from his poker game. Your massive financial overcommitment. Your awareness that once a big enough sum of money was staked you were obliged to accept the consequences, good or bad, and to enjoy those consequences as paid-for experiences in their own right. With the luggage packed (with Joel stowed beside Téo in the back, with Vic made comfortable under a blanket in the passenger seat), Ben started them on the next stage of their journey.

Patchwork fields bordered the road on both sides. Hedgerows, like track hurdles, staggered away into the distance. Ben saw toppled tree trunks, their middles crumbling and their ends covered in moss or mould. This was nature then. Traditionally, he felt most comfortable near concrete and glass, backgrounded by traffic noise, burglar alarms, the murmur of crowds. Ben was a man of the suburbs and his version of nature had for decades been that version kept fenced inside Enfield parks. He noticed the air tasted different up here, colder as if fridged. Were Ben to offer a complaint about the air at home he would say it was a tad heavy on particulates, your scorched rubber pieces from the roads, your

dust. Besides which you sometimes got the feeling that a mouthful of Greater London had been in and out of everyone else's
mouths already. Ben let himself appreciate the local product. The
Scottish air slammed him in his gob and he swilled it, sampling.

Vic was delighted by what he saw. He kept saying they were
better off, weren't they? Being out of London, being away from
Enfield?

"Why's that, Vic?" asked Ben. He was only scratching around
for more compliments. He wanted to be told, how kind all this,
how generous.

"They can't get at us," came Vic's answer.

Ben caught Téo's eye in the rear-view mirror.

"Who can't?"

"They can't bother us while we're up here. We'll finally have
some peace."

Ben grinned: an old man's paranoia. No wonder you daydreamed of enemies and the unseen, he thought, if your race was
almost run. It was sad.

For a while they played I spy with Joel. They took turns. They
were on a stretch of road that was walled in by bracken and for
a few rounds of the game they were reduced to "S" words, your
skies, your steering wheels. Then a view opened out and they
were treated to postcard peaks, a waterfall that winked.

It was Joel's turn. "Eyes pie," he said, "SOMEthing . . . beginner will . . . blue."

Téo corrected him. "Beginning with 'S' you mean."

"Uh-huh," said Joel.

"Sky?"

And he put a hand to his head, defeated, he couldn't believe it.

"Have another turn."

They'd emerged into a valley. On its far side there was a village. They saw a church, some chimneys. Sheep grazed in a field.

"Er-r-r."

"Anything will do. Look over there," Téo encouraged.

"Challenge us, Joel. Express yourself."

"Eyes pie . . . something beginner will . . . 'S.'"

"Sheep. It's gotta be sheep."

"No."

"It's not sheep?"

"No!"

"Spire?"

"no."

"Smoke?"

"no!"

"Oh God," said Téo.

"Not sky," pleaded Ben, "not again."

"Is sky," Joel purred, chin lifted, their champion.

They drove past lakes. Vic narrated what from what, explaining that these were some of the region's famous lochs. Banks of reeds and gorse dipped steeply towards the lochs, which in places looked shallow enough for wading. "Oh, yes," agreed Vic, who was recognising more and more landmarks, all shrunken, he said, but much the same. Overtaken by nostalgia, he gripped the passenger door. He kept reaching to do the same with the handbrake. Ben had to shoo his fingers away.

Vic told them he remembered individual river bends. The smell they were getting in the window, that was pine. They could see a wide wall of mountains ahead. On the other side, Vic said, was his village and the site of his old cottage. "Gone in an afternoon," he added for Joel's benefit. "I can still see it burn, clear as anything." He directed Ben around a gentle turn. They stopped the car on a slope.

Everybody bent forwards.

It didn't look like enough land for a home.

When Téo said as much, Vic nodded. "It was nothing."

"Do you want to get out, Dad, have a snoop around?"

"This is fine, this is perfect for me. You boys stretch your legs."

Joel ran ahead to the banks of a river. Ben kicked stones as he followed, football moves, some deft work. The river was noisy. It ran between boulders bigger than they were. Ben and Téo stood beside each other in silence with Joel between them, the chatterbox water talking instead. Humped on the horizon were more mountains, their tops wigged with snow. Lacking picture-book crags or any serious peaks, they were not mountains that impressed you with their height or their lines, instead, thought Ben, they gave out a sense of inertia, that they wouldn't negoti-ate, they were here and static and staying. He felt an urge to prove himself. He picked up a stone and he threw it as far as he could. He picked up another.

"Watch this," he said to Joel.

He sent the stone flying way out into the river, making a splash.

Joel wanted to try. Téo had to help him sift pebbles from the shallows. Before long they were all hurling in stones of every size.

They devised a points system with bonuses for technique, the majesty of a splash, your range. Ben disappointed himself with a couple of efforts back to back; and after that he searched around for a stone that was small and sleek, something he could really *launch* . . . Bent over the water he pulled out an excellent speci-men. Oh, she was the one! Sensible weight. Smooth-surfaced, almost blue. He showed Joel what he'd found. "This one's my winner for sure."

Joel kept his gaze on the lovely stone.

He licked the sides of his mouth and he said, "I want it."

Téo had just thrown in another. It broke the surface a good distance out.

"What," said Ben, distracted, "this one? We'll find you another that's just as good."

"Want that one. Please, Ben."

"There are loads. This is a country chock-full of stones."

"Ben. Please, Ben."

Wind came over the water. Their eardrums smacked like sails. Ben was being judged by these mountains, he felt sure. "We'll find you another stone," he promised Joel. And rearing back, he threw the one in hand as far as possible.

The kid had to be hurried back to the car. He was allowed to stand on the driver's seat next to Vic and press any button he wanted, as long as he agreed to stop crying. Ben was enjoying a victory smoke by the water. He was joined by Téo, who asked, "What's wrong with you?"

"It was only a stone."

"It wasn't only a stone, you cunt."

"*You* cunt."

They hushed themselves, moving along the river out of earshot. A path led them into a small birchwood. They went downhill. On the other side of the wood, the Scottish countryside was changed, they were in a different film, one with forest bandits, soldiers wearing chainmail, ambushes. "I'm trying," Ben complained.

"Are you?" said Téo.

The river was muddier here and tinged with red. Téo examined the water. He took off his coat and he rolled up his sleeve, pushing his arm in elbow-deep. "What did it look like anyway? This beloved stone. What shape was it?"

Ben said, "Stand up."

"Why? The boy's upset. I'm trying to make him feel better."

"Stand up."

"It's called trying to help someone. You might pay attention."

"I won't suck up to him. Not like this, not ever."

"It's not sucking up. It's care."

"You couldn't impress her in life. So impress her in death. That it?"

Téo clenched his jaw. Ben wondered if they would fight soon.

"How about this one?" Téo asked eventually. "Is it similar?" He held out a stone that was shiny and blue-touched, near enough the same as the one that Joel had taken a liking to.

"Looks good, lemme see," said Ben . . . and as soon as he could he stepped back, whipping forward the stone, releasing it and sending it out into the water. Téo stamped and swore. Whenever he was agitated he waddled as he walked, moving as though the soles of his feet were sore, as though the tightness of his jeans had suddenly come into account. He waddled away from Ben and he waddled back, snatching Ben's kappel off his head and throwing it in the river. They shoved each other, wrestling, playground business. Soon Ben had Téo's neck in its familiar hold under his armpit. "Fainites?" he asked.

This was a truce term they used at school. Ben remembered Lia questioning the word, like she questioned so much of their nonsense. What does fainites even mean, she asked them, often enough that Téo went away and looked it up. Fainites originated from Old French. It meant to wimp out of a challenge. "No," panted Téo, "no fainites."

He struggled and he rested. He struggled again.

"Say fainites and I'll let go."

"Fainites."

Ben stepped away. Téo rubbed himself where it hurt. He said, "You're letting me have Joel too long. You're making it more difficult for all of us."

"So keep him. I can't do it like you can, I'm not built for it."

"How do you know?"

"I'm not equipped."

"Nor was I. It meant learning how."

"You're different, more normal."

"And you're not as special as you think. You've heard my dad, how he talks about *his* parents, those circumstances he was dealt in childhood, he feels them now. He's seventy and he's stuck as a boy whose dad never acknowledged him. You gonna do that to Joel? Leave him to wonder where he came from, who his dad was?"

"I don't know."

"Figure it out."

They wrestled again. Téo got an arm around Ben's neck, trying to apply the same hold as before. He wasn't strong enough. Ben unfastened himself. They fell on each other, hurting each other for real, thumping and catching hold where they could. Ben controlled his breath and he paced himself. Soon he had Téo's face against the ground. Parity was at an end. Téo curled his body in anticipation of the two, three punishment blows. "All right," he said.

"Say it though."

"Fainites, fainites."

They stayed where they were on the ground. Ben said, "You gave her too much of the benefit. You never wanted to know she had flaws like me."

"What flaws?"

"Here's one. You ready? Lia was selfish."

"Lia Woods?"

"We can say this stuff, T, she's not hallowed now, she's not a statue, she's not a scroll we keep inside an ark. Lia had a bit of selfish in her. And I know this because I've got radar, we all do, people like me and her—we can detect each other across spaces. The minute there's another selfish person nearby, our own needs spike. We want to rush to be first and have the most, because we know there's someone else around who won't back down and let us."

Téo seemed surprised. He worked the information over, forming shapes with his mouth like someone sucking on a sweet. "What else then?"

"Lia could be boring. On occasion. She could be obvious."

"Nah."

"She was the cleverest out of us lot. But think about us lot."

"I never saw any of this."

"You *saw* it."

"I never took any of it in."

"I used to listen to you praise her and think, Lia's cool. But not for the reasons this guy's saying. I'd think, if this is love I'm good, cheers, I'll keep my clarity, cheers."

"When people are dead," Téo said. He took a moment. He started again. "When you love someone and they're dead, you're meant to remember the best of them."

"What's the best is what made Lia Lia—the worst included, I'm sorry to say. If I didn't believe that I wouldn't be able to stand myself."

". . . She could be condescending. About types of music."

"Okay. Keep going."

"She could be dismissive if you didn't straight-away agree with her. Like, if you didn't share her opinions, that put you beyond saving."

"What else?"

"She didn't leave me enough advice. I didn't get enough

instructions for Joel. She didn't give me any help. Neither did you."

Ben said, "She hated being kept in the dark, Lia, she hated there being things she couldn't see end to end. I guess I thought: she couldn't have done this to herself, or not on purpose, not without a plan." Ben gestured at the birchwood they'd passed through, the car beyond. "But if she chose that weekend for a reason, it must have been because you were back home. I think she wanted you to look after him."

Téo said nothing.

Ben went on, "She was clever enough to be suspicious of dickheads like me, dickheads who don't change, or not enough, and not in time."

"It's not change, Ben. It's . . . aiming your energies."

"At the kid?"

"Away from yourself."

Téo spat some dark phlegm on to the ground. He was maybe bleeding in his mouth after the fight. Reminded of the fight they both spat.

"I'm sorry about your kappel."

"Sorry I haven't helped you more."

They stood and they started walking through the wood. Téo said, "Do an afternoon with him on your own. While we're up here."

"Joel."

"Do it properly, committed, where you listen to him and look at him. Leave your phone behind. Run around after him, buy him his choice of food. Let him exhaust you for one afternoon. Let him drive you mad and make you laugh. Find out those feelings first, before you decide whether you can do this or not."

Shouts found them through the trees. "Tay-oh. Beh-hen."

The car horn sounded. "Where." *Bip.* "Are." *Bip.* "You." *Bip.*

Vic must have shown Joel which button to press. They were out of the woods again and waving at the car, saying we're here, we're coming, there's been a change of plan.

Bodybuilders and wrestlers, Ben was thinking, as he drove Joel towards the coast. Your action stars of the old days, your muscle men . . . there was that spate of movies from his youth, movies in which well-known action men were recast as fishes-out-of-water, as *dads*. There was meant to be comedy in it. Because they had their muscles. They had their reputations. Now they'd been left with a son or a daughter to care for! And what use were muscles, what use prestige? Ben thought of a film in which a boy was raised by wolves. Another about a ginger orphan in a mansion. There was a brilliant one about a lethal sniper forced to babysit.

The hire car purred along. From the back, raising his voice to be heard over the music, Joel called out a question. Could he sit in the front as well? No objections from Ben. They'd left Téo miles behind at the Highlands hotel. He made a snap decision and steering the car off the road he invited Joel forward, between the seats, asking him, "That better? That suit you?"

"Change this for loud," Joel said.

"Even louder? You madman!"

Windows open, they let all of Scotland hear their excellent taste.

Ben was a wayward follower of any map. A sat-nav's instructions he took as optional. Having noted there was a lot of pixelated blue ahead—the sea—he aimed the car in that direction, improvising a route. After an hour's driving they missed Aberdeen, arriving instead at sand dunes on an empty stretch just south of the city. Cars ripped by, veering inland towards town or else continuing along the coast to an amusement park, the big wheel of which Ben and Joel could see on the horizon.

"We'll head that way after. Try out the arcade," Ben promised.

He had no idea what was or wasn't plausible. He watched Joel carefully, trying to fathom what the tiny brain would credit. "First though, I wanted to show you my favourite sand dune. Uh, this one here." They approached it. Joel took Ben's hand. The dune seemed a lot steeper than Ben had bargained for. They lingered for a while on the cusp, wind-buffeted, neither of them ready to run it yet. Sand fell away to reeds and rubbish below. "Steady GO," shouted Joel without warning, and he ran them over the side so that Ben was pitched on to his front and blinded right away by kicked-up sand. He was turned around and around and ended up heaped at the bottom, beside Joel, in fits. "You're pleased with that bit of work," Ben said.

"Again!"

Ben remembered Vic's mention of crabs. They were supposed to be plentiful along this stretch. You only had to start overturning rocks near the water. They tried crab hunting for a while but neither Ben nor Joel's patience lasted long enough. Nature had performed all right, Ben explained. Nature had impressed them with its mountains and its lochs, its dunes. Now that nature'd come up empty regarding crabs it was time to let civilisation have a turn.

They climbed back in the car. Joel rode in the front again. "Think you were meant to put your belt on," Ben complained, noticing too late. They were already up the coast and parking.

"Hurts."

"Doesn't matter. Téo would be fuming at me."

"I *miss* Téo."

"Yeah? He would've made you sit in the back though."

Joel considered this and said, "I *miss* Ben."

"Nice. Cunning."

They crossed the coastal road, pushing in through the doors of a seaside arcade. They were met inside by a terrific din, that distinctive nowhere-else chug of motorised dispensers that shat out coins and a mishmash of digital tunes and sound effects from the games machines. Joel was excited. He ran in circles, overcome by the racket. They pondered a row of cabinets, each more muscular and with more plastic appendages than its neighbour. They tried a game that had holstered pistols, then a game with a mounted chain gun. There were games that mimicked for them the experience of guitar playing, horse-riding, dancing . . . activities, it occurred to Ben, they might have tried together for real and might yet.

At a change machine he pushed in another £50 and they filled their pockets with coins. They played a motorbike game then a space game. Stupid and screen drunk, they only stopped when all the money was spent. Ben wondered if an afternoon in Joel's company felt like months, what would months have felt like? He led them out of the arcade and straight to a fish and chip shop. It was on the front. It faced the inbound tide. "Ketchup?" he asked.

Joel couldn't remember.

"Plenty on both," Ben told the proprietor.

Legs swinging, they sat on rocks and looked out over Aberdeen's beach as they ate. When Joel complained about the ketchup Ben tutted; but he pared away the top layer as well as he could, showing Joel the undoused virgin chips beneath. The tide stole closer, covering more of the beach with every inward wash. "Sea's coming for us. Sea's greedy for our dinner," Ben said—and Joel, inspired, tossed the sea a chip. He had lots of uneaten food left over. So did Ben. They surrendered their trays to the seagulls, which hopped and cawed beside them on the rocks, petitioning for a share.

TWELVE
SIBYL

Rabbi Challis, they called her today, which was ominous. She met with the synagogue's leadership committee every Monday, often in the borrowed basement room of an office block in Enfield where somebody knew somebody who held the lease. This was a low and cramped-looking building that kept its magnitude below, in the rump, like the map of England. The painted walls of the underground conference room were a blinding white. Blue and green carpet tiles had been laid out in a pattern on the floor, not quite the precision chequerboard though close enough for anyone concerned about order and symmetry to wonder what went wrong. Since Sibyl's first meeting here, everybody had kept to their same seats, an unspoken contract like that which children adhere to at school. There were only the high letter-box windows for distraction, windows that looked out on to the road at pavement level. Paired ankles beat by.

"We have voted to terminate your appointment," she was told.

So that was that.

Hilda, the chair, gave the impression she would do them all

the favour of blunt truths. "It was a mistake on our part, no doubt," she said. "As a committee we have decided to take Enfield Progressive in a different direction."

"As I understood it, when you brought me in, I *was* the different direction."

"We have decided, not."

"The old direction then."

There was some squirming at the table. Sibyl had her allies here. The part of her brain that planned ahead tried to imagine how she would feel about this tonight, tomorrow, would she sleep at all? Another part of her brain asked questions of these people and formulated complaints. She was being sacked for trying to see through promises that had won her the job in the first place. She had tried to open the doors of the shul a little wider. "How long do I have? Without the residence I'll have to find somewhere else to live."

"It has been suggested as a compromise . . . that is, certain members of the committee have asked that you be allowed to stay on in an interim role."

"Until you choose my successor."

"This was always an experiment," said Hilda. "I'm sorry if you feel you weren't properly warned." She neatened an agenda on the table in front of her: "To other business."

It was a quarrel with the centuries, Sibyl told herself afterwards. Her chances of success were only ever slight. But rejection was indifferent to logical argument. Rejection wouldn't be haggled with. She came away feeling winded. She shook her hands at the wrists like someone stung. Unable to bear being recognised on the high street and without a specific destination in mind, she walked the back roads of the neighbourhood, she picked new routes, never tried. Conspicuous in the centre of the sky was a wrong note, a September blunder: the chalk-white thumbprint of the moon. She thought about phoning one of her sisters. She fantasised about running off and never a word. She wondered about the price of flights, skin already prickling, she imagined foreign sunlight on her shoulders. She thought about Ben. She wondered what he was doing.

While falling in love, while feeling the impossible beneficiary of that love returned, any other crisis took on a thinner, more provisional texture. The love got into the weave of everything else. Sibyl smiled suddenly. Then frowned then swore. She smiled again. She felt open to risk and detour, which had to be a consequence of all the time she'd spent with Ben, faulty Ben, who for every maddening quality had pushed on them both a gift, magicking up the possibility of love out of impudence and imagination. Him in mind, wandering in circles around the neighbourhood, Sibyl considered other audacious ways she might alter her life. Different work. New pieties. There was always more she could do to help Joel.

Her walk took her past the Erskine home.

Sibyl recognised it for the huge, unsuitable trampoline that was just visible from the pavement. The Erskines were away with Ben. Scotland was all she'd been told. It had been that rare Saturday at shul when Vic was not in attendance. Standing around his garden, now, were Joel's social workers. They were with two others, strangers to Sibyl, perhaps other council employees. The quartet carried with them an assortment of folders and laptop bags and briefcases. Sibyl watched as they tried Vic's doorbell.

She entered the garden and greeted the two she recognised.

"Rabbi."

"Hallo, rabbi."

They were awkward; there was something wrong. Sibyl was introduced to a solicitor, as well as to Gil and Alistair's colleague, who described himself as their team leader. "What's the matter?" she asked, having shaken the offered hands. "The Erskines are on holiday. Until midweek I think."

"Know where they've got to?"

It was the team leader who spoke. He was suited, he looked a pedant, a hand-up-in-the-audience sort of man, rarely wrong. His tone made Sibyl resist answering. She had Lia Woods in mind, her anti-authoritarian streak, the instinctive distaste for unearned bluntness. "I don't."

Gil said, "It's serious I'm afraid."

"I could try calling Téo for you."

"We've tried calling."

"I could leave a message."

"We've tried."

Sibyl was waved closer. Gil explained, Téo's viability as a carer had been put in doubt. They had received a tip-off, some breach, they were reluctant to say more. They had been able to bring forward the date of Joel's transfer to a foster home in the north. He would move there while matters in Enfield were resolved one way or another. Could Sibyl see to it that Téo made contact with their department?

"I'll do what I can."

The group lingered, as if waiting for her intervention right away.

"I'll let you know," Sibyl assured them, "I will."

She saw the visitors out of the garden and after a decent interval of time she sat down on Vic's front step. She took her phone from her bag and tried calling Téo and Ben in turn. Both numbers went to voicemail, the recorded instructions running counter to each other in attitude, Téo's a sheepish request for callers to leave

a message, Ben's a briefer command: "After the beep." Feeling
the need to be occupied, Sibyl moved about Vic's garden, collecting some of the seasonal debris that had fallen down from
his trees. She found a broom and she swept up leatherish leaves.
She dragged into a pile all the twigs, some of which had gathered
inside the netting of Joel's trampoline. Teenagers went by on the
road, laughing and tripping each other up. Parents with smaller
children came next, a fleet behind pushchairs. Sibyl sat on the
step.

It was easier to sink into prayer after the completion of a task.
Slowly, deliberately, she made herself more alert to her surround-
ings, the air around her, the sounds. There was birdsong and the
busy obsessive scratching of squirrels. She heard the crackle of
cars on gravel, the hum of a plane that disturbed the upper atmosphere. She felt the cold polished stone of the doorstep beneath
her, then brickwork, brass, whatever materials were near enough
at hand to touch. Prayer for Sibyl had become as passive an act as
recording a voicemail. She hadn't much trust she'd be listened to.
There seemed little likelihood of reply. But she prayed even so,
asking that Joel come through this, asking that Joel be all right
and still himself, a boy with fire, perpetually on the move, a boy
who'd faced so much already and would soon face more.

THIRTEEN
TÉO

There had been another visit from the hotel cleaners while they were downstairs at lunch. The beds were squared, the towels replaced at angles, a little boy's mess (if not quite expunged) made neater. Téo sat on his bed on the side nearest the room's landline telephone. He took up the receiver. He had grown so used to the compressed pistol-weight of his mobile phone, this one felt plasticky and far-fetched by comparison. He dialled the synagogue in Enfield, reading the number off his neutered mobile, which hadn't worked properly since they crossed into the mountains on Friday night.

It was Tuesday now. Téo listened as Sibyl's phone rang and rang and when he was put through to her answer machine he said, "Rabbi? This is Téodor Erskine, Téo, listen. I wanted to leave word. We don't get the reception up here. None whatsoever, zero bars. And the hotel wi-fi is down. I figured you'd want an update. How we're doing."

Téo slid off the bed as he spoke. He idled to the window, landline with him, its cord stretched to maximum give.

Glam enough to boast two swimming pools, one indoors,

one out, their smart hotel had a golf course and a putting green within its grounds as well. Their top-floor rooms, paid for by Ben, overlooked everything. When Téo pressed his nose to the window he could look down and spy on the others, who had finished their lunches and were heading outside. Ben as boss, Ben with a borrowed golf putter under his arm, they made slow staggered progress down the hotel steps. Victor needed help to make his way but Joel raced from the top to the bottom and back, wanting it demonstrated that steps were nothing to him, a piece of piss, he could manage *steps*.

"I've been friends with Ben a long time," Téo was telling Sibyl's answer machine. "I could see it drove him mad at first, this problem of the phone signal. He couldn't check the weekend scores from his pocket or pound out messages as and when . . . Actual fact, I think it's been good for him. Joel's got more of his time. He hasn't had to compete.

"They took a trip to the seaside together," Téo was saying, "did you know that? Just the two of them. Something happened there. Ben: he's in deeper now. He forgets himself. Oh, small example, rabbi. Doesn't sound much. But we're eating lunch today. You know those free-for-alls, like buffets, with salads and cold meats and no-limit garlic bread? Ben's taking ages over his choices. He's curating a plate. He returns to our table loaded. And when Joel says hm-m-m-m. About a potential swap. When Joel says *act*ually. About how he might want to eat off Ben's plate instead of his own, Ben accepts the situation. He slides over his plate. He swaps."

Téo remembered them both in the spring, how self-consciously Ben chatted to Joel, as if waiting to be admired for doing so, as if he expected to be scored out of ten.

"I can't tell you, rabbi, what it is to see Ben Mossam surrender a present, a lovely present, and one he's prepared for himself."

He had lapped the room while he spoke, moving as far as

the phone would let him before returning to the window again. Outside, Victor was sitting in a deckchair. Ben putted on the manicured lawn. He bent to peer after a rolling ball that was promising, promising—then he straightened, showing the distance of the miss to Joel with two fingers. On his own part of the lawn, the boy sat cross-legged. He was arranging into mysterious order a dozen loose golf balls. Téo felt sure that no adult would readily be told which order or why.

"I know I should be pleased," he said, "seeing Ben and Joel get closer. It's what I've wanted, even schemed for. I've been desperate to get back to my old life. I dream about the company of anyone who can help themselves. Only that! People who have the knack for reaching high objects. Dressing.

"So I should be relieved watching Ben and Joel get closer," Téo was saying, "but I watch them, I'm watching them as I speak to you, and I can see what pain I'm due." He sniffed. "I'm the Jew from a joke. I see prices."

When he peered down again he saw they had abandoned the green. Ben and Joel were playing on the garden steps instead. Joel had challenged Ben. Or Ben had challenged Joel. They were to climb as many of the steps as they dared then leap on to the grass below. Joel was in imperial mode, a viceroy, squandering energy on orders. Should he be allowed to sleep in the car? That was the question in the back of Téo's mind. And even as he said to himself, "Let Ben figure it out," he was pondering other specifics. Whether Joel ought to be bundled up in a blanket; whether there ought to be shushes and encouragement for him to doze as soon as they drove off for the station. *Or.* Whether they should try to save Joel's precious sleep and do questions on the journey, play loud music, reintroduce the games of I spy, anything to keep him awake and so heighten the chances of an instant knockout once they were on the train.

"Where was I?" Téo asked the phone. He hadn't meant to leave Sibyl such a long message. Only update her, explain about the difficulty of keeping in touch. He considered ending the call but didn't, because of how pleasurable this felt, the growing lightness with each confession that left his mouth. There was medicine in the voicing. She had taught him that.

"You wanted to be told how we managed on the Victor front. Our effort to find those graves of his mum and his dad . . . So on Saturday, while Ben and Joel were at the seaside, me and Victor went off on our search. We're scouring a cemetery behind the church in his village. And I'll admit I'm thinking, Victor won't hack this for long. He gets a sheen of sweat on his face, as you're aware. His breathing turns ragged. He's been getting more and more Scottish since we've been up here, rabbi, as if he's shedding Enfield, shedding the adoptive Jewishness, as if he's shedding marriage, widowhood, becoming more childlike. I remember how Joel, when he came to us, how overwhelmed he would be. Every morning was like a new affront. Now Joel wakes up with such confidence. For my dad it's the opposite, it's like he gets out of bed and he's gained another enemy overnight.

"We're searching this cemetery. And we do find one of the graves we're after. We come across his mum.

"And Victor says that's her, Annie Erskine, the dates are right.

"He's this terrible colour, rabbi. He's yellow from tiredness and he's shaking, the tired-tears coming on, how they do now. We sit for a rest and he's trying to hide his face from me. He can't seem to get his throat decently clear.

"I'm sat and I'm thinking, what's coming next, what's he about to say?

"I'll be gone soon myself, Dad admits. And I'm all, I suppose so, yeah.

"We're looking at these graves. We never did find the other

one, of Victor's father, my grandfather. But I say to him, wherever he is, this man, whoever he was, you've been a better dad to me. Do you know that?

"And Victor says oh. Like he's shocked. Like this is news.

"So now it's me crying. That this would be a surprise to him. That I ever let this information turn into a surprise."

Téo was at the window. He rested his forehead and he cooled it on the glass. His voice had been water, it had a current of its own, the vocabulary there for him, the words surfacing and awaiting his fishing-out. Now he was spent. He breathed a shape on to the window and he rubbed it off with a sleeve, saying to Sibyl's answer machine, "I best go now." He said, "I wonder if you'll listen to this."

Down in the grounds of the hotel he could see Ben and Joel jumping from steps that were already too high. And they urged each other higher. Victor no longer paid them much attention. He was sat forward in his deckchair, intent on whatever patch of grass he could see between his feet. He rocked as if trying for a burp. While Téo watched, a uniformed employee, the hotel manager perhaps, walked by on the path. He stopped to talk. Though Téo couldn't hear what was said he saw a vivid flash of dismay on Victor's face, because here was another stranger, forcing him to rally. Victor was able to raise up a smile. He answered a few questions, playing the conversation game. When he was left alone again his face turned slack. He removed a handkerchief and he dabbed a drip of something off his nose.

Téo hung up the phone. He stood and he moved between the suites of interconnected rooms, putting Joel's strewn possessions into a suitcase, no sort of strategy about it—a first pass at packing. He worked at speed, aware of dwindling time, then he went through to start packing for Victor. He was thinking how his dad's appearances in public were getting more dismal by the week. As though he was aware of a subtle joke at his expense, Victor flinched from strangers' kindnesses. He smiled wryly at their well-meant offers of help. Lately only Joel brought out his unguarded warmth.

Soon as Téo had a full bag of luggage for Joel and another bag for Victor, he heaved them on to his shoulder and he went down in the hotel lift. He was thinking about the pitiful frowns that Victor put on . . . how, under his breath, he whimpered to himself like the tyrannised. These habits were expressions of his illness, Téo supposed. They were also manifestations of new freedoms, those available to people who were too far gone for pretences. Manners could be abandoned. Pride too. Victor as a younger and healthier man would have felt any public bids for sympathy beneath him. He grew up alone. He grew up in one institution after another, the world leaving him to wing it almost from Joel's age. He pushed through till he was an adult himself, at which point he tried on identities like clothes, finding a few he was able to tolerate, as office worker, married-over Jew, son-in-law, homeowner, a dad who drove you to fury with his meddling. It was almost over. Victor was letting go of defences he'd hauled up around himself decades ago. When he looked at Téo now it was with the blank entreaty of a child.

Luggage in the boot of the car, Téo padded over the grass to join them, appreciating as he went that pliant lunar feel of a well-kept lawn underfoot, then gravel's crunch, how it shifted like the unreliable floor in your dreams.

"Joel?" he said as he passed. "Don't do it, mate. Don't keep jumping from those steps."

His warning was half-hearted. Already, as if something had

been agreed on paper, Téo could feel his authority starting to shift over to Ben. Already a double sensation, the longed-for respite from responsibility and a dread at not mattering so much to the boy.

Joel would move on. Maybe he would live with Ben in time. After Joel left, Téo would have to stay on at Victor's flat, help *him* to live. Téo's head swam, it could all last years. He squatted by the deckchair.

"That's most of your packing done."

"Did you remember my medicines?"

"Pretty sure. Yeah."

"And my pyjamas?"

Téo sighed. "I'm going back up in a minute. I'll make sure."

Victor rolled his shoulders as if he was cold. He said, "Wait a minute."

His scarf was loose. Téo leaned over to fasten it again, taking care over the knot where it rested on the hollow of Victor's throat. The skin there was thin and fragile, like something you might tear without meaning to. "What's the matter," he asked, "what's got you agitated? You've barely said a word all day."

Victor had been worrying, he said—something about a mix-up back at home, some confusion in Enfield that he might be responsible for. He didn't want this holiday of theirs to end. He didn't want to go back, he said.

"I get that. It's been good up here. But listen, whatever it is, this confusion, we'll fix it. We've got a journey ahead of us. Have a rest on the train. We can discuss it tomorrow."

There was the difficult work of getting Victor out of his chair. His feet had to be put firmly on the ground before they tried anything more. Then Téo grasped both his forearms and pulled. On the undersides of Victor's arms (both his palms as well) the skin was warm, baby-like, soft enough to stun you. Those times he needed help pulling up his socks you bent, you folded back the hems, you found: Victor's ankles were as slender as a young woman's.

"One, two, three . . . there."

Téo kept a hand on his back, lying, "You're doing brilliantly. Take it a step at a time. You're nailing this."

There was a level of trust a person needed to keep putting the left foot in front of the right. In Victor's case that trust had evaporated, reduced to nothing by recent falls. Focused on every move, he scanned the coming patches of grass, gravel and tarmac for possible treachery. Téo used his Joel voice, malice-less and practical, to encourage Victor forward. He used his old nappies voice, that sing-song . . . When the roof of the car was in reach, Téo took away Victor's stick and tossed it in the boot with the luggage. He brushed down Victor's shoulders and his chest. This man wasn't shown how to be a father, he thought, but I was.

Left to themselves all this while, Ben and Joel had been conferring. They admitted it when Téo passed by again: they were wondering about their stomachs.

"But we had the big lunch," Téo protested.

Joel said, "Oh, but no, but Téo, but listen." Apparently there was a whole different meal called fish and chips. Joel called it "fisher chips." There was something about seagulls too, though this part of the explanation was told through hysterical laughter on the boy's part and Téo could not follow his meaning.

"I've got to dash up to our room," he said, "and pack the last of our stuff. We'll eat on the way to the station." He would help Ben apply for guardianship, he thought. If Joel ended up living with Ben, and Téo had to hang around with Victor after all, they could still be close, around the corner from each other, a short walk apart. He imagined himself answering Ben's texts and pop-ping over late, sharing his tricks and his know-how. It might be all right. Téo would be an extra. Nobody's main anything. But he would get to orbit Joel a while longer.

From around the room he gathered tiny T-shirts, some bought new for this trip, others older, dating from back before the summer. The older clothes had turned cardboard-like and beige from scorching washes. Téo took up handfuls of worn socks and pants and the elastic-waisted shorts that weren't too tight round Joel's middle. He gathered bears and a fox and about a dozen plastic men, also storybooks, a tennis ball, a rubber ball, some pocked and patterned marbles and a pile of stickers that were held together by an elastic band. He'd be an uncle figure. A mentor for Joel. Someone who came-and-went from the house, joining them for Sunday double-headers on TV or for kickabouts in the park. Téo would be that vague relative who took control of family barbecues. One day he would say to Joel, do you remember what we went through that year? And Joel would say some of it. Yeah. Some.

The sound of a car horn brought Téo back to the task in hand.

He checked the time. He hurried between rooms to collect final scraps, a comfort blanket of Joel's, a sword, treasured pebbles. He went belly first on the floor to check for objects that'd snuck under the furniture, one plastic spoon, a small trumpet. He stood at the door, propping it open with his heel, looking back— anything else?

The landline phone was illuminated. A little orange light winked for his attention.

Be a voice message, Téo guessed. Maybe Sibyl had made a note of the hotel number and called him back with news of her own from Enfield. There wasn't time to listen. They would be back there by morning. Téo was summoned from outside again, the car horn sounding three times in succession, *bip, bip, bip.* He let the door swing closed and he went down the stairs at a sprint, quick as he could manage them. Outside, bags stowed, he hopped in the back of the car next to Joel. Ben had the engine running. Warmth flooded out of the dashboard vents.

"Not like you to cut it fine."

"I was distracted. Let's go."

"Enfield-bound. Bye bye, Scotland," said Ben. "You were decent, you were better than I expected."

"Ben," Joel petitioned, "a little bit of beeps?"

"I think he's done enough beeps," said Téo.

They weren't yet out of the hotel grounds. "I'm doing beeps," Ben said. And he mashed his hand on the steering wheel, sounding the horn again and again.

On board the train they divided themselves between cabins as before. Victor went to bed early. The other three agreed—Ben would tuck in Joel tonight, Ben would lead the ritual, with Téo showing him how.

Their train left the station and started to push free of the mountains. When they moved into flatter land, their phones made contact with local masts. Buzzed at, chimed at, they took receipt of a load of unread texts and voicemails. "Oi, try to concentrate," Téo said. "Leave the phones charging. I'm showing you this, it's important."

The train kept skimming and rattling south. The scenery outside had disappeared in darkness; instead they saw reflections of themselves, dancing Joel in and out of his pyjama legs, arranging his stuffed animals by pecking order around the pillows on the floor. With effort they persuaded Joel under a blanket. He shut his eyes. They waited.

"What now?" asked Ben.

"Now we're patient. And we whisper."

"How long do we have to stay like this?"

"However long he needs. You'll learn. It gets to be a part of you."

"What if it doesn't? What if I don't learn?"

"You'll learn."

"My phone's going mad over there."

"Mine too. Ignore it. Concentrate on Joel. What I do now, I wait another ten minutes, even if it seems like he's definitely asleep. Cos sometimes he sits up. You have to start over."

"Weird question . . . how d'you know it's happened for real?"

"Sleep? You listen. The rhythm of their breathing has to change."

"I mean, how d'you know if you've started to love them or not?"

Téo hesitated. "I wouldn't know that."

"Be serious," said Ben.

Something did change in Joel's breathing. His exhalations were longer, more complete. "There," Téo said, "can you hear the difference? You will soon. When Lia first asked me to do this I had no clue either."

They stayed where they were on the floor of the cabin. They leaned against the fixtures in the dark, talking about her in whispers. There was a mode of weather, bright and intense, a sensory attack, that always put Lia in mind. And they agreed that sometimes the circumstances of her death threatened to overpower the wholer memory—that Lia, when she first came to mind, would be wearing one of the more mysterious expressions in her repertoire, she looked secretive, freighted by what was to come; it took effort to bring to mind those images of her when she was in adventure mode, relaxed, Lia's arrival in rooms, the sudden departures, certain scars and nicks, her vocabulary, her dancing.

"Man, her dancing."

"Lia dancing," Ben agreed.

They decided the brain must be compelled to prioritise certain impressions of a suicide, the melancholic memories first, the brain foreshadowing in these remembered moments the one desolate decision that would define her for Joel but only if they let it. Time was helping. Some honesty was helping. In Téo's mind, it was as though a building had been knocked down, a tree had shed its leaves, he saw her more clearly, he wondered he hadn't been as curious before. Removed by time and events from an obsession—finally able to free Lia's ghost from his bludgeoning admiration of her—Téo had started to think instead of the friendship that fastened the two of them, an affinity as rare and precious as romantic love. Tonight, on the floor of the train, he thought of Lia's knack for quoting books she'd read only once. He thought of her tearful, flu-struck, snot on her sleeve. He remembered how patient she was with Victor. How she paid Victor the respect of arguing back—arguing passionately. He thought of her sleepy, raging, he thought of Lia next to him on a park bench, butting her shoulder against his in platonic affection, not speaking, not needing to.

They played a new game of Ben's, right there on the floor.

As with all of Ben's games it was competitive. You won by excavating a statement or a gesture or some cheek of Lia's that made the other person reel at its accuracy, its caught and distilled Lia-ness.

"Year nine," said Téo. "School play. Her robot voice, remember?"

Ben said, "The Christmas when she swore she was really into snooker."

Téo said, "The summer of the fez."

"Oh-h-h-h-h!"

"Oh-h-h-h-h!"

They flapped their fingers at each other in recognition. It was hard to see in the cabin, the only light their illuminated phones in the corner. Joel stirred. He settled. "Anyway. Shush," said Téo.

"You shush."

"I am shushed."

"Be honest here, T, admit it. You think Lia wanted it to be you. You think she chose you."

Téo was worn out, too tired for second-guessing or the normal diplomacy. He was distracted by the activity on their phones. He nodded, yeah.

"Then do it with me. Stick around. We'll raise Joel together."

"Together would only mean me doing it."

Ben was bouncing where he sat. "Help me till he's eighteen and I swear, I'll do what I can for Victor in return. We'll be teammates. Same as at school. Let's try it and see."

They touched fists: maybe. Ben said, "You don't look happy."

Téo could be honest. "I'm happy."

WINTER
TO
SPRING

FOURTEEN
VIC

One day there was frost on the leaves and the air was smoky and close. All around the neighbourhood the trees were cut back. This work was done a road's length at a time, the fallen branches shredded by tow-along chippers that rumbled and whined at the base of the trunks. For a while, until winds came, Vic's part of Enfield was covered in threads of yellow and gold, this woodchip so thickly carpeting the byways that they became impassable, at least to somebody being pushed from place to place in a wheelchair. One day there was frost on the ground as well. Between the barer branches of the pollarded trees, views announced themselves, forgotten since last winter. Enfield was started on its sundowns as early as the mid-afternoons. Windscreens, wing mirrors, the small square panels in the doors of old phone boxes—all this glass flared white, reflecting a brilliance. Shadows lengthened in the park. Whenever Vic shut his eyes against the bright he saw patterns, threaded veined shapes; he believed he saw colours unknown to him before. He understood something important. This was his only winter, the last of his life.

He spent more and more time in the synagogue. Encouraged to by Sibyl, he sat for hours in a sanctuary that was hers to watch over, at least until her replacement arrived. Always choosing the same chair (right of the aisle, middle row) Vic inched the weeks. He saw out the autumn then most of winter. He listened to choirs and bands in rehearsal. He sat through preparations for the Hanukkah celebrations. Study groups gathered around him, shyly at first, and although he never contributed to their discussions he was made to feel he might, any time. It was understood by everyone at the synagogue that Mister Erskine was down on his luck. He wasn't well—he struggled to make coherent conversation now. Rabbi Challis had taken a hand in his care. The Mossam boy, Ben, was helping too. It was understood that Vic's son was no longer around. People were curious what happened there. They didn't ask. Instead, visitors glanced in Vic's direction, registering who he was and who he'd been when he weighed two or three stone more. Some of them smiled in recognition and they offered Vic their best.

This morning there was nobody around.

Vic passed the time by watching a burning candle that flickered above the sanctuary stage. He learned early in his membership that they referred to these candles—suspended in the air, enclosed by glass—as everlasting. They kept them lit and replenished, a symbol of respect for the scrolls in the cupboard or the ark at the back of the stage, their bimah. Vic moved his gaze between the sheening criss-cross patterns that were cast on the wooden surfaces of the bimah. The flame in the jar was made to dance compulsively by invisible aggravations of air. It was skittish and rooted at once, restive but stuck in position.

He believed he might doze.

Later, out of the synagogue's higher windows, Vic watched a plane glimmer and grow. It cleared a cloud and disappeared. He strained, listening to noises from the road, the goods lorries, an ambulance, somebody's trainers as these were cheeped across the pavement tiles. In with a steady clack (which would be heels or leather-soled shoes) he heard the distinctive purr of a wheeled suitcase. Focused, lingering over every sound, gratified at his range, Vic allowed himself a fantastic thought: that he could listen further, out beyond the suburb and the North Circular Road, as far as Téo in his flat by the river. It was the longest Vic had gone without being visited by his son—without hearing from him at all. Vic's chin touched his chest. He napped again, moving between the skins of dreams. When he resurfaced he looked about for landmarks, reminding himself, the sanctuary, the candle patterns, the street sounds, yes.

He licked his dry lips. He was able to rouse up some saliva to wet his mouth. At its business end, the sanctuary had four stained-glass windows. These windows were set into brick on either side of the stage, each depicting a scene to represent a season. The colourful glass let in a beautiful treated light, browns through the autumn panel, blues the winter, greens the spring, yellows the summer. Around these elegant windows a decision had been made that the sand-coloured brick should be left exposed. It must have been a whim of the architect's, Vic thought . . . the fellow's notion, perhaps, was to let a sense of industry contrast with all the colour. Utility was set against brilliance; and for those who came here to pray there was a subtle suggestion that in order to reach a technicoloured religious bliss they must work.

Alone in the sanctuary, Vic clutched the edges of his seat. He levered his body forwards and backwards, a jerking motion that from a distance might have made him mistakable for someone in communion with God. He knew they sometimes rocked their bodies in prayer, those stauncher Jews from other cultures and countries. His involuntary spasms were harder to resist each day. Sometimes he stopped resisting! He dared the disease to take hold, even exaggerating the see-saw motions and rowing through one convulsion after another, letting relief and defeat flood him together.

Everything had gone wrong on the day of their return from Scotland.

Vic was still pinching the sleep from his eyes when he was led from Euston station to a taxi to his garden and there to a scene of strangers, arguments and procedures. They went indoors with the social workers. Sibyl hurried over to try to mediate. Téo was asked to find some text messages on his phone. Hurt, he swore that he would never speak to Vic or trust him again. Joel had been sent to play upstairs. He kept coming down. He couldn't understand what was happening. Téo shushed him and stroked his hair. He said, "At least you won't be around old meddlers." He said, "At least you won't be around people who can hurt you." Eventually, Vic spoke.

"I didn't want this, Téodor."

"Shut up, you old fool. You've done enough now."

"Téodor, please."

"It's not about you, it's not about forgiving you for this."

"Téodor, please."

It was Sibyl who stepped in. She prevented Joel from being taken away. It was agreed she would take him till Christmas or the new year, another stopgap, for as long as she had a home at the synagogue. After that, they would have to reconvene. Téo sat dumbstruck, like someone out of a wreck. He had been told he was a danger to Joel. He got in his car and he left for the city that night. Vic rarely reached his phone in time, but whenever it rang he was sure in his stomach it was never Téo who called.

He must have slept again. Blinking, comprehending, Vic took in the everlasting candle, the prayer books they called siddurs, the stage they called their bimah, yes. To index this, to push around the Hebrew words in his mind brought a measure of peace.

Along the east–west walls of the sanctuary, the iron radiators gargled up a stomach-ache sound. The first snap of the winter had found them out as late as December, like a lie of omission they were hoping to get away with. The cold came heralded by vicious winds, hoolies, Vic used to call them. When he tried to recall the spring and summer months and their time looking after Joel, the memories were not so distinct, Vic was at a loss for days at a time, imagining he'd forgotten the laughter in the flat, angry at himself, that he could no longer recall Joel's mangled phrases over breakfast or lunch, phrases he'd sworn he would write down and keep.

In the sanctuary, the radiators trickled some more. They made a tutting sound. It was as though these radiators were aware they had failed people, exactly when they were needed most. When Vic woke from another doze, a crew of uniformed plumbers were crouching down by the radiators with their tools. One of them advised Sibyl to cross her fingers. "You too, chap," Vic was told.

Crossed fingers, he thought. In a synagogue.

He used to make the same mistakes. Touching wood, knocking wood. How hungrily he had revised their names for things! The rules and what was forbidden to Jews. As a tourist might in a foreign town, latching on to words and meanings not only for ken but inclusion, Vic used to think that by learning their language he would become less conspicuous, he would bob along better in conversation. "By the way you'll be bored," Sal had said before Vic's first service. But no, he wasn't bored, he loved her, he meant to love what she loved. He remembered, they swapped from Saturdays to Friday nights, preferring the intimacy of it, the changed charged warmth of prayer when the rest of the neighbourhood was out drinking or at the pictures. Under the regime of the old rabbi, senior congregants were often asked on to the bimah to read during services. They were invited in deference to their status, how long they'd been members, how much money they'd donated over time. It was Sibyl who put a stop to that. When she came she arranged a looser system whereby students from the Hebrew school were waved on to the stage unwarned. Marginal back-row congregants were asked to volunteer as readers as well. She did a fine thing, Sibyl. That was just Vic's opinion. She opened the doors of Enfield Progressive to the wavering, the half-ins and half-outs. Vic had been made to feel he belonged.

Now he watched the plumbers as they wiped away excess water from the valves, taking pride in their work. As the radiators began to warm under their palms they muttered at each other, satisfied. Warmth returned to the sanctuary and this put Vic in a mood of groggy consent. He slept and he woke. My time dwindles, he thought, but I can take pleasure in the warmth of a room, in other people's usefulness, in naps. I might get one useful thing done.

"Are you awake?" Sibyl asked him.

Vic stirred. He nodded: oh yes, yes, awake.

"There's a visitor coming to see me. About half-past. I'll be showing him around in here. But you stay right where you are."

"New," Vic managed.

He tried again: "The new rabbi."

"That's right. We've got some time before he comes. Can you manage a sip of this?"

She had brought them coffees. Carefully, Sibyl put Vic's fin-

gers through the handle of a big mug. He could no longer manage the daintier cups and saucers. He took his coffee mild, plenty
milked, they had tried him drinking stronger brews—and no,
never again. Sibyl sat with her trainers on the spindle of the chair
in front. She'd been learning to look after Joel while preparing
to leave the synagogue and she looked exhausted, overwhelmed.

Vic held up his drink, dipping his head and meeting it part
way. He inhaled the immortal smell. There was pleasure in this
ritual as well. Quite some time had passed since Vic had dared
enter a pub. His Sunday roasts he'd abandoned of course. Even the
daily newspaper was too much of a trial, its wavering print . . .
but he enjoyed his coffees. He appreciated the insight afforded,
the emotional tumble-downs, all of it welcome to someone
whose existence was limited to rooms and chairs and a bed. I say
goodbye to all this, he thought again. I tell myself of a place or
a flavour or a sight, that was fine, but will I get another? Have I
paid the proper attention to everything, to atmospheres, moods,
did I remember to see it all and smell it all? Gingered by the last
of the coffee, Vic was hopeful again, that he might have one more
thrust in him, a chance to set things right.

At half past the hour Sibyl took away his mug.

She said, "Wish me luck."

Vic was aware of the rumours. Sibyl's replacement had been
found after months of searching. The rabbi that Sibyl was showing around today was said to be a traditionalist. Most likely, he
would undo her reforms. He wore a suit and a kappel and he bore
himself with the suggestion that you were better off leaving him
room to manoeuvre. He had a bee-stung nose; those small and
tablet-like English teeth. A growth of beard did not fasten con-
vincingly at the joins between his whiskers and his chin. For a
moment Vic felt himself scrutinised. This rabbi, he'd be thinking . . . he'd be thinking, there'll be no more idlers hanging
around on my watch. And how would Vic ever explain to some-

body new that he wasn't idle, he was defeated? The synagogue was another pleasure he'd soon surrender. He would leave here when Sibyl did.

She was crouched beside him. He wasn't sure how long he'd been asleep.

"I've telephoned Ben. He said he'll be here to collect you when he's finished working. He said it twice—the part about working."

Vic moved his head, a gesture after laughter.

This was a joke of theirs. Ben and his job. Ben and his outsized pride about earning money for the first time. Vic wanted to say more. He wanted to speak about the jolt they'd all had when Joel was removed from Téo's care, how Vic's illness had quickened in its aftermath, how Téo had retreated into his former life, how Ben had been bumped towards responsibility or at least an awareness that responsibility was an attribute he lacked, that lives were being upturned because of this lack, that a thirty-one-year-old wasn't yet too old to become grown up. Trying to hold together his powers of concentration, Vic made a shape with his lips. It could be helpful if he surrendered to the rocking motions of his body, if he allowed the illness a fuller hold, that way he could gather together whatever determination he had and supply it direct to his clouding brain. No good. A sad, quartered sound came out of him. He was always tiredest in the afternoons.

"Sit. Be at peace. You don't need to impress me," said Sibyl.

"Joel!" he managed.

"You're right. Joel handles that, the impressing."

"School," he managed.

"Joel's at his nursery. Yes."

Sibyl was good at guessing what Vic wanted to say to her.

She figured out what he might be curious about and she spoke to these matters. When they sat together like this, she would try to save Vic the effort of forming questions. Once (it can't have been long ago), they were sitting in the sanctuary and Sibyl had said, "I've decided. I've made my last mistakes as a rabbi. So no," she said, "if you're wondering, I won't be trying for a post anywhere else."

She had smiled. But it wasn't your true or valid smiling. Vic was amazed by Sibyl's mention of mistakes. He set much store by his own and he could feel ungenerous when other people made claims. "What mistakes?" he managed to ask. It was a forcing-out of words, exhausting every time.

"For one," Sibyl had answered, "I let you walk into that meeting with the council in September. Even though I was fairly sure it spelled disaster. I let you go in alone, without me, so there's two mistakes. I could carry on and on, I could make a list. I let Joel dangle for months when he needn't have."

They sat quietly after that. Vic had brushed his knuckles down his cheek. He had moved a thumb from his chin to his nose, as if he would switch them to a distant dormant language made of gestures instead of words. He had patted her hand.

"Is the patient ready to go?" asked Ben, sweeping into the sanctuary. He wore his pilot's sunglasses. He wore a cold-weather coat and parts of a football kit.

"You called him a package yesterday," Sibyl protested, "a patient today."

They were hobbling up the aisle together. Vic said to Ben, "No sun."

"That took you long enough. Pleased with it?"

Outside the synagogue, Vic asked to be turned around. He liked to do this after a departure, he liked to look back and see. Opening and closing his mouth, he issued a final grunt of affection. Enfield Progressive.

"Ready to be put in the car?"

Ben took his arm and led Vic forwards, repeating the encouraging rubbish he'd once heard Téo use, "that's it, that's right, that's it." After a few attempts they got Vic in. Ice had formed in pools on the road. It filled depressions in the pavement wherever the stones met at odds. People were heading home themselves. They folded their arms waiting for buses and they stamped. Some of the cafés they passed had fiery red lamps outside, the heat aimed obliquely at outdoor tables. Vic watched as a motorcycle courier rushed in and out of a café without removing his helmet. He was blinded by the change in atmospherics and his visor clouded over quickly from the sides, a preview of a death. Further along the road, Vic saw people rubbing their hands together, the same as plotters. They made ohs with their mouths. When they were parked outside Vic's flat, he recognised his kerbstones, scarred and chipped by tyres, his browning and chewed-looking bushes, his blemished brickwork. Some days, if Vic did not have the energy to climb stairs, Ben drove on to the Mossam house.

"Can't."

"My place again, is it?"

Ben restarted the car. "Might as well move you in at this rate."

One day there was a downpour. Vic watched it through the window of his new room at Ben's. All week there was rain so routinely that Ben took to styling his hair each morning in the hallway mirror—with the understanding, he shouted through to Vic, that there would need to be another styling session after lunch. One wet day Ben rushed in to say there were snails on the drive, their shells patterned with rust colours, their underbodies bloated and trimmed with mushroom-like lips. The snails must have kept to an isolated suburb of their own through the worst of the winter. Now, free and giddy, they were out graffitiing the walls and floor with their translucent script. They were making their danger-runs from under hedges. They were racing across the pavements against coming sets of feet.

Vic had trouble keeping a grip on time. He slept a lot. He knew it was the longest he'd gone without seeing Téo.

One day the snails had vanished from the drive, or so Ben reported. Instead there were spiders everywhere, spiders stringing their webs in corners and lolling at face height to booby-trap the alleys and paths of Enfield. Vic slept and woke, and when he got his wits together again he saw that Ben was arranging chairs in the room. January sun raked in through the windows, revealing suspended dust, blinding Vic as he tried to focus on the others as they came in and sat. He was curious to see how they greeted each other, what they were saying. He reminded himself he had to listen to other people's words, try to fathom their sentences . . . it was not enough to follow along with their actions, which was easier.

Ben sat with a hand in the pocket of his football shorts. He kept it there while he talked. His other hand wheeled around, making shapes, at all times in motion, this free hand on mime-duty and contributing punctuation to go with his speech.

When it was Téo's turn he spoke with his arms folded. He would not look at Vic.

As for Sibyl, she chopped the side of one hand into the palm of the other. She rubbed her eyes. This was a summit Vic had waited for. But now he was too tired to take part. Listen then, he ordered himself, listen to them properly. "We should talk through the options again," Sibyl was saying.

"It can't be me," Téo said flatly. "Thanks to him and his meddling I'm considered a safeguarding risk."

"Easy," Ben interrupted. "Be gentle."

"Can't bear," Vic said. He tried again, "Can't bear to think. You and Joel, apart."

"Good," said Téo. It was the first time he'd addressed Vic directly. "You shouldn't be able to bear it. This is your fault."

Ben repeated, "Be gentle."

"Why?"

"He's frailer than when you last saw him."

"You his minder these days?"

"Someone has to be."

"Excellent, perfect. Ben Mossam's decided he wants to do some looking-after. The rabbi as well! This is beautiful timing."

Sibyl said, "One option, Ben steps forward and looks after Joel on his own. Another option, we both look after him."

"Both of you? Together?"

"Yes. What would you think of that?"

"Does my opinion matter?"

"But of course. You're closer to Joel than anyone alive."

Téo was stopped by that. He moved his mouth. He appealed to Sibyl, "Why couldn't you have volunteered like this at the start?"

"I was scared to," Sibyl said. "I persuaded myself I had to put my congregation first. I was scared," she repeated.

"You could have done something, before me and Joel got turned and turned around each other. Before this became undeniable for me."

"I was scared of that, I think—the undeniable."

"Sibyl and Joel can move in here," Ben suggested. "We'll do the forms or whatever. We'll make the applications. You'll come back to Enfield," he demanded of Téo, "cos we need you here, and you'll become a part of Joel's life. Everyone's happy."

Téo said no. "When I was with him, when he was mine to watch out for every day, and I was knackered, and I was resentful, I thought it would be easy to step aside. I told myself, I'll live around the corner. I'll drop in and see him after meals."

Téo continued, "I see how stupid that was. Cos I hadn't been apart from him yet. I hadn't spent a minute by myself. And those were shit minutes, I'm telling you, when they came. They're still shit minutes. I'm having to learn to live alone as if it's something I've never done before. I'm waiting for my food to taste—to sleep through a night. I can't start it all again. So do whatever you decide," Téo said. He was standing. He was ready to go. "Do what's best for Joel. But I can't be involved."

Sibyl said, "Stay and talk. Help us settle the plan."

"You've settled your plan. It's obvious. Everyone's happy."

" 'Cept you."

"I'll be happy enough. If you leave me alone."

Vic was agitated, excited by an idea, that if and when he spoke he would look at Téo and be seen to be looking. He would use his last request. People did that: he would make over his final allotment of words and ask for what he wanted most. Vic tried to speak. He sat there and he rocked. Reduced to pure intent, down to the grains of himself, he was picturing Téo in retreat through the years, old enough to be granted a beer, young enough he could have his nose wiped.

Téo was at the door. He made a show of indifference, bending to neaten a shoelace, clapping his palms over his pockets to check that he hadn't left anything behind.

Vic was reminded of Téo at school, fussy about leaving for the day without his pencils and pens. He was thinking about Téo making friends for the first time, real friends, keeping secrets about them even from his mother. Mind your beeswax. That's what Téo used to say whenever they asked about some latest episode of trouble involving Ben or Lia. Vic was thinking of the afternoon that Téo was born. How they kept the sun off his cot, their care with the curtains. What a gift. Vic understood that now. Everything had been a gift.

FIFTEEN

Ben's one rule. His students had to train with him however bad the weather. He told them, do your duty to football: "Show up." Oh they griped. They questioned Ben's judgement, especially the senior boys, seventeen and eighteen years old already, who dragged their feet to practice whenever it was raining. By nagging at them and humiliating them if necessary, Ben was able to make the point that to skive meant being wrapped in a damper, sadder mantle than any soaked-through kit. Skiver's shame was a shame that clung to you; he could tell them so from experience.

Come the spring, when it started to get warm again for the first time since Ben started working as a coach, he was convinced that his students were better footballers for their wet-weather trials. He swore that he wouldn't forget their loyalty to the sport or to him. Everywhere around Enfield the vibes picked up, improving with the weather. Their park became greener, the mornings brighter, strangers were more inclined to say yo to Ben in reply.

In the door at home he shouted, "Which of you are in?" He glanced at the roster of carers, reading their names, matching a few names he recognised to faces. "Just picking up my football gear," Ben shouted as he jogged upstairs to a bedroom. From a wardrobe he pulled out another tracksuit, more socks, the slippers he could step from as soon as he was over on the pitch. He would carry his boots and the rest of his gear . . . Where was his whistle though? Ben clapped his hands, searching. Where was. His fucking. Whistle though. "Got you."

Downstairs, two of the carers were trading shifts in the hall. They compared notes on Vic's condition, speaking in muted voices outside the room that used to be a lounge. Both of the carers wore casual clothes. One of them was about to put on a disposable apron and disposable gloves. There were hellos, high fives, then the carer starting his shift went through to the kitchen to clean the morning's equipment. Vic had moved in during the winter. It was a choice between the Mossam house, with its spare rooms and its passenger lift, or a care home: somewhere miles away. Ben surrendered half the ground floor. He covered bills. Pay me back next year, he joked with Vic, on those rare occasions the old man was lucid enough to be teased.

Ben knelt by his kit bag in the hall. He checked that his boots were packed as well as his stack of cones, the clipboard with the paper and pens, a notebook he used for a student register. Another bag bulging with footballs waited in a heap beside the boxes of Vic's medical supplies. Téo used to say, weary but appreciative, that Joel supplanted any alarm clock. Joel stood in for seasons, because your rhythms adjusted so completely to his schedule of care. Vic's presence had had a similar effect on Ben. For hours at a time he crept around trying not to disturb the old man's sleep. He looked in on Vic when he could. Téo used to say of Joel, the moment he arrived to be looked after, that was Moment One, the point in time from which subsequent events were measured.

Ben frowned, trying to remember the former life of this house, when there were parties here, frequent contests of cards, when his mates fell down drunk and slept wherever they landed.

Vic was too ill to venture between rooms. He existed in his bed and except for when he was hoisted out to be changed or washed he lay on his back. Mostly he lurked a layer beneath coherent conversation. But he could murmur, he could exclaim in a voice turned rough from disuse, making sudden efforts to explain himself, his dreams, whatever visions he'd been a witness to. Declines in Vic's health had been steep. Ski slopes, Ben thought of, whenever a carer made the gesture to explain his latest deterioration.

Among the nurses and the carers sent to Ben's house by an agency, there were older hands who carried themselves with the poise of long experience. They took note of Vic's position in the bed, they saw how he slept with a backwards tilt of his head, and they started to offer Ben their condolences. They gave him advice on what would happen next.

Today's carer said, "He will be with God soon." He was Italian, this carer, and religious. Ben knew that he supported a rival football team.

"Yeah? I'm not familiar with any of this," he admitted.

"You must gather your family."

"It's not my family. But I'm trying, I'm trying to gather whoever I can . . . Give me a break, you!" He left the house to laughter, after a final rush of chatter about the weekend's stand-out goal, *bellissimo*, they agreed. "I've got to get to work. I've got to go to my job." He loved saying this to people.

He walked to the park, carrying his gear himself, enjoying the burden, relieved to be in charge of limbs and muscles that answered to command. When he arrived on the turf he spread around cones. He put out balls and nets and coloured bibs in piles. While he did so he hummed, turning over ideas. "Gather the family," he was thinking. Ben scowled at his boots for a full minute.

Lately he'd been trying to put this talent for persuasion to better use. He took out his phone and he starting sending off a few messages to friends. He wrote to close mates in the group, those who were always invited to communal activities. He wrote to second- and third-tier mates as well. He wrote to transients, hangers-on, poker acquaintances, he even wrote to a couple of the employees at his favourite casino. Ben took time over these messages. Everybody got their sunbeam. The gist of what he said to them all was the same. Party. Big one. Tonight.

His football students were arriving. They slung down gym bags and bottles of water, widening their eyes at Ben in non-committal greeting before they skulked off to jog laps around the pitch. They were familiar with Ben's expectations. Obedient enough. Despite this, he put his whistle between his lips and he harangued them, becoming a pest, over-particular about details and hard to satisfy. After a while he blew three short bursts to gather them in for a lecture. Steaming, sweating already, they gave off a mixed smell of underarm spray, washed nylon and minty gum. "Who's chewing?" Ben demanded. He glared at a few likely culprits. "Share the wealth," he ordered.

He wasn't a conventional teacher, being erratic and enough of a show-off to ball-hog during their practice games. He could be impatient with the duller students and over-enamoured of the prodigies. But as long as Ben was himself, he found, as long as he didn't try to fake a maturity that wasn't there, a mutual trust persisted. Honestly it amazed him: how the kids responded best to Ben when he let them see who he was, and what a handful. "So listen," he was telling them, "I've got a scheme brewing. Extracurricular. I'm putting the finishing touches on a little plan for tonight. Who here's eighteen already, remind me?"

Some hands were raised.

"Seventeen-year-olds as well?"

More hands.

"You lot who are seventeen and eighteen, gather over that side of the pitch. The rest of you are on triangles . . . Yes, yes," said Ben, over their belly-aching. "I hated triangles myself. But your passing's been crap lately." He whistled at them. He panthered around as they passed to each other, harsh in his criticisms but timing the encouragement for effect. Then he went over to the older players. "Target practice for you," he said, "something different." Ben had arranged a row of balls on the ground. He waved an arm at the graffiti-covered wall that ran along one side of the pitch. "See the sign near the top?"

This sign, much appreciated by those who noticed it, said NO CLIMBING.

You'd have to be wearing crampons. You'd need super sticking powers.

"Anyone who can hit that sign from here, three times in a row, gets to join me on a mission tonight. Your time paid for, plus one free can of beer. Yes, even you," he told the seventeen-year-olds. He blew his whistle. "What you waiting for? Fire at will."

Later, one of his mates from the group asked Ben on the messages: "Where are we supposed to be meeting?"

"Top of the escalator," someone else answered.

"Which escalator?" someone said.

"Don't you read instructions?"

"Which escalator!"

Ben was there early, standing at the top of the designated escalator inside Aldgate station. "If you're not at the meeting place soon," he wrote, "you'll be left behind. I'm serious. Mission starts at 7 p.m. sharp."

Someone asked, "Does Téo know what's coming?"

"Does he fuck. It's a party-bomb. Like the old days. That right, Benno? A party-bomb?"

"We party-bombing him?"

"Just get here by seven," Ben wrote.

Soon he was joined in the station by his football students, then his poker acquaintances, those real keen types who never turned down an invitation to a high-stakes game. As the footballers and the gamblers raised fists to each other, Ben waved in another pair: a croupier from his casino and one of the bar staff. They had the night off and Ben had agreed to pay them for their time. In ones and twos more Enfield friends arrived. There were cross-intros. Hands were reached for between bodies. People whistled, giggled, asked questions of each other. Then the doors of a lift slid open and Ben's heart moved a little inside his chest.

Joel stepped out on to the concourse, Sibyl behind him. Ben went down on one knee and he wrestled with the kid, quickly and violently, right there on the station floor. Joel had the traces of an evening meal on his face. His tongue moved out in exploration, probing the sides of his mouth for flavour. Ben jabbed a finger at him. "You know we're on a mission tonight?"

"Is it top secret?"

"*Oh* yeah."

"It's top secret," Joel confirmed to Sibyl. There must have been discussion about this on the journey. Ben rose, a hand on Sibyl's arm, introducing her to the crowd. Before they left the station together, Ben heaved Joel on to his shoulders. Hot hands gripped his forehead; his fringe became reins. They set off as a gang or a posse in the direction of Téo's flat, with reminders passed backwards from Ben—that they could make whatever noise they liked on the journey, but closer to their destination it was black-ops rules, lowered voices only please.

Their procession passed a row of modern restaurants then an ancient London pub that gave off a browner burn through its frosted glass. In this part of the city you passed in and out of history, a cobbled alley then factory flagstones, crooked Tudor houses before the dead-straight concrete avenues. Wearing team kits, casino uniforms, special-occasion sleeves, clothes casual enough to sleep in, their group looked weird and drew glances. Between them they carried footballs, packs of playing cards, beer cans, supermarket ice, cocktail equipment, speakers. Ben muttered a command to Joel, who raised his arm from on high, ordering quiet. They were on the side of a public square, well concealed by shrub-topped planters. The windows of Téo's flat were in sight. Thin U's of light leaked from around the edges of his lowered blinds.

Ben explained to Joel, they would watch some of the comings-and-goings from the building. "Recce the situation first."

Home-bound residents, they noticed, took out key fobs that had to be pressed against a sensor by the building's entrance. *Buh-BLINK* went the sensor, admitting them. "*Buh-blink*," said Joel, in decent imitation.

A can of beer clicked open. Someone in the group was playing music already. Ben ordered quiet . . . but even as he did this he knew their expectation of a party could not be deferred indefinitely. Joel had been tasked with keeping watch on the windows of the flat. "Think he's up there?" Ben asked.

Joel nodded.

"You sure?"

Joel shook his head.

"*I* think he's up there. C'mon let's go."

Ben turned, explaining to the crowd the next phase of the plan. When he'd done so he said to them, "It's an honour by the way. To be working with a hand-picked unit like this." He crouched in front of Joel. "You ready?"

Joel shouted yes.

"Woah, woah, keep your voice down. Copy me remember."

Joel whispered, he was ready.

Ben glanced over at Sibyl who said, "Just don't let him out of your sight."

"No chance."

He grabbed up Joel in his arms and he hustled them over the square. "You're heavier since this morning," Ben complained.

"Two lunches."

"Again? Listen, I need that tantrum. You got a tantrum in you? On the count of three?"

They stood in front of Téo's building, the full racket. Ben danced around and waggled Joel as if to calm him. Joel wailed, screaming for a wee, turning himself pink from effort. He was even able to wring out a tear, leaving Ben speechless, as if from an excessive tackle in a football match or from some maniac's unwarranted slap in a pub. Disorientated by love, Ben even forgot his own part in the performance, right as a resident with a key was approaching. It was Joel—improvising—who got them inside.

Ben had to apologise. They were upstairs and hiding in a stairwell, one turn above Téo's corridor. "I nearly scuppered us there."

"Uh-huh."

"You saved the day there," Ben admitted, after which Joel's mouth did strange things, the upper lip contorting over the teeth in an attempt to stopper his pride.

"What for next?" he asked.

"Next I cue our footballers . . ."

Ben took out his phone.

"I saved the day? Actually?"

"Yeah, you're the hero of the hour. But don't get a big head all right, we've got the hardest part to come. We'll need to be quick. You're quick, aren't you?"

"Uh-huh."

"Quicker than me?"

"Uh-huh."

"We'll see."

"Will see."

"Don't copy me."

"Doan copper me."

"You're infuriating."

"You're fury aching."

Faintly, from outside, they heard the sound of footballs slapping against the side of the building. An irregular noise at first, it became a patter, faster and more consistent as Ben's young trainees found their range. He was confident they'd be hitting Téo's windows as requested—and here came Téo himself, rushing along the corridor, clattering into the stairwell beneath them, taking the downward stairs two at a time, intent on chasing the teenagers away. Speedsters, all of them, Ben didn't fancy Téo's chances of catching them. He had given orders for his friend to be lured as far as possible.

"Go," he said to Joel.

They hustled out of the stairwell together.

Encouraging each other on, laughing, they reached Téo's door just before it locked shut. They collapsed inside his flat, out of puff. Joel rolled on to his back on the floor and pushed a thumb in his mouth. Ben made a phone call.

"Up you come," he said, "we're in."

Mates disposed themselves around Téo's lounge and his kitchen. They stood talking in the space in front of the coat hooks; they perched on the end of his bathtub. Lamps were trialled for mood potential, the overhead spots dimmed, a string of fairy lights attached to the mains and fastened over pictures and furniture, switched to psychedelic flash mode.

Joel was rewarded with ten salt-and-vinegar crisps, a bounty agreed in advance with Sibyl. He counted the crisps out twice to ensure he was being fairly paid. When the footballers had looped around and returned to the flat they were granted their promised beer, one each. Ben was in the kitchen helping his barman tear open bags of ice. The croupier had begun to clear Téo's table of clutter, directing volunteers in the careful spreading of a baize. When Téo did stagger in, he was mobbed. His collar was messed up, his arms squeezed, his name shouted. He'd been gone a matter of minutes and during that time his flat had capitulated, utterly, to a party. The room was thick with sugar fumes, music, yelled chatter. When Téo was handed a cocktail he seemed to move out of shock, through crossness, reaching a reluctant acceptance. Ben had pulled off an enormity. Nobody could deny it. When Téo found him in the kitchen he swore at Ben, he shook his head; he could only say, "Well played."

"Ta."

Someone had taken on the music as a project. Beats quickened. Lyrics became gnarlier. The musicians they were listening to had sharper teeth. Smokers began to stick their heads out of Téo's bathroom window instead of trooping outside. The footballers were sent home, each with a £20 note in their pocket. Joel would have to leave soon as well. "No-o-o," he complained when he was told. "You carn been serious." He was quoting some cartoon.

"Ten more minutes," Sibyl said.

Joel's game tonight was accumulation. He'd sourced stray clutter from around Téo's flat, a toothbrush sealed in its packet, then a glossy magazine, years out of date. He carried these treasures to a part of the flat where Téo stood talking to friends. Joel seemed to want Téo to notice what he was doing. Perhaps he was expecting to be told not to touch things. Once, when the boy was in reach, Téo put a hand on Joel's head: as though this was a resting post, Ben thought, or some waypoint on a journey, a landmark you visited once, to see it, to touch it, to be able to say so. Otherwise Téo seemed to ignore Joel. He never looked again.

"This isn't even a cool flat," Ben protested. More people were leaving. Mostly it was the poker players who hung around. "All these years of wondering what it looked like and I'm not impressed."

Téo shrugged. "Mine though."

Joel had fallen asleep on a sofa. Sibyl managed to lift him without waking him. Even now, Téo wouldn't look. He kept his focus on the other guests till Sibyl and Joel were gone.

"I don't know what to make of you like this," Ben said, "this mercenary version."

"Why're you here, Benno, what's this about?"

"You know what. Victor hasn't got long now. You have to come home."

A poker game was getting started at the table. Téo nodded at it, saying to Ben, "Let's join."

Seats had been saved for them. They sat down on opposite sides of the baize, each submitting money to the croupier. She was almighty here, in charge of everything for the next few hours; she was their bank, their umpire, the charm to whom all the players appealed for luck. She moved money between them as they won or conceded hands. As usual, wealth began to gather in conspicuous places.

After a period of silent concentrated play, the standard teasing began. There were ironic congratulations sent towards the richest players. Once in a while someone's temper popped. There was bitter commentary, a phase of name-calling. Underneath this, everybody was occupied by the one ambition, to annihilate everybody else. Both Ben and Téo were winners tonight. Both played with nerve, some fortune, emerging as the authorities of the game: Téo with his patient sawing-away at you, Ben with his gumption, the superbly timed risks. They were like statesmen, they had all the influence, their every decision changed the landscape. "Fold," someone said in response to Ben's latest move. Someone else laid flat their cards and conceded the hand as well: "I fold."

Seated opposite each other, Ben and Téo were left alone by the others to fight over money that was moving between them constantly.

A hundred quid was at stake. Ben put in more.

"Fold," someone said.

"Fold."

"Fold."

It was left to Téo to decide. He had to choose whether to risk more money or fold himself, surrendering everything he'd wagered so far. He pushed in what he had, a large amount. Ben didn't have enough to match it.

"What now?" someone asked.

"It's fine. I can make up the shortfall," Ben said. "I'm gonna come away from this the winner anyway . . . Here," he said.

He took a key from his pocket and he laid it on the table.

"I don't want your car," said Téo.

"It's a key to my house."

"I don't want your house."

"All right. I'll stake you two sugars as well. I'll stake you a Scottish shortbread. What do you want?"

"I want your promise," answered Téo, "that if I win this you'll leave me alone."

"Done," said Ben.

He pushed in his money. He pushed in the house key too. With a finger he drew a signature on the baize, his promise, to leave Téo be. "That enough? You satisfied? Can we settle this?"

Téo nodded.

The other players held their breaths.

Ben said, "Cool. I fold my hand. You win everything."

"What? What are you doing?"

"I fold."

The croupier swept away Ben's money and his key, his sworn promise as well, depositing everything in front of Téo, who sat there as surprised as anyone.

Yawning, Ben stood up out of his chair. He patted crisp crumbs off his lap. He circled the table to say goodbye to people. He was off home he told them. He had an early start in the morning. He felt about ready for bed.

SIXTEEN
SIBYL

They were living together in the Mossam house. Sibyl and Joel had been here long enough to become acquainted with certain quirks of the property, such as the arctic chill in the big entrance hall, abiding, whatever Sibyl tried. They had lived here long enough that they could agree whenever they returned,

"We're home."

"Is home."

"Nice to be home."

"I'm sleepy."

"Joel, the time! How did it get so late?"

"It's so time."

Sibyl clicked her tongue. They should have left Téo's party much earlier. She followed Joel upstairs, letting him set the pace. They visited the bathroom first, Joel reminding her it would be his wee, then teeth, then stories. Joel pointed out which was the tap for cold water. He showed Sibyl that his toothpaste was patterned with stripes.

"See?"

"It's pretty."

"Is factory," he corrected her.

She waited to hear more. Joel only blinked. There would be no further explanations about toothpaste tonight. Instead he marched himself to his room. When they had first arrived here from the synagogue residence, Joel had been asked: where would he like to sleep? After a dash around every bedroom he made his choice, the biggest one please. Maybe he regretted choosing scale over intimacy. Maybe his truer tastes were similar to Sibyl's, shaped by time in smaller flats where a solid wall was never far from reach. Disavowing his king-sized bed, Joel had lately been camping under a window. He'd built a den using cushions and bedsheets, into which he crawled each night with a torch. He had his books in there and a changing roster of toys. "Knock knock," visitors had to say before crawling in after him.

"Who's there?"

He could speak wholer sentences. He could be arch, he could tease.

"It's Sibyl."

". . . Sibyl who?"

Joel's bedroom had belonged to Ben's parents once. It contained a large gilt mirror, a freestanding bathtub, an antique writing desk, luxurious irrelevancies to a boy. But the Erskine flat was up for sale. Vic had a few smaller pieces of furniture that Sibyl hoped to bring over for Joel's use. She thought that by importing the narrow bed he slept in when he lived with Téo, he might be persuaded off the floor. Ben had promised to salvage it the next time he drove over on another packing mission. It was still impossible to know which of Ben's promises Ben would keep. He seemed to be trying to remember every rash commitment he made; and if he only saw some of these commitments through, remembering was a start.

When Joel was asleep, Sibyl went to bed herself. She read for an hour. Books had been vital during transitions of the past. After

reading an assured book, whatever the subject, she felt embold-
ened, she carried away with her some small inherited piece of
the author's courage in writing the effing thing. Tonight she had
one stack of books beside her bed about raising children. Another
stack, not yet touched, told of the lives of women and men who'd
founded charitable missions. She wanted to learn more about
those who'd made spaces in busy cities for the lost or the overlooked. It was only the beginning of an idea, a support group
(but not a support group), a synagogue (but not a synagogue), she
might want to call it a shul or a church for the excluded, somewhere that a person such as a Lia or a Vic could go to find the
consolations of a religion without preconditions, without being
told what else they must be. It was private for now: like a small
sum of money put away. Joel first. Joel today.

She heard the front door open. There was a good deal of noise
as Ben tried to move around down there without disturbing anyone. He thumped up the stairs.

"Yo."

"How was the rest of the party?"

"Decent. I left before the others . . . Téo has a house key anyway. It's up to him whether he uses it."

"Will he, do you think?"

Ben was working a finger around his teeth, trying to pick free
a scrap of food. He pulled off his shoes. "Can't be sure of him
these days. I can't even tell if we like each other."

"A lot has happened."

Ben was down to his T-shirt and boxers. He climbed into the
bed beside her. "What you reading? Same books? Where you up
to? I don't know how you can handle the self-help stuff. Doesn't
seem like a business you can cheat-code, parenting. Not so far."

"I like to know what worries other people. It comforts me to
know they worry at all."

"Me, I'm winging it."

"Yes. That's why I think it's probably a wise idea that we're doing this together."

Ben rolled over to face her. "Téo said something to me once. We were fighting. We were up in the Scottish mountains. He said to me, he said point your energies. Your appetites. The football player in you, the poker cunt, direct all that at a *target*. Till recently, I swear I didn't understand what he meant. In my head I'm thinking, change? A person changing, becoming a better version of themselves? A flake and a greedy piglet one week, a plausible parent the next? That would mean *deciding* to change. Then following through on a change. That would mean remembering to *be* changed, every minute you were with a kid, every second of those minutes. And because of that . . ."

"You thought it unlikely."

"I thought it would have to be faked. I didn't ever see myself putting up a hand, saying, 'Joel's mine to look after.' Because I didn't ever see myself saying, 'I'm done looking after me.'"

"What changed?"

"Whenever we speak to them now—Joel's social workers— I feel like I can admit the two things at once. That I'm his dad. And I'm an imperfect candidate to be his dad." Ben yawned. "Is it me getting up in the morning. Or?"

"Yes, it's you. You know it's you."

"Right. No, that's what I was hoping! I'm—"

He yawned again.

"I'm looking forward to a nice, early—"

He was asleep. Sibyl opened her book and found her place. The child is always in motion, she read. The child advances forward, urgent and rapt and changing at a rate it will never experience again. The parent is in motion as well: but only some of the time. The parent moves at fitful speed and whether in stride, keeping pace . . . whether ahead and turned about, shouting encouragement . . . whether lagging behind and shouting wait, wait, WAIT . . . all that matters is to keep the child in sight.

Sibyl closed the book. This was how Vic had put it once: "Your gaze." Since leaving the synagogue, she felt further from God than she'd ever been. And yet she felt she was kept in sight; at a distance but in sight. She turned off her bedside light and she lay and she thought of Joel, how he smelled, of skin and cereal and earwax. The soles of his feet were beginning to putty and harden. She would check them again tomorrow. Whenever Joel addressed you from a distance his shrill voice carried, cleaving air. But talking alone he muttered to himself in lower tones: confessional. He giggled in his sleep. Anybody who heard this giggled too. In front of the television, Joel would find a trough in Sibyl or Ben's abdomen and rest his whole weight there. Joel would talk and Ben would talk. They would babble at once, like two pots of water, set beside each other to boil. She would clean his fingernails. Those fingernails.

SEVENTEEN
TÉO

Days after the party, it was still on its knees, the Aldgate flat. Téo recovered beer bottles that had rolled under his furniture. He found cups and glasses put out of sight, their dregs contributing to a sweet rancid smell that he couldn't shift. The toilet seat was loose. He bought more bin bags and inflated them with matador twitches of his wrists. Dishwasher on and set grumbling under the kitchen counter, he went over his surfaces again: an indiscriminate bleaching.

Ben's house key, surrendered at the end of their poker game, he put aside. Tidying everywhere else, tidying around this key, he had tried ignoring it since the night of the party. Now he put the key in his pocket and he left the flat.

It was a weekend morning. Start of spring. Téo collected his car from its underground bay and he inched up an exit ramp. He drove north out the city on the A10 and eventually he crossed the North Circular Road, after which he had to pass through the laddered junctions of Enfield, waiting at light after light, those that were understood by locals to be cruelly sequenced and those deemed kinder. There were quilted white clouds that hung over the neighbourhood and trapped down a thick and soupy warmth. He used Ben's key to let himself in.

Medical supplies were stacked in the hall. Téo could see more boxes of supplies in the rooms beyond. Someone had put out a jug of fresh flowers. He took in their pleasant smell, that upside-down sense of something outdoors brought in. He was smiled at by a carer on duty and told that Ben and Joel were out this morning, Sibyl as well.

"I'm here to see Victor," Téo explained.

He was shown where to go. Mister Erskine has lost a lot of weight, the carer warned. The problem of the weight loss was only halted when they were able to start feeding him through a tube.

Which would make sense of Dad's appearance, thought Téo, who had to turn away and regather himself before he could look at Victor square. The face was almost a stranger's. It was too grey and too narrow. Victor's hair had retreated over the prow of his forehead and away from behind his ears, uncovering skin that shone and even looked youthful. Victor lay under blankets. He was sleeping though not, your instinct warned, at rest.

"What sort of discomfort's he in?"

"We can't be sure. The new medicine seems to help."

"How bad did it get?"

"Poor man," said the carer. "I'll leave you two alone."

Téo found a chair. He carried it over to the bed. For a while he sat without saying a lot, only inspecting a troublesome fingernail, only fiddling with the frayed pocket of his T-shirt. He tried to remember what room this had been before. He listened to Victor's breathing, rapid and feral as a rooting mammal. Victor's chin was queerly tilted, perhaps because of some reflex to open the widest possible channel for air. "Be weird," Téo said, "sitting next to you and finishing every sentence I try. Without one complaint! Without one grunt of your irritation."

Téo stroked the old man's hair.

"I was never much good at being honest with you. Let's see if this helps, you being quiet for once, without any choice."

He had been sitting up straight like someone from the olden days, like someone trained to fret about their posture. Now Téo made rolling movements with his shoulders and his elbows, working loose the cramping muscles. He checked his teeth with the tip of his tongue and he put two fingers to his neck, timing his own pulse.

"Yeah and by the way," he said, tapping his dad on the elbow, "I found out second-hand, from the rabbi, what it is you've decided to do with our flat. How you changed your instructions. How you're leaving the money to Joel instead of me. I've got to admit, my first reaction, I'm wondering, is this spite? I'm wondering is this my punishment? Because I've punished you, staying away these last few months? Now I'm taking the different view. I think your decision releases me, Dad. I think it undoes a final tie. I'm seeing this as permission, like a blessing—for me to make the next moves as I want to."

Téo leaned against Victor's body. He nudged him, rocking him. "I'm happy for Joel though. I'm comforted. Cos he'll have something, won't he? Something firm and fixed that belongs to him. He'll have a back-up plan, won't he? In case Ben lets him down again. Which we can't discount, you and me, which we hope won't happen but which you and me as Erskines will not discount. Yeah, I think I understand what you were up to, Dad, I think I can see how you schemed that one out for yourself while you could."

Téo wondered then if his phone had buzzed. If there was a message or something.

He checked, welcoming any distraction, but no. There was a sudden compulsion to find out if he had missed new news since he entered this stifling room. He wanted to know how long he'd

been visiting and what sort of weather they were due this afternoon, if the nice spring day would hold. He made himself put
away his phone. He made himself look at Victor.

"Did you hear about this? Ben filled my flat in Aldgate with a
party, and why? Because he'd decided it was the only way to get
my attention. Because when Ben has an idea he mistakes it for a
decision. They seemed different, Ben and Sibyl, when I was with
them. I still recognise it, Dad—how someone looks when they're
worried about that boy."

Téo stood. He windmilled his arms. He flexed the fingers
which felt numb.

"Listen. I'm gonna leave now," he said. "I can see you're well
set up here. Spending money was never Ben's trouble. I'll take
away this idea that you're comfortable. I'll be an optimist about
it. You try being an optimist too, yeah? If you can hear me, try
this. Try picturing Joel in ten years' time. Joel as a teenager. You
got that, you picturing it? Isn't it good?"

Téo neatened the blankets he'd disturbed. He nodded again at
this stranger's face and he kissed it goodbye.

Afterwards, Téo drove to the old flat. He parked where he could
and he walked to the garden gate. The neighbours' windows
reflected back a sunny afternoon, inverting Enfield, drafting it
a second population, everybody the wrong way around, everybody ghosts. Joel was playing outside: Téo could hear as much
from the pavement. He hung back, hidden by Victor's shrubs.

Ben was out in the garden as well. Together, they were invent-
ing little games on the fly. They messed about with a rake, calling
this Joel's spear. They had a tennis ball: in fact Joel's last grenade.
They played at war then they played at peace, resting in a pile
on the grass. They spent time evaluating Joel's noises and secre-

tions, a crumb of dirt brought out from between his toes, whatever was available from a nostril. Without warning Ben snatched up one of Joel's toys, demanding to know its biography. He was exasperating.

"Who's this one again? Alien, isn't he?"

Joel's voice got higher, his radar for adult teasing going haywire.

"No-o-o," he said.

"He's got walrus powers then. He's part bird part man."

"No-o-o."

"Cyborg: has to be."

"This one's called leopard-boy."

"Ah," said Ben.

"You keep him, Dadder."

"Yeah? You sure?"

"He's too babyish."

Between their playing and their teasing, Ben was trying to dismantle the garden trampoline. Téo remembered them building it the spring before, when everything was only getting started. Since then the big trampoline had dominated Victor's lawn, its mesh walls clogged with leaves and cobwebs, its steel frame beginning to discolour and rust. Ben had some inadequate tools beside him. He was tackling the disassembly in fits and starts, with a logic incomprehensible to Téo, who had to restrain himself from rushing through the gate and taking charge. He kept out of it, watching.

Joel demanded whatever money was in Ben's pocket. "The metal money," he stressed. He started to order Ben's coins on the ground, not by size or by value but by shiningness, he said. Téo noticed that Joel's limbs (doughy not so long ago) were hard and taut as clubs these days. His spine had straightened. He was cresting towards the waistline of the adults in his world. Sparing no feelings, he seemed to fidget inside his body even as it grew and improved. If you knew him you could tell he was tired of this, a boy's limits, his obsolete model. Téo did picture him as a teenager, then. He saw Joel clogging corridors at school, rushing in early to be punctual . . . no, a foot-dragger, attending every day on sufferance. Joel might turn out compliant or he might turn out the opposite, an ordeal, you couldn't predict.

Joel also had some questions about Ben's faltering effort to take apart this trampoline.

When would they be finished? he asked. When could they *only* play? Ben called a halt to more inquiries. Some limit of his was reached. One particular rusted joint was beyond him. He tried a few more times with his screwdriver, finally losing his temper and swearing.

"It's a bad word."

"I keep forgetting not to use that eff one, don't I? Long as you keep reminding me I'll get there," said Ben.

Joel did go inside. He waddled off, burdened with interesting finds from the garden, leaving Ben alone. "You gonna help me?" he asked Téo. "Or stay hiding?"

Téo approached. "Doesn't he wanna bounce any more?"

Ben wiped his forehead. "He reckons the trampoline's too babyish. A lot of things are now. We play loads of football. He prefers football."

"Makes sense . . . What's your system here? For dismantling the trampoline."

" 'System.' Hello, mate. Welcome home."

"I'm not home. I'm not staying. What's your system? Keep removing pieces till it falls down around you?"

Ben ignored this. But he had started too far down the structure, he must see that. "Let me help," Téo said, crouching beside him. Together they got away part of the trampoline's upper body. They started to work on the lower frame. "I came here to give you back your house key. The carer you've got looking after Dad today, he told me where to find you." Another large piece of the trampoline came away in their hands. "Seems decent."

"The carer? They all are."

"Thank you for arranging that, Benno. Must be costing you a fortune."

He said nothing.

"You'll have to get a job soon!"

They were trying to untether taut springs, dozens of them, one after the other. The effort left them gasping and rubbing their wrists.

"So you visited."

"Yeah."

"Bad."

"Yeah. You ever try speaking to him, when he's like that?"

Ben said: "He hears parts of it I think. What did you talk about?"

"This and that."

They peeled off squares of rubber mesh. Each square was tacked to metal studs. They held on and heaved, tug-of-warring the material away.

"Keep the key," Ben suggested. "You'll want to visit him again."

They had the trampoline dismantled. "What you planning to do with all these pieces," Téo asked, "lug them to the dump?" They stared down at the broken-apart trampoline. Ben didn't seem to have thought that far ahead. "Load everything into my car," Téo sighed. "I'll find somewhere in the city that could use a trampoline."

"You sure?"

They carried it out bit by bit, a job of stages, backwards and forwards from the garden to the road.

"You gonna look in on Joel before you go?"

"I don't know."

Téo's hands were covered in a translucent grease. It must have come from the disassembly. Ben handed him a tissue. "Oh. Cheers . . . Tissues, Benno!"

"I keep loads. Come out *armed*. Hey, listen. Why don't you visit us at the house next weekend? It's been a year. We'll raise a toast to her."

Téo wasn't sure.

"You could bring someone."

"Maybe. We'll see."

"I'll hassle you during the week. Come thirsty though."

"Come thirsty," Téo repeated, shaking his head.

"Just come." They clasped each other goodbye. "Go in and see Joel."

"Bit scared to," Téo confessed.

"If Lia was here she'd have no time for that. She'd be all—"

"Lia would say—"

" 'Go in, dickhead.' "

"It would be more like 'Go *in. Dick*head' . . ."

They flapped their fingers at each other, recognising her. "Oh-h-h-h-h!"

Packing boxes filled the old front room. Some of the boxes were swaddled under such a lot of twisted brown tape, Téo figured that Joel must have petitioned for the job of sealing them himself. Some were still open, half or three-quarters filled with Victor's possessions. Téo waited to feel guilty. He'd done nothing to help with any of this. He waited.

Joel, he saw, had toppled one of the half-filled boxes on to its side. Spread over the carpet now were various household items, takeaway menus, broken remotes. Reimagining these as danger-ous obstacles, Joel moved his toy figures around, voicing the dialogue of a strenuous and costly expedition. Over here. This way. Behind you. No-o-o-o. Avenge me.

"What are you playing here, explorers?"

Joel shrugged.

"It's okay. You don't have to talk to me."

Eventually he said, "The baddie ones don't like the goodie ones."

"Do they have powers or are they normal people?"

"They have powers."

Téo really could imagine him older: a ten-year-old, a teenager, a young man in love with some impossible choice. "Don't know if you'll remember this," he said, getting down on his heels, "but you and me, we used to play with these toys. A lot. Every morning for a while. You probably don't remember."

Joel still wouldn't look at Téo. Instead he inspected the toy he happened to have in hand, a thick-waisted monster or demon type. He dragged this monster's legs backwards and forwards on the carpet. It was maybe not actual play, more a performance of play. Téo wondered if the boy was simply waiting for him to leave. He got up on one knee.

"I'll come," said Joel.

"What?"

"Tay-OH. I'll come with you."

Joel was staring at his toy.

"Oh, mate, no—you're with Ben now. With Sibyl. You live in the big house."

Into the following silence, Téo added: "It's better like this."

He thought, I might have to scowl or even shout at him. I might need to scare him straight. Téo sat again, cross-legged this time, and he picked up a toy of his own. Neither of them said much. Instead they clicked their toys against each other in wordless combat. Téo was remembering a family story that his mum used to tell about *her* dad, Téo's granddad, how he got out of

Europe in time. He was small. He was barely older than Joel. There was some opportunity, a berth on a train or a boat. He didn't want to go by himself and in the end he refused to leave. His parents told him there is nothing for you here, we don't love you here, unbearable things. Those lies might have poisoned the rest of the life. There was no telling. The lies saved him though, that much was definite.

"I can't look after you like they can," Téo said. "You're better off with Ben and Sibyl."

Joel was quiet again. When Téo nudged him, asking if they were mates yet, Joel said: "Your one has leopard powers."

"Yeah, I remember him."

"And leopard *skills*."

"Ah."

"Can we keep playing?"

"For now? Sure."

"For long though."

Téo decided, "I'll come and see you next weekend."

He saw Joel as an eighteen-year-old. He saw him lingering in front of an open fridge. He saw him styling his hair.

Joel was asking, "What are Ben's powers?"

"Ben's? Football maybe. His energy. He makes stuff happen, yeah. What are mine, d'you reckon?"

"Téo's powers?"

"Yeah."

"*You* know."

He laughed. "Guess I do."

Joel said, "You're un-die-able."

It was his word for immortal. Téo said, "Ah, no, afraid not."

"What are Leeyer's powers?"

"Your mum?"

Joel went still, as if to move again might distract Téo from answering.

"Lia's *powers* . . . okay. She had this power to make us laugh. Like, really laugh, a surprised laugh, not to be forgotten."

Joel hadn't moved.

"She was clever like that, she was original. Bit selfish? I don't know if I've admitted that before. She hated polite small talk. She called out bullshit—sorry." He was out of practice. "She wouldn't let anyone sugar-coat. I think . . . I think she'd want us to tell you about all of her, without shying from the complicated parts. I think she'd want it given straight. Cos that was one of Lia's powers too."

Joel was ready to speak. He closed one eye, confirming, "I *do* have powers."

"Bet you do."

"I have ten."

"Are they all secret or can you tell me one of them?"

"Um, they secret."

"Joel!"

"I can tell you one."

He made Téo wait. He whispered it, "I grow."

Téo squinted at him, it was true.

"Joel, my friend. I will keep your secret."

They played.

ACKNOWLEDGEMENTS

Writing for a living is only possible when you feel confident at least some of the time. For their conferred confidence, I am grateful to my family (the Lamonts, the Carnes, the Dotschs, the Elmhirsts) and my friends (in particular the TFs, Jimbo and my Latymer and City Uni crowds), as well as the magazine and newspaper editors who have shaped me on the page and kept me employed for twenty years: Tim and Emma; Clare, David and Jonathan; Chris and Geoff; Melissa, Merope and the desk; Jane and the desk; Eva and the desk; Guy and Sarah.

Further thanks are due. To Tom, for showing me your beautiful poems and getting me started. To Sam, for better arranging my players on the stage. To Hannah, Mark and Fenella, for advice (variously worded) to trust myself. To Fran, Felicity, Sarah and Prema at L&R, Lucinda at Casarotto, Francesca at Phoenix, Juliet at W&N, Sophie at Scribner, Sarah at Rowohlt and Louise and Liv at Sceptre for renewing that sense of trust at different times. To David at Inkwell, for crying. To Jenny at Knopf, for picking out my book and for explaining with such passion and eloquence why. To Reagan and Tiara, for supporting Jenny in this. To Helen, Katherine, David, John and others, for championing a stranger. To Anna, for the perfect cover. To Malvika and Lucia, for suggestions on legal aspects of the story. To Jess, for helping me grow up. To Fede, for your faith and guidance and for opening a door, giving me the funnest year of my professional life. To Holly, for helping Fede improve the book we had. To Jane, for agreeing to meet me all those years ago and for becoming my agent, engine, editor, therapist, co-conspirator and friend—cheers, JF.

This novel is dedicated with bottomless love and gratitude to my mother, Joanna Lamont, and my father, John Lamont, who died before I finished it, somewhere in the middle of chapter 10. I have borrowed aspects of Pa's biography and applied them to an invented character: he was no meddler.

Last of all, thank you to Daniel (my boy in motion) and to Cleo (my still, observant girl) for your patience in waiting for dedications in books I hope will come. Thank you to Soph, for everything, the lot.

Tom Lamont is an award-winning journalist. In 2015 he became one of the founding writers on the *Guardian*'s Long Read desk, and since 2017 he has been a regular correspondent for American *GQ*. His long-form stories in both publications have been optioned for film and TV and have been read millions of times online. He lives in north London with his wife and two children.

A NOTE ON THE TYPE

This book was set in a version of the well-known Monotype face Bembo. This letter was cut for the celebrated Venetian printer Aldus Manutius by Francesco Griffo, and first used in Pietro Cardinal Bembo's *De Aetna* of 1495.

The companion italic is an adaptation of the chancery script type designed by the calligrapher and printer Lodovico degli Arrighi.

Typeset by Scribe, Philadelphia, Pennsylvania

Printed and bound by Berryville Graphics, Berryville, Virginia

Designed by Anna B. Knighton